I didn't get far before I heard someone call my name.

I turned to see Mulhouse striding after me. "Do you have a moment, Rufus?"

"Not really," I said. "I have to get to the prison."

"I'll be brief, then. I think I may have a . . . what is the word you Americans use? A *job* for you."

I blinked at him, baffled. "I was to work for you if I *lost*, not if I won."

"This has nothing to do with our wager. I thought you could use the money."

"I could. What kind of job? As I said, I'm not very strong."

"It will take some time to explain—more time than you have just now." He handed me a calling card. "Will you meet me tomorrow morning around nine o'clock, at this address?"

I glanced at the card. It read:

JOHANN NEPOMUK MAELZEL

AUTOMATA • DIORAMAS • CURIOSITIES

———— MASONIC HALL ————

SEVENTH & CHESTNUT STS. PHILADELPHIA

Other Books You May Enjoy

GARY BLACKWOOD

CURIOSITY

PUFFIN BOOKS
An Imprint of Penguin Group (USA)

For Michael,
my Book Buddy

PUFFIN BOOKS
Published by the Penguin Group
Penguin Group (USA) LLC
375 Hudson Street
New York, New York 10014

USA * Canada * UK * Ireland * Australia
New Zealand * India * South Africa * China

penguin.com
A Penguin Random House Company

First published in the United States of America by Dial Books for Young Readers, 2014
Published by Puffin Books, an imprint of Penguin Young Readers Group, 2015

Copyright © 2014 by Gary Blackwood

THE LIBRARY OF CONGRESS HAS CATALOGED THE DIAL BOOKS EDITION AS FOLLOWS:
Blackwood, Gary L.
Curiosity / by Gary Blackwood.
pages cm
Summary: In 1835, when his father is put in a Philadelphia debtor's prison, twelve-year-old chess prodigy Rufus Goodspeed is relieved to be recruited to secretly operate a chess-playing automaton named The Turk, but soon questions the fate of his predecessors and his own safety.
ISBN 978-0-8037-3924-6 (hardcover)
[1. Chess—Fiction. 2. Apprentices—Fiction. 3. Poverty—Fiction.
4. Robots—Fiction. 5. Mälzel, Johann Nepomuk, 1772–1838—Fiction.
6. Philadelphia (Pa.)—History—19th century—Fiction.] I. Title.
PZ7.B5338Cur 2014 [Fic] —dc23 2013013438

Puffin Books ISBN 978-0-14-242448-3

Printed in the United States of America

1 3 5 7 9 10 8 6 4 2

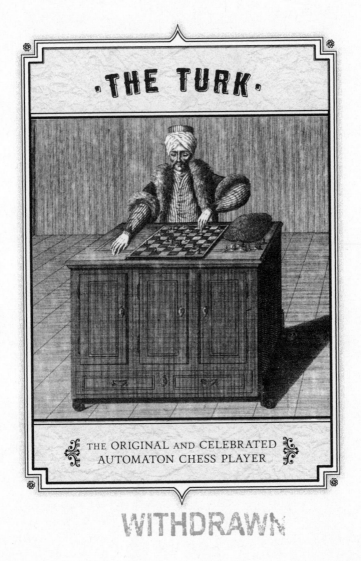

·THE TURK·

THE ORIGINAL AND CELEBRATED AUTOMATON CHESS PLAYER

WITHDRAWN

CURIOSITY

CHAPTER I

OUT OF ALL THE BOOKS IN THE WORLD, I wonder what made you choose this one. Perhaps you're a chess fanatic and you saw that the game figures prominently in the plot.

Or perhaps not. It may be that you know nothing at all about chess, and care less. You may just be hoping to read a rousing story.

In either case, I feel confident that what follows will satisfy you. If that sounds as though I'm boasting, I assure you I'm not. I make no pretense of being a clever or accomplished writer. I'll simply recount the events as they happened to me and trust that they're compelling enough to keep your attention.

I suppose I should mention before I begin that there's a certain amount of unpleasantness involved.

Every person's life has its dark corners, of course, but I suspect that mine has had more than most. I'm not crying "Oh, poor me," mind you; I'm only warning you, in case you're easily upset.

Actually, some parts are more than just unpleasant. There's a good deal of cruelty, as well as poverty, illness, and imprisonment. Not to mention murder, madness, deceit, obsession, resurrection, and unrequited love. In fact, at times it resembles a tale penned by Mr. Dickens or Mr. Poe—though I wouldn't presume to compare my storytelling skills to theirs.

The passages concerning chess may mean more if you know a little about how it's played—the names of the pieces, for example, and how they move—but even if you're completely ignorant of the game, it shouldn't matter much. I'll keep those bits as simple and straightforward as possible.

However little you may know about chess, you've no doubt heard of the celebrated chess-playing automaton known as the Turk—unless you've been living in Siberia or Darkest Africa for the past several decades. (Actually, it wouldn't surprise me to learn that the Turk's reputation has reached Siberia; after all, they say that the Russian empress Catherine the Great played against him—and lost.)

Certainly I was familiar with the Turk long before I encountered him in the flesh—or in the wax, I should say, since that was what his fierce, exotic countenance was made of.

Ah, but I'm getting ahead of myself. I know you're curious, perhaps even eager, to learn more about that marvelous and mysterious machine. But if you don't mind, I'd like to begin by telling you something about my life before the Turk entered it. Well, perhaps "like" is not the proper word. Some of my early experiences are quite painful to recall. Still, I believe they're essential to the story.

If you're not a chess fancier, I hope you'll forgive me for starting right off with a scene that revolves around the game. I will keep it simple and straightforward, as promised.

I remember clearly the moment when I first saw a chessboard. It must have been sometime around 1826; I know I was not more than four years old. At the time, my father, the Reverend Tobias Goodspeed, was in charge of a small but prosperous parish in Philadelphia. Since his duties weren't very demanding, he had plenty of leisure time to indulge his two main passions—natural science and chess.

On this particular day, he was playing a game with Father Barry, in the library of the Parsonage. This was before Philadelphia was swamped by the great wave of Irish immigrants, you know, and people saw no great harm in a Methodist minister keeping company with a Catholic priest.

The two made every round of chess into a sort of cheerful crusade. When my father won, he claimed it was because God was on his side, and when Father Barry won—which was rarely—he grew ridiculously righteous. "There, you see, Tobias?" he would say. "You can never keep us Catholics down; we will always triumph eventually!"

The library was normally forbidden territory for tots with grasping, grimy hands. But I begged my father so piteously and gave such sincere promises of good behavior that at last he allowed me to enter the *sanctum sanctorum*—under the eye of my nanny, of course. Like Father Barry's Catholics, I always triumphed eventually.

I'll be the first to admit that I was a pampered, coddled child. In point of fact, I was spoiled quite rotten, both by my father and by Fiona, my Irish nanny. Mainly, I think, it was because I was such a sickly little fellow. According to my father, my birth was a hard one, and the doctors didn't expect me to live an hour, let alone several years. I suspect that, in his heart, my father resented the fact that I had survived and that his beloved Lily had not. But he also seemed to see something of my mother in me, and I think that made me precious to him.

In some ways, I must have been a difficult child to

love; in addition to being sick more often than not, I had a slight deformity of the spine—no doubt a result of being wrenched into the world by a doctor's forceps. I was not a pint-sized Quasimodo, by any means, but I had a bit of a stoop. I think I must have looked rather like an old codger in need of a cane.

I've been told, though, that my disposition made up for my many *indispositions*. Despite all that spoiling, I wasn't a demanding child, or given to tantrums. By all accounts, I had a sweet temper and a ready laugh, and didn't complain much, no matter how ill I was or how much my back pained me. Though of course I enjoyed being pampered, I wish now that I hadn't been. It did nothing to prepare me for the hard times that were to come.

There I go again, getting ahead of myself.

As I said, I was only four when I saw my first chess match, but somehow I grasped the essence of the game almost instantly, instinctively. The bumptious Father Barry didn't have the patience to play slowly or methodically, so he insisted on a limit of half an hour per game. I sat utterly motionless through the first game, like a cat watching at a window.

This seemed to worry Fiona, who sat nearby with her needlework. "Are you feeling poorly, Master Rufus? Shall I take you up to your room, then?" She was a good, earnest girl, and as solicitous of my welfare as any mother, but she was not blessed with brains. She could never have understood what I was feeling, even if I could have explained it. I was like a person under the influence of mesmerism—hypnosis, as it's now called.

The men began a second game; still I didn't stir. As my father was about to take his opponent's bishop, I spoke up at last. "No, Father, you mustn't. If you do, he'll attack your king with his horse."

My father stared at me in astonishment, then at the board. "By thunder, the boy is right."

Father Barry was clearly peeved at having his clever strategy foiled. "How long has your father been teaching you chess, my lad?"

"Is that what it's called?" I said.

"Oh, so you're teaching him to lie, too, Tobias? He pretends to know nothing about the game, when clearly he knows a good deal."

My father put a hand to his heart. "Upon my honor, Barry, we've never even discussed the subject."

"Then how can he begin to grasp such a complex game? I'm still struggling with it, and I've been playing for twenty years."

My father shrugged. "Well, my friend, if you'll pardon the expression, I'd say that God only knows."

My understanding of the game didn't seem odd to me, of course. I thought it perfectly natural, like the ability to walk or talk, and I couldn't see why it would take anyone twenty years to become good at it—or, in Father Barry's case, to become mediocre at it. Now, of course, I realize that it was a rare gift, one that I can't begin to explain.

I've had only one other experience I can compare it to. Years later, when I was traveling through Europe, I stopped overnight in a picturesque town in Austria. Its narrow, winding streets were like a maze; when I went out for a stroll, it took me an hour to find my way back to the inn. But the next morning, I climbed to the top of a tall church tower. With the town spread out beneath me, suddenly I could see clearly where each street led and exactly how to get from one place to another.

That's the way it was with the chessboard. Up close, it appeared to be just a grid of identical light and dark squares. But I seemed able to look at it from another vantage point; I could see patterns, the best way of getting from one place to another. I'm sorry, I promised to keep this simple and straightforward, and here I am getting mystical and metaphysical on you.

My father was delighted to find that he had a *bona fide* curiosity on his hands. The 1820s and 30s were, above all else, a time of curiosity-seekers. Everyone and his brother—and often his sister—fancied himself a budding naturalist. My father was one of the most avid of these amateurs. He was convinced that, if he searched long and hard enough, he would discover some previously unknown species or fossil or set of bones and earn for himself a sort of immortality.

I think he saw me as a kind of glorified science experiment. I don't mean that he treated me like a laboratory animal. He was always very kind and patient with me, and careful not to overtax my frail body. But from that day on, we spent at least two hours each afternoon at the chessboard, testing the limits of my newfound skill.

There seemed to be no limits. By the time I was six, I was winning more games than I lost. When I was nine, he took me to the Philadelphia Chess Club and pitted me against some of the city's best players. I created something of a sensation by defeating most of them. I even showed off a bit, playing three or four men simultaneously, sometimes with a blindfold over my eyes. I considered this more of a parlor trick than a serious challenge, but it impressed everyone.

I loved these outings; they gave me a rare chance to see people and places outside the walls of the Parsonage. My father didn't think it wise for me to attend school. He wouldn't say why, exactly, but I know now that he was trying to spare me from the jokes and pranks and torments that are always suffered by children who are different.

Though he hired tutors from time to time, most of my education came from his extensive collection of books. I had inherited his avid curiosity, and there probably wasn't a single volume that I didn't delve into. My father fed my hunger for knowledge, borrowing or buying books on whatever subject interested me at the time. Many of them were about chess, of course. The best was a manual written by the great French chess master, François-André Philidor. It was in the original language, so in order to understand it, I spent a year learning French.

When I was twelve, my sheltered, privileged life came to an abrupt end. At least it seemed abrupt to me at the time. I realize now that my father had been sowing the seeds of his downfall for a long while. Somewhere along the way, his harmless dreams of being a respected naturalist had gotten out of hand. He was paying less and less attention to his duties as a minister and more and more to his scientific pursuits, which also ate up a growing amount of his modest income.

For years he'd been working on a book that explained—to his mind anyway—how all the different species of animals and plants came to be. He even financed an expedition to South America to gather evidence for his theory. I don't think it ever occurred to him that he was treading on dangerous ground. The church taught that all forms of life had been created exactly as they were; to suggest that they could change, all by themselves, was akin to heresy.

He paid for the cost of printing *The Development of Species* out of his own pocket, which by now was all but empty. The sales were, of course, dismal. Even worse, the church dismissed him, and we had to move out of the Parsonage—the only home I had ever known. Of course we also had to let poor Fiona go, who was the nearest thing I had to a mother.

We were reduced to a single room at a boarding-house in Southwark, a neighborhood that was even less appealing then than it is today. The streets were strewn with garbage, sewage, and dead animals. But it was the live ones you had to look out for: the ill-tempered pigs, some of them as big as I was, that feasted on the heaps of foul waste and would just as soon feast on you; the drunken sailors with their smelly tarred clothing and their exotic tattoos; the young toughs who hung around the firehouse, hoping for a blaze or a battle with a rival gang to add excitement to their day.

Our room and board was only two dollars a week, but it was two dollars more than we had. My father was forced to sell off his precious library, one volume at a time. In the meantime, the collector of South American specimens and the printer of the ill-fated

book grew tired of waiting for their money and took him to court. I believe the magistrate, who was also a church deacon, held a grudge against my father, too, because of the ideas contained in *The Development of Species*. Ironic, isn't it? Though no one bought the book, everyone seemed to know what it said.

Rather than give my father a chance to pay his debts—which he surely would have done in time—the magistrate sent him to the debtors' apartment at Arch Street prison. Don't let the word "apartment" fool you; it was nothing more nor less than a jail cell, made up of five rooms, each occupied by eight or ten other debtors of all stripes, from habitual drunks to failed businessmen. Some had friends generous enough to buy them a few amenities: a bed, hot meals, a plug of tobacco now and again. The rest got only two scanty blankets and a daily loaf of questionable bread. My father was one of "the rest." When he was the respected Reverend Goodspeed, he'd had no shortage of friends. Now they wanted nothing to do with him, not even Father Barry.

We had no family to turn to, either. My grandparents on the Goodspeed side were Methodist missionaries, who had been living among the Ojibwa people of Upper Canada since before I was born. My father seldom talked about my mother's family, the Raybolds, but I gathered that they disapproved of their little Lily's

choice of a husband; after her death, they had broken off all contact with us.

In all the times I visited my father at his new and Spartan lodgings, he never uttered a word of complaint about his own condition; he thought only about how I was faring. That was his way. For a minister, he wasn't much good at giving advice, but I've always remembered something he told me when I was very young: "I've come to believe," he said, "that the secret of life is to accept with good grace whatever befalls you."

I would have paid his debts myself, or at least bought him decent food and bedding, if I'd known how. But I'd never done a day's work in my life, and in any case who would hire a weak, sickly boy with no skills except a freakish prowess at chess?

CHAPTER

2

ASIDE FROM THE OCCASIONAL TRIP TO the prison, I stayed holed up at the boarding-house. I had grown up with no company but my own and Fiona's and Father's, and it had made me shy of other people. Most of the boarders gathered in the parlor in the evening; I remained in my cramped, musty room playing chess against myself—that is, I made the moves for both Black and White, an arrange-ment with one big advantage: I always won. I had to show up in the dining room twice a day for meals, of course, but I timed it so that I arrived as everyone else was leaving. The food was all cold by then, and there wasn't much to choose from, but it kept me alive.

I went on paying for my room and board by selling off what remained of our little library. Our only other possessions worth anything were the chess set and my father's treasured microscope. I knew that, if I asked, he would tell me to pawn them and use the money for my own needs. But I couldn't sleep nights, thinking of him lying on that cold stone floor and eating stale bread laced with sawdust and plaster of Paris.

With my sheltered upbringing, I knew nothing about money matters, so I consulted Mrs. Runnymead, who owned the boardinghouse. It took some courage, for she was an imposing, intimidating figure. She didn't just look large because I was so small, either. She loomed over all her other boarders, the way the chess queen looms over the pawns. "Please," I said, in what I'm sure was a pitiful voice, "can you tell me where I might go to pawn something?"

She peered down at me as though I were too far away to see clearly. "What sort of something?"

"A microscope," I said, feeling much the way a tiny bug on a microscope slide must feel.

"Like a telescope, you mean?"

"Not exactly. It's more for looking at very small things."

"Oh. Is it worth much?"

"I think so."

"Hmm. Why don't I show it to my friend Mr. Wheelock? He'll take most anything, and give you the best price."

I was only too glad to let her handle it. I surrendered the microscope and waited for her return, hoping it would fetch enough to at least buy my father a straw mattress. To my delight, Mrs. Runnymead came back with ten dollars in crisp banknotes. "Mr. Wheelock snatched it right up," she said. "It seems them things are in great demand."

"He won't sell it, though? You told him not to sell it?"

"Of course, he'll sell it, you gilly. For twice what he gave me, I've no doubt."

"But—but I only meant to pawn it," I protested feebly, "and buy it back later."

"Oh, dear." Mrs. Runnymead made a *tsk*ing sound. "Ah, well, what's done is done. Anyway, a Michaelscope is no good to your dad if he's locked up in prison, now is it?"

Though I felt as if I'd betrayed him, I had to admit she was right. Just now my father needed nourishing food and a warm bed far more than he needed a "Michaelscope." I sighed and held out a hand for the money. But instead of giving the notes to me, Mrs. Runnymead folded them briskly and stuffed them into her already overstuffed bosom. "There. That'll pay your room and board for a good while, I guess. I'm not running an almshouse here, after all."

I had always managed to get my own way with Fiona and with my father, but I knew somehow that no amount of pleading or coaxing would have the slightest effect on Mrs. Runnymead, except perhaps to make her angry, and I didn't care to have her angry at me. My position was precarious enough.

I had tenaciously held on to the chess set and the Philidor chess manual, partly because they were a way of filling up the long, solitary days, but more, I think, because they were familiar and comforting, the only relics that remained of my old life. The fact was, though, I didn't really need them. I had the Philidor book all but memorized and, if it came to it, a person could just as well play chess on a checked tablecloth, with pieces of dried bread.

Father's set was a fine one, brought back from China by some Methodist missionary. The board was ebony and maple and the ivory pieces were of an Oriental design; the king and queen wore kimonos, and the knights resembled dragons. When we played at the Chess Club, many of the players had admired it. If one of them were to buy it, perhaps we could get it back when our fortunes improved—which I had no doubt they would. As I told you, I had a sunny disposition.

The Chess Club gathered at a coffeehouse in the Earle and Sully Exhibition Gallery, which was on Chestnut Street. With my twelve-year-old's sense of humor, I thought it hilarious that a group of chess nuts should meet on Chestnut Street. It was only fifteen minutes' walk from Sassafras Alley, where the boardinghouse lay, but for my short legs and milk toast constitution that was quite a hike. Still, I would have managed it well enough if I hadn't encountered the two young rowdies.

They were no older than I, but considerably larger, and so dirty and so ragged that I was sorry for them. At the same time, I felt somehow akin to them; if my situation did not improve, in six months I might be every bit as dirty and ragged.

They clearly had no feelings of kinship toward me. At first it seemed they might be content just to poke fun at my skinny frame and hunched back. But then they noticed the package under my arm, which I had wrapped in brown paper.

One of them seized it and, when I refused to let go, he punched me in the face, hard. I toppled over like a checkmated king. As I lay there amid the refuse and garbage, the other boy, laughing, kicked me in the ribs; fortunately for me, he was barefoot. It was fortunate, too, that my feet were so small, or he would surely have had my boots. The two of them hurried off with their prize; they hadn't even looked to see what it was.

The boy who had kicked me was limping—not from the kick, of course. Even in my dazed state, I noticed that his other foot was black and swollen, probably with gangrene. I feared he would not have long to enjoy his ill-gotten gains.

I was left with nothing to sell now but the clothes on my back. If I said I sat there in the dirt and cried my eyes out, it probably wouldn't surprise you. But for all my frailties, I was not a weepy sort. Though I wasn't accustomed to being beaten up and robbed, I was accustomed to pain and to bearing it as best I could, without feeling sorry for myself.

I got gingerly to my feet, knocked off the worst of the dirt, and went on. Why I still headed for the Chess Club, and not back to my cheerless room or to the prison, to tell my sad tale to my father, I'm not sure. Perhaps it was because I didn't want to burden him. Perhaps it was because I was so stubborn. One thing I do know: I had learned from playing chess that, if your strategy fails, you don't concede the game; you come up with a new strategy.

During my visits to the Chess Club, I had seen men play for money. Each player put up a stake, and the winner took the lot. I had no money to put up; I didn't even have a chessboard. But there were plenty of wealthy businessmen who fancied themselves crack players and who might find it amusing to be pitted against an undersized twelve-year-old.

Many of the regulars at the Club had seen me play, of course, and when I stood in the center of the coffeehouse and called out, in my piping voice, "Who'll wager fifty cents that he can beat me?" they glanced knowingly at one another. But there were several newcomers at the tables, playing or just drinking coffee and observing. A portly, red-faced man called out, "I'll be glad to beat you, my lad; just let me go find a stick."

A slim, well-dressed fellow with a French accent spoke up. When you're twelve, it's hard to know the age of adults; they all seem old to you. But I'd say he was a bit younger than my father—perhaps thirty-five. "Beat you at chess, you mean?" he said. When I nodded, he raised an eyebrow skeptically. "Are you a good player?"

Since I so seldom spoke to anyone outside my little circle, I had never learned to be either modest or tactful. "Yes. If I'm not, why would I bet money on myself?"

He laughed. "I know many men who are not nearly as good as they think they are."

"Well, I guess you won't find out unless you play me."

"I could watch you play against someone else."

"No one else has taken the bet."

The Frenchman glanced around the room. "No? Then I shall." He gestured to the chair opposite him and I sat. "What happened to your face? You look as though someone *has* been beating you with a stick."

"On the way here, I was knocked down and robbed."

"Ah, *quel dommage*. So they took all your money?"

"I didn't have any to take. They stole my chess-board."

"Why, the deuced scoundrels!" put in Mr. Peach, one of the regulars, who was playing a game at the next table. "Was it your father's Oriental set?"

I nodded glumly.

"Did you report it to the gendarmes?" asked the Frenchman.

Mr. Peach gave a humorless laugh. "You're not in Paree, monsoor. We have a total of twenty-four constables to patrol the entire city; they're not likely to bother with anything so minor as the theft of a chess set." To me he said, "I hear the Reverend Goodspeed has fallen on hard times."

"He's in debtors' prison."

Mr. Peach shook his head sadly. "I wish I could help him, but I don't dare. If my customers got wind of it, they'd take their business somewhere else."

The Frenchman gave him a disdainful glance, then turned to me. "*Eh bien*, if you've lost your board, we shall have to rent one, shan't we?"

"You can use ours," said Mr. Peach. "I was about to lose, anyway."

"No, no, m'sieur. It might distress your customers if you helped the son of such a notorious criminal. I am sorry, my boy; I don't know your name."

"Rufus Goodspeed."

He shook my hand. "They call me Mulhouse. *Excuse-moi*." He sought out the proprietor and returned with a simple wooden chess set. "Pardon me for being blunt, Rufus, but you say you have no money and your father is in debtors' prison. How will you settle the wager, if you should lose?"

Like any good chess player, I had my next move already planned. "I'll do a week's work for you, whatever kind you want, without pay."

"Hmm. Again, pardon me for saying so, but you don't look very strong."

"I'm not. But I am very clever."

Mulhouse grinned wryly. "Yes, I've no doubt you are." He swiftly set up the board. "Do you prefer Black or White?"

In case you don't know, White has the advantage of the first move. But I didn't want it to seem as if I *needed* the advantage. "Black, if it's all the same to you."

A move-by-move account of a chess game is like a blow-by-blow account of a bare-knuckle boxing match. All you want to hear about are the knockdown blows, and perhaps a little about the style of each fighter. Did he dance around the ring, feinting and dodging, like Country McCloskey? Or did he pound steadily, relentlessly at his opponent, like Yankee Sullivan?

Mulhouse's style was nothing like mine. He was all

flash and daring, sacrificing pieces without a qualm to further his ends. My strategy was straight out of Philidor's manual. I was methodical and careful, and reluctant to part with so much as a pawn. According to Philidor, pawns were not expendable; they were crucial. Instead of putting my big pieces into play, I concentrated on advancing my pawns, using them as a sort of protective wall. Mulhouse seized a few, but one made it all the way to White's home row where, like some poor girl from a fairy tale, it was transformed into a queen. From that point on, the game was mine.

Like my father, Mulhouse accepted his fate gracefully. He seemed more surprised than upset. As he slid the coins across the table, he said, "Another game? With a larger stake, *peut-être*?"

The second game was much like the first—daring versus doggedness. I expected Mulhouse to be a bit more careful and calculating this time. But he seemed less concerned with winning than with dazzling the crowd that had gathered around us. Looking back on the game, I think that, in fact, he had no intention of winning, that this was his way of helping me without seeming to help.

During both games, he displayed an unfortunate tendency to cough just as I was considering my next move. At first I thought it was deliberate, but then he offered a sincere apology. "I assure you that I am not trying to distract you, Rufus. I have an irritation of the throat, as a result of—well, never mind that." He fished a packet of lozenges from his pocket and slipped one in his mouth. "That is better."

On the twelfth move, I put my Black queen in a position to be captured by the White knight. A sympathetic murmur went up from the crowd; they naturally assumed that, if I lost my most powerful piece, it was all over for me. I could see Mulhouse hesitate. But with all those people watching, there was no way he could refuse to take her; it would be obvious that he was letting me win. He shrugged and gently toppled Her Majesty.

It was all over, all right, but not for me. Everyone thought that, in my eagerness to win, I'd made a fatal blunder. But they'd forgotten about my rook, which had sat patiently in its home row all this time, waiting for its chance. When I slid it across the board to checkmate the White king, there were gasps of surprise; then the observers burst into applause.

Mulhouse shook my hand again. "Well played, my young friend." He fished in his pocket and came up with a silver dollar. "Now you may buy yourself another chess set."

"I've got more important things to spend it on," I said, and hurried from the Club. As always happens when I'm caught up in a chess match, I'd lost all sense of time. The afternoon was almost gone. But if I paid the keeper at the prison right away, my father might have a bed and a good meal before the day was out.

I didn't get far before I heard someone call my name. I turned to see Mulhouse striding after me. "Do you have a moment, Rufus?"

"Not really," I said. "I have to get to the prison."

"I'll be brief, then. I think I may have a . . . what is the word you Americans use? A *job* for you."

I blinked at him, baffled. "I was to work for you if I *lost*, not if I won."

"This has nothing to do with our wager. I thought you could use the money."

"I could. What kind of job? As I said, I'm not very strong."

"It will take some time to explain—more time than you have just now." He handed me a calling card. "Will you meet me tomorrow morning around nine o'clock, at this address?"

I glanced at the card. It read:

JOHANN NEPOMUK MAELZEL

AUTOMATA • DIORAMAS • CURIOSITIES
—— **MASONIC HALL** ——
SEVENTH & CHESTNUT STS. PHILADELPHIA

"But you said your name was—"

"Never mind that, now. Can I count on you to be there?"

"I'll be there." Not only did I need money, I wanted to know more about this Maelzel and his Automata, Dioramas, and Curiosities.

"Ah, *bon, bon*." He shook my hand once more. "Go, now."

I headed for the Arch Street prison as fast as my puny legs could carry me. I could hear the coins clinking in my pocket—a sound that cheered me no end. Suddenly my prospects were looking up. Not only could I help my father out a little right away, in time I might even earn enough money for his release, if the job Mulhouse had mentioned actually materialized.

I had no idea what it might involve, or what the wage might be. But whatever sort of work it was, and however much it paid, it was bound to be better than my current miserable situation.

Or so I thought.

CHAPTER

3

THOUGH THE MAIN STREETS OF THE CITY were wide, the brick sidewalks were narrow. I often had to step off the curb or flatten myself against a building to avoid being run down by self-important businessmen anxious to get home to their comfortable town houses and their decanters of whiskey and their suppers of roast beef and pickled oysters.

But I was weary from all the walking, not to mention the chess playing, and I didn't always dodge fast enough. When I was nearly to the prison, a well-fed merchant, bent on catching an omnibus, knocked into me and sent me spinning. I don't believe he even noticed.

As I picked myself up, I spotted an object lying on

the bricks next to me. It was an ornate gold pocket watch, with a short length of chain attached. I suppose that, when we collided, it was yanked somehow from the merchant's vest pocket and the chain snapped. "Oh, Lud!" I said (an expression I'd picked up from novels, and one my father disapproved of). Snatching up the watch, I turned toward the omnibus the man had boarded. But it was already pulling away from the curb and, in my dazed and exhausted state, I couldn't dream of catching it.

And then I saw the policeman. It gives you some sense of how bad my luck was at the time; with only twenty-four constables spread out over the whole of Philadelphia, what are the chances that one would happen to walk past at the very moment when I was holding another fellow's ridiculously expensive watch in my hand?

The constable must have had a bad day, too, for he had no patience with me. He wouldn't listen to a word I said in my defense. He seized the watch, then my ear, and dragged me bodily before the nearest magistrate— the very same God-fearing fellow who had sentenced my father. When the magistrate learned my identity, he nodded grimly, as if this were exactly what you could expect from the son of a heretic, and muttered, "The sins of the father shall be visited upon the son."

A few years earlier, being arrested for theft would have gotten me three or four months in prison—perhaps the same one that held my father. But the Society of Friends—the Quakers, you know—had recently established the House of Refuge. Its purpose was to reform what they called "juvenile delinquents." Throw a young offender in with adult criminals, they said, and he will learn nothing except how to be a criminal. At the House of Refuge he would be educated and trained, and eventually might become a regular apprentice. At least that was the theory.

I couldn't wait for eventually. My father needed my help now. I tried to tell the magistrate that I was no thief; I said that I'd been offered a job and that, if they put me away, I'd miss my chance at it. He paid me no more mind than if I had been a small stray dog, yapping at him.

He assumed that the coins in my pocket were stolen, too, and confiscated them. Then he had me put in a holding cell with three other so-called delinquents: a pair of scrawny sisters who were younger than me, and a boastful older boy named Ezra, who claimed that he'd broken out of the House of Refuge three times and would do so again. "My last name's Dunaway," he said. "But the other boys call me Runaway." His latest attempt had involved cramming himself into a shipping crate that he had addressed to a fictional person in Baltimore.

Curious as always, I asked, "Why Baltimore?"

Ezra shrugged. "We read about it in our lessons. It sounds like an interesting place."

"Did you get there?"

"Nah. When they were loading the box onto the freight wagon, they dropped it." He rubbed his shoulder. "Nearly broke my arm. 'Tis just as well. If they hadn't, I probably would have suffocated. Next time I'll remember to cut air holes in the box."

"Why do you want to escape so badly?"

He gave me a scornful look, as if I'd asked the stupidest of questions. "You'll see," he said.

After dark, we were loaded into a police van and treated to a bone-rattling ride that ended in a suburb known as The Vineyard. I saw no vineyards, nor much of anything else. When we emerged from the van, we found ourselves in a large courtyard dimly lighted by oil lamps. "Welcome to the House of *Refuse*," said Ezra sarcastically. There was nothing house-like about the building that stood before us. In fact, it more nearly resembled a prison—a bleak, three-story structure of rough stone surrounded by a twenty-foot wall with a tower at each corner.

A plainly dressed woman appeared and led the two

sisters, whose names I never learned, to the girls' dormitory. Ezra sighed. "I'm too tired to escape tonight. Come on." He shouldered his small sack of belongings, approached a thick oak door, and pounded on it. A bony, grizzled man opened the door; he raised his lantern to get a look at our faces, and gave a mostly toothless smile. "Well, if 'tisn't Brother Runaway. Had a good holiday, did thee?"

"Not bad. A bit shorter than I planned."

"Who's thy friend?"

"Oh." Ezra turned to me. "Thee never—*you* never told me your name."

"Rufus Goodspeed."

"Welcome to the House of Refuge, Brother Goodspeed. I'm Brother Bunsen. Brother Dunaway, one of the big boys took thy room. We'll have to put thee in this one." Calling it a room was being far too kind; it was more in the nature of a cell, perhaps four feet by eight, with a single bed and a narrow window, and nothing else. Well, I thought, it's more than my father has.

"Good job I took my belongings with me," grumbled Ezra, "or somebody'd have had them, too." He dropped his bundle and, sitting on the mattress, bounced up and down a few times. "Not much stuffing. I been here longer, so I get to choose, and I'll take the outside."

My side of the bed was right up against the rough wooden wall. As we had no nightshirts, we just removed our shoes and stretched out in our street clothing. We slept head to foot. Ezra's feet were not quite as bad as those of the boy who'd kicked me earlier, but if cleanliness is next to Godliness, as my father always claimed, I'd have say they were ungodly filthy. It had been a trying day and I was ready for it to end but, as I was drifting off, Ezra said, "Does it hurt?"

"What?" I said, drowsily.

"Your back." He had made no mention of my infirmity until now; I had fooled myself into thinking that perhaps he hadn't noticed.

"Yes," I said.

"You never let on."

"My father says that, whatever our fate is, we should accept it with good grace."

Ezra grunted dubiously. "And what was *his* fate?"

"Right now, he's in prison."

"Mine, too. What's yours in for?"

"Debt. And yours?"

"Murder," he said matter-of-factly. "What about your mother?"

"She died when I was born. Yours?"

"The consumption got her." There was a silence, then he said, "Rufus?"

"Umm?"

"You ain't got head lice, have you?"

"No."

"Good. If you do, they shave off all your hair. Even your eyebrows."

"Umm." I dozed off for a few moments, and then I heard Ezra's voice again. "Time to get up, Rufus," he said.

"Very funny," I murmured.

"No, really. The five-o'clock bell just rung."

I sat up and peered at the window; there was no trace of daylight. "Five o'clock? Who gets up at five o'clock?"

"Juvenile delinquents," he said.

Like the words "apartment" and "room" and "house," the term "refuge" is misleading. It suggests a place of safety, a retreat from the cares and woes of the world. The Parsonage had been a real refuge. This place was merely a compressed, claustrophobic version of the larger world, with all the same troubles and tiresome tasks but without the comfort of family and familiar surroundings.

The only thing my new life had in common with the old one was the emphasis on prayer and religious services. The first order of the day was morning worship in the chapel. This was followed by an hour or two of studies; our textbook was something called *Moral Recreations in Prose and Verse*. Dickens, it was not, or even Catherine Sedgwick. I still recall one bit of doggerel that we committed to memory:

Whatever your diversions are
Pursue them all with proper care
And never till your task is done
To any play attempt to run.

It was accompanied by a woodcut of two boys. I remember it clearly because one of the boys had a bit of a stoop, and at first I thought, Well, there's another fellow like me; I'm not the only one. Then I realized the reason for his hunched posture: The two were playing leapfrog, and the other boy was about to vault over him.

At seven we finally broke our fast with porridge and butter bread, then worked at our appointed jobs until dinner. Some of the boys did bookbinding, some made brass nails or umbrellas or furniture; I was fit only to wind weaving yarn onto bobbins. It was such a repetitive task, I had plenty of time to think.

I thought about my missed meeting with Mulhouse; whatever he had in mind for me, it must be better than winding bobbins. Certainly the money would be better, for here we received no pay at all. I thought about my father, who told me how much he looked forward to my visits; I could not visit him now, nor could I provide him with a bed or food. And I thought about chess. I had played it every day of my life from the age of four, and I keenly felt the loss, the way a drunk must feel when deprived of the bottle.

After dinner there were more lessons, then four more hours of work, then supper, then even more lessons, followed by evening prayers. Oh, I nearly forgot: Before the evening classes, we were given a full half hour for recreation.

Naturally, the older boys' favorite recreation was to torment the younger ones. They reserved their meanest pranks for the colored boys. The place held perhaps a hundred lads of all ages, from six to twenty. Only a dozen or so were black, and most of those were quite young; I believe it was usual to treat Negroes above the age of thirteen or fourteen as adults and send them to prison, no matter how minor their crime.

On my third day there—or it may have been my fourth; I lost all track of time—while the other boys played noisily at catch and tag and torment-the-coloreds, I sat alone in a corner of the courtyard, playing chess. Since I had no board or pieces, and no means of making any, I was reduced to conducting matches in my mind. This isn't as difficult as it sounds. Remember, I'd played blindfolded many times at the Chess Club, sometimes against three or four men simultaneously. A single unseen game was no great effort, especially when my opponent was myself.

I must have been unconsciously moving the invisible pieces with my hands, for I heard a brash voice

chance. Get out of here now, and you'll escape having your stupid knob knocked off."

"I can take it," said Ezra, then nodded toward me. "He can't. So why don't you—" He broke off as Duff raised a fist and clubbed him alongside the head. I expected Ezra to go down, but he only staggered a little, shook his head, and drove a fist into the bigger boy's gut. Duff doubled over, gasping for breath. I don't know whether or not Ezra would have finished him off, for the other three boys fell upon him, then, flailing at him with fists and feet.

Eventually one of the keepers came to break up the fight—if something so one-sided can be called a fight—and help Ezra to the infirmary. As the Quaker nurse tended to his cuts and abrasions, I sat by the bed and watched; it seemed to be all I was good for. Although, while Ezra was being beaten up by the big boys, I hadn't just knelt there in the dirt and watched. I'd closed my eyes.

When the nurse departed, I said, "Why did you do that?"

Ezra's lower lip was so swollen that the words came out sounding strange and slurred. "I couldn't stand to see them knock you around, that's all."

"So instead, they knocked *you* around."

"Like I said, I can take it. You can't."

"They never would have beaten me up the way they did you."

"Oh, so you'd have had me just stay out of it?"

"Yes."

He glared at me for a moment, then laughed and shook his head; the movement made him wince. "I know you try to accept things with good grace, Rufus, but I reckon you're going a bit far. It don't mean you have to just give up. Sometimes you got to fight back."

"Why?"

"*Why?* Because you can't let a blunderbuss like Duff just walk all over you, that's why!"

"You fought back, and he walked all over you anyway."

Ezra stared at me, as if this were the stupidest thing he'd ever heard—or as if he'd just never thought about it before. He shook his head again and gazed up at the soot-stained ceiling. "I got to get out of this place."

"*Now?*"

"No, you ninny. But soon. Duff already had it in for me; now he'll really be out for my blood. I got to think up a better escape plan." He carefully turned his face to me. "You can come with me." When I looked down at the floor, he said, "Oh, sorry; I forgot. You'd rather just stay here and take it all with good grace."

By the time Ezra was released from the infirmary, he had a new escape strategy. "'Tis foolproof," he whispered to me at supper. "You see, I hide next to

one of the workshops till dark. When the police van comes in with a new crop of delinquents, I just grab a hold of the underside and let the coppers carry me to freedom. Nice touch of irony, ain't it?"

I wished him luck, and half wished that I had the strength and daring to join him. But even if I managed to break out, where would I go? It would be an easy matter for the authorities to find me and bring me back.

As it turned out, they brought Ezra back, too. Long after I was in bed, I was wakened by Brother Bunsen. "I thought thee would want to know, Brother Goodspeed. Thy friend has had an accident."

"Ezra? What's happened?"

"Well, as best I can gather, he tried to escape by hanging underneath the police van. It must have hit a bump and shook him loose. One of the wheels ran over his arm."

"Oh, Lud. Is it broken?"

"Worse than that. They've brought in a doctor. I expect he'll have to take it off."

I gasped. "*Amputate* it, you mean? Can I go see him?"

Brother Bunsen shook his head. "'Twon't be a pretty sight." This was before ether and chloroform, you know; the only thing a surgeon could do to make his patients suffer less was to cut as quickly as possible. "Perhaps thee may look in on him in a few days, when he's recovered some."

I never got the chance to visit my unfortunate friend. The next afternoon, as I was winding bobbins with my hands and playing chess games in my head, one of the keepers appeared and escorted me to the superintendent's office. "What have I done?" I asked. "Am I to be punished?"

"I don't know," said the man. "I was only told to fetch thee."

Though I had never before seen the superintendent, I was well acquainted with the man who sat across the desk from him. "Hello, Rufus."

"Monsieur Mulhouse! How did you find me?"

"It was not easy. When you did not keep our appointment, I consulted the gentlemen at the Chess Club. None of them knew where you lived. But nothing stays secret for long in a city of this size." Before all the immigration, you know, Philadelphia's population was less than half what it is now. "One just has to ask the right people. It seems that the keeper at the debtors' prison is the brother-in-law of the constable who arrested you."

"So," said the superintendent, "thee will take responsibility for the child, Brother Schlumberger?"

"I shall watch over him like a brother, Brother. I promise you that he will sin no more."

And just like that, I was free to go. As we rode in a hired cab back to the city, I said, "Why did he call you . . . whatever he called you?"

"Schlumberger? Because that is my name."

"You said it was Mulhouse."

"*Mais non;* I said they *call* me that, after the town in France where I was born." His throat was clearly irritated again, as it had been when we played chess. He retrieved his packet of lozenges and took one.

After a time, I said, "I didn't steal that watch, you know."

"I never imagined you did. What became of the money you won from me?"

"They took it. I was going to buy bedding and food for my father."

"No matter. You'll have a chance to earn more."

"You mean I may still have the job?"

"If it were up to me, you would. But we shall have to convince Maelzel."

"What will I be expected to do?"

The Frenchman gave me a wry smile. "Why, to play chess, of course."

That's all he would tell me; for the rest of the ride, I was left to wonder what lay in store for me. I knew that top players, including the great Philidor, were sometimes paid by chess clubs to be a sort of resident chess master. But I couldn't imagine any club hiring a scrawny and socially inept twelve-year-old. Though I had plenty of skill, I had precious little experience.

Maelzel's headquarters occupied nearly the entire

first floor of Masonic Hall. It was obvious at a glance that the place was no chess club. It looked more like a factory. Half a dozen men in work clothes and carpenter's aprons were engaged in a bewildering variety of tasks: One was carving what looked like a doll or marionette. Another was chiseling teeth into a wooden gear a foot in diameter. A third was constructing a miniature house, laying bricks the size of split peas. Next to him was a fellow crafting a wagon so small it could have been pulled by snails.

On the back wall hung a sheet of linen some four feet high and ten feet long, on which two men were painting a landscape as true to life as a daguerreotype—though of course the daguerreotype hadn't been invented yet. These odd activities stirred my curiosity, and I might have stood there gaping for a long while, but Mulhouse led me across the sawdust- and shavings-strewn floor and into an office with a large glass window that gave a clear view of the whole workshop. The desk was cluttered with books and drawings and clay models and dirty cups and overflowing ashtrays, but no one sat there.

On one wall of the office was a heavy door; Mulhouse approached it and knocked—not as you or I would knock, but in a certain pattern: three raps, then a pause, three more, then a pause, then two more. After a moment, a little panel in the door opened and I saw dark eyes peering out. "Oh, it is you," said a voice. The door opened slightly—not enough for me to see inside the room—and a man emerged, swiftly pulled it shut behind him, and locked it.

This, I supposed, must be Maelzel. As I've said, when you're young it's hard to judge an adult's age, but I suppose he must have been sixty or so. His hairline had receded considerably; the remaining hair—which was worn long, in the manner of men who wanted to appear artistic—showed no trace of gray. No doubt he dyed it with silver nitrate and henna, but I didn't know about such things then; I noticed only that it seemed unnaturally black.

I later learned that, when he made public appearances, he wore a corset to contain his ample belly, but at the moment it was contained only by a carpenter's apron, like those worn by the workmen. Otherwise, he was dressed like a gentleman, in a brown linen jacket and trousers. His face had an aristocratic look, too, with a long nose that was nearly as straight and sharp as a knife; his arched eyebrows, which looked as if they'd been plucked, were raised in surprise.

"What have we here, Mulhouse? You said you would bring me a chess player, not a street urchin." He had a European accent, too, but it was heavier and more guttural than Mulhouse's.

Mulhouse smiled smugly. "Ah, Johann. You, of all

people, should know better than to let appearances deceive you. The boy may look a bit shabby, but I assure you, his chess playing is not."

"Have you played against him?"

"Of course. I am not a fool."

"That is debatable." The man approached me and, to my astonishment, placed both hands on my head and began exploring my scalp, much the way the keepers at the House of Refuge had when they were looking for lice. Alarmed, I glanced at Mulhouse. He smiled slightly and gave me a reassuring nod.

After a full minute of massaging my skull with his blunt fingers, Maelzel said, "Hmm. His organ of Locality is well developed; so are those representing Order and Calculation. A good sign." The fingers moved to a spot directly above my ear. "I note that he is also better than average in Cautiousness and Agreeableness." The fingers probed the area behind my ear. "He is lacking in Combativeness, which is a good thing . . ." They crept across my crown, making me shiver. ". . . but also in Deference, which is not so good."

"If I'm to play chess," I said, "why don't you test my skill?"

"There, you see? The boy shows no respect."

"He has a point, though," said Mulhouse. "Instead of playing phrenology with his head, why don't you just play him at chess?"

"I hardly think he could be very accomplished, at his age. How old are you, boy? Nine?"

"Twelve."

"All the same. The best we can hope for is that he may be taught to play passably, and that could take many months—years, even."

"I told you I'd found a chess player, Johann, not a *prospective* chess player."

"All right, all right, have it your way. Help me find the chessboard."

CHAPTER

5

THEY SPENT THE NEXT LITTLE WHILE searching the cluttered office for the board, and another while locating the scattered chessmen—most of them, anyway. We had to substitute a thimble for one of the rooks, and cigar stubs for two of the pawns.

It was clear at once that Maelzel was a strong player, and one who was used to winning. When it was my move, he drummed his fingers on the desk, as if I were taking far too long. I did my best to ignore him and to play in my usual careful fashion. Each time his turn came, he took only a moment to consider, then made his move quickly and confidently.

But halfway through the game, when I took his thimble with my cigar stub, his confidence began to falter. When I captured his queen, he gave a low whistle. He knew it was over. Many players—and I admit, I am one of them—will refuse to accept defeat; they go on stubbornly fighting to the last man. But, though Maelzel might dislike losing, he had sense enough to see that it was inevitable.

"I concede," he said, and held out his hand. I shook it cautiously, knowing that his thick fingers could easily crush my spindly ones. Maelzel turned to the Frenchman. "Did he defeat you that easily?"

"Oh, yes. Twice."

Maelzel stared at me for a time, drumming his fingers as if he were again waiting for me to move. But the next move was clearly his. Finally he stood up, took off his carpenter's apron, and draped it neatly over the back of his chair. "Very well. You may begin by picking up the chess pieces and putting them where I can find them next time."

"Does this mean I have the job?"

"Perhaps." The man turned to Mulhouse. "*Was hast du ihm gesagt?*" I knew enough German to understand the meaning: What have you told him?

"Nothing except that chess is involved."

"*Sehr gut.*" Maelzel leaned down and put his face close to mine. "Before I take you on as an apprentice—What is your name?"

"Rufus."

He pursed his lips in a disapproving look. "Did no one teach you to address your elders as *sir*?"

"No."

"Well, they should have. Before I take you on as apprentice, Rufus, there is one thing you must know." He spoke to me with exaggerated care, as though I were a young child, or an idiot. "Inside that room—" He gestured toward the inner door. "—is a closely guarded secret, a secret known only to myself and Mulhouse and my craftsman, Jacques. Once you step into the room, Rufus, you will become a party to that secret. But—and this is the important part—you must *never* breathe a word to anyone about what goes on there. Do you understand?"

"Yes."

He peered into my eyes as though trying to read my thoughts, and I had the uneasy feeling that perhaps he actually could. "Hmm," he said at last. He placed a hand on my head again, only this time his fingers did not massage it; they closed upon it like the claws of some giant raptor. "I found one other spot on your skull that seems quite prominent—the one denoting Secretiveness, or Discretion. I hope for your sake that I am not mistaken."

If my cosseted childhood hadn't taught me how to relate to other people, neither had it taught me to fear them. Even in the House of Refuge, I hadn't felt truly afraid, not even of Duff and his cronies; the most I was likely to suffer was a little pain, and I lived with that every day. But, though Maelzel's words were neither harsh nor threatening, there was something in his voice that sent a chill through me, and for a moment I considered backing out, before I was in too deep.

Then I thought of my father and his plight, and I pushed the unfamiliar feeling of fear aside, as I had learned to do with the familiar feeling of pain. I must admit, I had another feeling, too, even stronger than the fear. As I said earlier, for better or worse I had inherited my father's compulsive curiosity. I had to see what lay beyond that door. "I won't tell anybody," I said. "I don't have anybody to tell."

"Good." Turning to the inner door, Maelzel unlocked it. "You wait here, Mulhouse. Rufus?" He beckoned to me. "Come inside and close the door behind you—and bolt it." The door was so heavy, it took all my strength to push it closed. The iron bolt was heavy, too, but well oiled, and it slid easily into place. What could be so valuable or so secret, I wondered, that it must be kept in such a secure room?

And then I turned and saw, for the first time, the Turk.

Perhaps you've come upon one of the many engravings that have appeared in newspapers and books and magazines, depicting the famous chess-playing automaton. This one was published in 1783 by a journalist named von Windisch. (The cabinet at which he sat was not a separate piece of furniture, you know, but an integral part of the machine):

Though the likeness is accurate enough, it doesn't do justice to the Turk, any more than, say, a brief summary of "The Raven" could possibly do justice to Mr. Poe's celebrated and chilling poem. No picture can begin to convey the uncanny feeling you got when watching the machine perform its delicate, lifelike movements, or the unnerving quality of the figure's unblinking gaze. Those coal-black eyes, rimmed all around with white that was startling in the swarthy face, seemed to look right through you. Some have found the Turk's expression rather menacing, but I always felt it held more of a challenge, as though he was engaging you in a contest of wills, and the loser would be the first one to look away.

At the time I met him, he looked quite different. For one thing, he had been decapitated. Wires and mechanical bits protruded from his headless neck. His wooden torso was bare—his ermine-trimmed robe and embroidered shirt hung from a hook on the wall—the white kid gloves had been stripped from his hands, and his left arm had been amputated.

My mind went to poor Ezra: How had he endured the brutal operation? Had he even survived it? And if he had, how would he stand up to Duff, or become skilled in any trade, with only one arm? Maelzel's voice interrupted my thoughts. "Allow me to introduce to you the world-famous chess-playing Turk, seen by more eyes than any other curiosity ever exhibited!"

Even sequestered as I was in the Parsonage, I had heard of the Turk; with all the chess books I had read, I could scarcely have avoided it. It was said that Napoléon himself had challenged the machine—and, to his disgust, lost. Other celebrated opponents included Frederick the Great, Voltaire, Ben Franklin, Empress Maria Theresa, even the great Philidor—who, of course, defeated the Turk. Its inventor, Wolfgang von Kempelen, had supposedly destroyed or dismantled the machine some time around the turn of the century, without revealing to anyone exactly how it worked.

Well-crafted automata were common enough; some were amazingly true to life, such as the mechanical musician who flawlessly played a flute, or the clockwork duck that quacked, flapped its wings, ate grain from people's hands, digested the food, and then excreted it. But a machine that could play a fearfully complex game, and do it so well that few human players could outwit it? It was nearly inconceivable.

There was no shortage of theories about the Turk. Some said it must be operated by a concealed dwarf, or perhaps a trained monkey. More scientific-minded observers insisted that it was controlled by magnets, or electrical current from a galvanic battery. Those who were mystically inclined suggested that there was black magic at work, or that the figure was not wood and wax, but an actual body that had been revivified in some fashion, as in one of Mr. Poe's stories.

The doors of the Turk's cabinet had been removed, revealing an impressive array of gears and cams and escapements and springs and wires, all of which indicated that there was some clockwork, at least, involved. I was so fascinated by the machine that I barely noticed the flesh and blood man sitting behind it until he let out a blistering string of French curse words (when I studied the language, I had made a point of learning as many curses as possible).

"What is the trouble, Jacques?" asked Maelzel.

"Ahh, one of the tendons in his arm snapped off."

"Replace it, then, and stop being so ill-tempered."

The man named Jacques grumbled something ill-tempered. With the help of a crutch that leaned nearby, he slid off his stool and approached us. He walked with a curious hobbling gait, as though he were slogging through mud. He didn't use the crutch for locomotion so much as just to steady himself. Aside from this peculiarity, he seemed a fine physical specimen—solidly built, with broad shoulders and arms as muscular as a blacksmith's.

His appearance was quite different from the fashion of the day: He had several days' growth of beard, though it was neatly trimmed; his sandy hair was even longer than Maelzel's, and pulled back into a queue, like those you see in pictures of Jefferson or Hamilton. Aside from a livid scar that divided one eyebrow, his face might have been pleasant enough if it had not been set in what looked to be a perpetual scowl. "Who the devil is this misshapen midget?" he demanded.

"This is Rufus—your new apprentice."

"*Vraiment?*" Jacques looked me up and down, like a plantation owner considering a purchase at a slave auction. "Well, he is certainly the right size for the job. But can he play chess?"

Maelzel gave a sarcastic smile. "You will soon discover just how well. Can you make up a bed of some sort for him here? I do not want him leaving this room."

"Am I to be a prisoner?" I asked in dismay.

"No, no, of course not. You will be able to go out occasionally, but not alone. It is too risky. Many people in this city know you as a chess player, and if they see you here, they will make the connection."

"But I need to visit my father."

"Your *father*? When we spoke of keeping secrets, you said you had no one to tell."

"I won't say a word to him about this."

"Hmm. Where is he?"

"In debtors' prison."

"Is he indeed?" said Maelzel. "For how long?"

"Until he pays his debts, I suppose. I mean to help him, with what I make here."

"Yes, well, it will not be much—not until I see how well you perform."

"Perform? What am I to do?"

"Jacques will show you. I have other matters to see to."

When Maelzel was gone, Jacques hobbled back to the half-assembled machine. "Well?" he growled impatiently. "Move your hunchbacked bones, *Bébé*."

"My name is Rufus."

"I will call you whatever I choose, and I choose to call you *Bébé*. And I will thank you to keep your mouth shut until I tell you to open it. *Maintenant*." He pointed to a small platform inside the machine. "This is where you sit." I nodded to show that I understood, but Jacques snapped, "Well? *Assieds-toi*! Sit!"

If I show you another of Windisch's engravings, it will help you understand how the interior of the Turk's cabinet was set up. (In this view, the center door has been removed.)

The platform where Jacques ordered me to sit was in that large, relatively open compartment on the right. Attached to one wall was a small chessboard that folded down into my lap. That was the board I actually played on, using a set of miniature chess pieces with pegs on the bottom. The pegs fit snugly into holes in the board; that way, if I bumped the board, the pieces wouldn't go flying.

As you can see, there was a full-sized chessboard on top of the cabinet, with full-sized chessmen. Hanging from the roof of my little compartment was a mechanical arm with a pointer on it. This was connected to the Turk's left arm (when his arm was actually in place) by a complicated system of levers and wires. It worked in much the same way a pantograph does—you know, those devices that let you reproduce a drawing in a larger or smaller size.

When I placed the pointer on a particular square of the small chessboard, it moved the Turk's hand to that same square on the big board. If I twisted the end of the pointer, it made the Turk's jointed fingers open and close, so that I could actually pick up the big chess pieces and move them around—well, not at first, of course. It took me some time to master that skill.

Alongside the pantograph-like arm were several levers. When the Turk was fully assembled, one lever moved his eyes; another moved his head. The third operated a bellows that pumped air through a mechanical voice box, enabling him to speak a few essential words.

As I said, people had been trying for decades to find out the Turk's secret, and in a matter of a few moments it had been revealed to me, just as I'm revealing it to you. "I am sure," said Jacques, "that Maelzel warned you to say nothing about this to anyone." I nodded. "Good. Make sure you heed that warning. If you do not . . . well, I am not sure what he will do. But I know what *I* will do." Next to him stood a sturdy wooden bench with woodworking tools lined up in neat rows. He selected a carving knife with a wicked curved blade and shook it like an admonishing finger, a few inches from my face. "I will split you down the middle like a stick of balsa wood."

For the second time that day, I experienced that strange and slightly sickening sensation—fear.

By the way, there's no need to worry about the fact that you, too, are now privy to the Turk's secret. You may reveal it to whomever you like. As you will discover in due time, it no longer matters.

CHAPTER 6

I WAS EAGER TO TRY OPERATING THE TURK, but of course I couldn't, since his chess-playing arm was out of commission. For the moment, all I could do was ask questions. "If I'm controlling the machine, what are all the gears and springs for?"

"To mislead the audience. Also, the noise they make covers up your farts and sneezes."

"But if the audience can see the clockwork, why can't they see me—" I broke off as one of Jacques's large-knuckled hands struck me alongside the head.

"I will tell you what you need to know, when you need to know it. In the meantime, shut your face." He snatched up a twist of chewing tobacco and bit off a hunk large enough to choke a horse. "Now get out of muffled by the wad of tobacco.

...d was sit in that room,
... the machine and playing
... amputated arm was reattached
...ly, he turned his attention and his
...k's voice box. Twice a day he crossed
...n his strange, hobbling gait and had
...or his supper at the Oyster Cellar, while I
...ut up in the workshop. Each time, he brought
...some food for me; though it was always cold
...d usually greasy, I was grateful enough to have it.

I slept in that same room, on a sack full of wood shavings. I didn't even leave to use the privy, for we had an indoor earth closet; once a week or so, the night soil men came by and collected the contents.

It didn't matter much to me that my life was limited to a single room. Thanks to my poor health, I had spent much of my childhood confined to my bedroom, so in a way this felt reassuring, safe. I only wished that I had better company, and a few books to read. Of course I also wished to visit my father, to see how he was faring, to let him know that I was all right.

Another thing I would have liked was to air the place out; the room was stuffy, usually hot, and always smelly—though Jacques washed himself regularly, he

also sweated copiously. But we weren't allo
the room's single window for fear some cu
erby might spy on us and learn the Turk's
long as the sash was closed, no one could se
the panes were made of frosted glass.

The one feature of the room that bothere
most, though, was the Turk's disembodied head.
on a high shelf, still wearing its turban. Though I
my best to ignore it, I fancied I could feel those dai
eyes staring at me. Sometimes they challenged me to
meet their gaze; other times they seemed to accuse
me of something, though I didn't know what. I often
woke in the night and peered at the shelf, thinking
that perhaps the eyes would be closed in sleep, but
they never were. In the little light that came from the
streetlamps, I could see the whites glowing like two
miniature moons, half eclipsed by the dark orbs of the
pupils.

Once, when I was feeling feverish—as I sometimes
did, for no good reason—I heard the head speaking to
me. The words were slurred and almost inaudible, but
I thought he was asking why the gift of life was wasted
on someone as frail and useless as I was, when he
clearly deserved it more.

I was most aware of the head when I was left alone
with it. One day while Jacques was at dinner, I climbed
onto a chair and carefully draped a clean rag over the

thing. "There," I murmured. "That's better." Then, for some reason, I added, "I'm sorry." There was no reply.

The head couldn't actually speak, of course; in fact, Jacques was still struggling to get the voice box in the neck to say a few words. In between bouts of cursing he revealed that, when the Turk put an opponent's king in check, he was supposed say *"Échec,"*; when he checkmated the other player, he said, *"Échec et mat."* But there was something amiss in the artificial vocal cords, and it came out sounding more like "A sheep say baa"—a phrase that I couldn't imagine having much use for.

Jacques was so obsessed with restoring the voice that he completely ignored me and the job I'd been hired to do. Finally I decided that I might as well educate myself, as I had always done. The next time I was left alone, I set up the board, climbed inside the machine, and tried my hand—or rather the Turk's hand—at moving the pieces about. At first, I was hopelessly inept. I can't tell you how many times I failed to lift the hand high enough and ended up strewing the chessmen all about the room. But after a few days, I began to develop a feel for it.

I still had very little idea what was expected of me. I assumed that at some point I'd be playing against another person. But if I couldn't see the big chessboard, how would I know what moves my opponent was making? Jacques hadn't bothered to explain this. As I got more adept at moving the chess pieces, though, the answer became obvious.

Beneath each square of the main board was a little pin with a thin metal ring on it. Each chess piece had a magnet in the base; when I picked up a piece, the magnet let go of the metal ring, and it dropped; when I set the piece down again, the magnet lifted up the metal ring on that square.

Von Kempelen, the Turk's inventor, had clearly been a clever fellow. I wanted to know more about him, and about how the machine had come into Maelzel's hands; I wanted to know who had operated it before me, and who I was to play against and when, and so many other things, but I didn't care to risk Jacques's wrath—especially after what occurred about a week into my apprenticeship.

At some small hour of the night, my already fitful sleep was disturbed by the sounds of someone struggling and crying out. In my stuporous state I imagined that it was the Turk's head, protesting the fact that I'd covered him up with a cloth. Then I realized the clamor was coming from Jacques's bed. Thinking that he must be ill or in pain, I rose and shuffled across the room, banging into unseen objects on my way.

Jacques was tangled up in his blanket and thrashing about as though assailed by demons. *"Non! Non!"* he called out, in a voice as tortured and indistinct as the Turk's. *"Laissez-moi tranquille, je vous en prie!"* Not knowing what else to do, I bent down and, catching hold of his shirtsleeve, shook it a little. There was no response. I shook it harder. His eyes sprang open and the look in them was wild, desperate; one huge hand shot out and seized me by the throat.

I tried to shout in protest, but his grip was so tight that I couldn't breathe. Frantically, I flailed at his arm with my fists; it had no effect at all. Just as I was on the verge of passing out, he seemed to come fully awake at last, and to realize what he was doing. He released me and I sagged to the floor, gasping.

Jacques swung his legs awkwardly over the edge of the bed and sat up, holding his head in both hands. *"Idiote!"* he growled. "Never do that again!"

In a choked voice, I said, "I—I was only—"

"Do not explain! And do not ask any questions! Just go back to bed. And in the future, when I am asleep do *not* come near me, no matter what I may do or say. *Compris?*"

A few nights later, his cries and struggles woke me again. I lay listening, wondering what sort of torments he was suffering, and why, until at last he grew quiet again.

After nearly two weeks of being cooped up with Jacques and the Turk, I was once again rescued—temporarily—by the amiable Monsieur Mulhouse. He convinced Maelzel that, if I was to stay in good health—as good as my health ever got, anyway—I needed fresh air and exercise. Maelzel reluctantly agreed to let me out, but only at night. No one was to see me coming and going from the hall, lest they guess what we were up to.

The streets were dark, except for the widely spaced coal-gas lamps, and deserted except for a drunk making his unsteady way home. "I imagine you would like to visit your father," said Mulhouse.

"Oh, yes! Will you take me?"

"*Oui*. But you must not let Maelzel know. I think he would prefer to keep you two apart. He likes his minions to have no loyalty to anyone but himself."

"Are you his minion?"

"I was. Until he no longer had any use for me."

"What did you do?"

"What was my job, you mean? Or what did I do to make him dismiss me?"

"Both."

Mulhouse took his time in replying. "I am so accustomed to keeping it a secret, it is difficult for me to say. But I suppose I may tell you. I operated the Turk."

"Really? How did you fit inside? It's close quarters, even for me."

As we passed beneath a streetlamp, I saw a pained

smile on the Frenchman's face—or perhaps it was a wince. "It was not easy. By the end of even the shortest game, I was stiff and aching all over. I don't know how I bore it as long as I did."

"When did you begin?"

He gave me a look of mock exasperation. "You ask many questions, Rufus."

"No one else will tell me anything."

"I am astonished. I supposed that you would have long, heartfelt conversations with Jacques nearly every day."

I laughed weakly. "No. And I seldom see Maelzel."

"He gives far more attention to his machines than to his human workers. Now, what did you ask me? Ah, yes, when I took over the Turk." Mulhouse sighed, as if it wearied him even to think about it. The sigh turned into a cough. He dug out his lozenges and let one soothe his throat as he spoke.

"Perhaps thirty years ago, Maelzel bought the machine from its inventor and restored it. It quickly became the main attraction in his exhibition of automata and dioramas. Around 1820, he brought his show to Paris. I was still young enough to think that it was my destiny to become the best chess player in Europe. The fact that dozens of others had played the Turk and lost did not worry me; I was confident that I could defeat a clockwork man.

"Imagine my shame when he checkmated me in

twelve moves. I knew there had to be a human player concealed inside; my pride would not let me think otherwise. But another six years passed before I found out for certain.

"A letter was delivered to me at the Café de la Régence, where I was the resident chess master. It was from Maelzel. He was touring America, he said, and he offered me a good deal of money to demonstrate the Turk for audiences in Boston and New York. It was not until after I arrived that he revealed the truth: I would be *operating* the Turk."

"What happened to his usual operator?" I asked. The Frenchman didn't reply at once. When we passed beneath another gaslight, I saw that his expression had turned grim. "Monsieur Mulhouse?"

He coughed again, but it didn't seem due to an irritation so much as to nervousness or a reluctance to answer. At last he said, "Well, the fact is, no one quite knows what became of her."

"Her?"

"A young woman named Mademoiselle Bouvier— not an expert player, I gather, but good enough for Maelzel's purposes. He hired her in France and brought her to America with him. But shortly after they arrived, she disappeared."

"She quit, you mean?"

"No. I mean she simply disappeared. No one has seen her since."

"Did you ask Maelzel about her?"

"Of course."

"And . . . ?"

"He told me to mind my own business and to never mention the woman's name again. I can think of only two reasons why he would despise her so much. One is that he made advances toward her, and she rejected him. The other is that she sold him out."

"Sold him out?"

"Revealed the Turk's secret. To some rival, perhaps, or to a newspaper. If she did, nothing came of it. Still, I can't help wondering . . ."

"What?"

"Well, whether Maelzel had something to do with her disappearance."

"You mean . . . ?" I drew a hand across my throat.

"I don't know. All I know is that, when it comes to business matters, he can be ruthless."

"But surely not *that* ruthless."

"To be honest, I would put nothing past him. Or Jacques, for that matter. I don't know much about the fellow, and I don't care to, but in France there were rumors that he killed a man; some say it was the reason he fled to America."

I shivered as I thought of Jacques waving that carving knife in my face.

"Are you cold?" asked Mulhouse. "Here." He draped his jacket over my thin shoulders.

"Thank you." We walked on in silence for a time, then I said, "Why did you stop operating the Turk? Because it was too cramped?"

"Partly. But also because of this cough of mine—a result of being shut up in that infernal cabinet for so long, with a burning candle next to me. It became such a problem that Maelzel feared the audience would hear me, and he let me go."

"You're not worried that you'll disappear? Like Mademoiselle Bouvier?"

"*Non*. I believe he trusts me to keep his secret." He leaned in closer to me and said softly, "Speaking of secrets, you must not let Maelzel know how much I've told you. He would be angry."

"Why did you tell me, then?"

"Because. Because I put you in this position; it is only right that I warn you of the risks involved."

"It's a bit late for that, isn't it?"

He shrugged apologetically. "*Oui*, I suppose it is." He patted my shoulder. "But not to worry; you're perfectly safe as long you do not make the mistake of telling anyone about the Turk. And in any case, I'll be around to make certain that nothing happens to you."

Somehow, I didn't find his reassurances very comforting. A chill went through me, but not the sort I was used to. This was not a symptom of ague; it was the sickening feeling of having fallen into dangerous, dark waters that were over my head. I shivered and pulled the jacket close around me.

Regular visiting hours at the prison were long past, but when Mulhouse slipped a banknote into the keeper's hand he readily let us into the debtors' apartment. My father was sitting on the stone floor of his cell with his blankets wrapped about him; he had a small notebook propped on his knees and was making entries in his meticulous handwriting by the light of an almost-extinct candle. His cellmates were asleep, two of them on stained straw mattresses. Softly, I called, "Father?"

He looked up muzzily, like a man waking from a dream. When he saw me, his face brightened. "Rufus!" One of the sleepers stirred and grumbled, "Be quiet, would you?" My father whispered "Sorry" and, rising stiffly, ushered us into the hallway. He embraced me carefully, as he always did, as though fearful of crushing my slight frame. "I'm so pleased to see you. I've been wondering how you were getting along. Is Mrs. Runnymead looking after you?"

"I'm not at the boardinghouse, Father. Monsieur Mulhouse got me a job with—with—" I remembered my promise to Maelzel, that I would reveal nothing to anyone. For the first time in my life, I had to lie to my father, and I couldn't quite manage it.

"With a firm that constructs dioramas and automata," Mulhouse finished smoothly.

"Really?" said my father, with obvious delight. "Like those at Peale's Museum?" Peale's, I should explain, was a popular attraction at the time. Billed as "An Encyclopedia of God's Wondrous Creation," it contained a dizzying display of exhibits and curiosities, from mammoth bones and Egyptian mummies to Siamese twins and a cow with five legs and two tails.

"Exactly," said Mulhouse. "Rufus is apprenticing to one of the craftsmen."

"Indeed! I always imagined he might become a schoolmaster one day, but this is far more interesting!" He grabbed Mulhouse's hand and shook it energetically. "Thank you for helping my son. As you see, I'm not in a position to do much for him at the moment. Do they provide him with room and board?"

"He sleeps on the premises. And I suppose they feed you well, don't they, Rufus?"

"Oh, yes," I lied. "I'm to receive wages, too. When I do, I'll pay the keeper to get you a bed and some better food, Father."

He smiled and patted my arm gingerly. "Thank you,

my boy, but it's really not necessary. I'd rather you kept the money for yourself. I'm doing well enough. I'm as strong as Brazilian tea. It's you I worry about. You're like your mother, I fear—too fragile for this harsh world. You're a good boy, Rufus, but Nature cares nothing for goodness. It's the most fit who are most likely to survive." He paused, and gave a sheepish laugh. "Sorry, I sound as though I'm promoting *The Development of Species*, don't I?" He held up the notebook in which he'd been writing. "If I keep at it, I'll have a second volume soon. You know, if you do have a few extra pennies sometime, you might just bring me some writing paper. It keeps my mind occupied."

As the keeper showed us out, Mulhouse handed the man several more banknotes. "Will you see to it that the Reverend Goodspeed is given a bed and regular meals? I shall come back in a week or so; if everything is satisfactory, you will have my gratitude—about a dollar's worth of it, I should imagine."

When we were alone on the dark streets again, Mulhouse said, "Your father seems a decent man. I wish I could pay his creditors and have him released. But, to put it as delicately as possible, I find myself financially embarrassed. Since I left Maelzel's employ, all I have is the little I make tutoring players at the Chess Club."

"Thank you for giving that money to the keeper."

"You are welcome." He coughed and reached for his lozenges again. "Actually, I suppose that, in some sense, the money was yours, anyway."

"What do you mean?"

"Well," he said, awkwardly, "it was what remained of the fee that Maelzel had promised me if I would find a new chess player for him."

So, though I had not yet seen a cent, Mulhouse had been paid for bringing me in, like a bounty hunter who is rewarded for capturing runaway slaves. But I am being overly dramatic. My situation, of course, was far better than that of even the most fortunate slave. Still, I didn't like the notion that I was some sort of commodity.

When I took the job, I had felt a certain amount of pride; I saw myself as someone who possessed a valuable skill and, like any good craftsman or artist, could use that skill to earn a living for himself. I was beginning to see that, in reality, I was no more than a curiosity that could be bought and sold and put on display, like the Feejee Mermaid or the Turk.

CHAPTER

7

AFTER CURSING AND POKING AT THE voice box for another two days, Jacques finally got it to speak proper French. When the still headless Turk clearly said the words *"Échec et mat,"* Jacques thrust his muscular arms into the air and roared, *"Enfin! J'ai triomphe!"* Then he burst into a horrible, rasping rendition of "La Marseillaise": *"Allons, enfants de la Patrie, Le jour de gloire est arrivé!"* I couldn't help laughing, but he seemed not to mind.

"Maintenant," he said, "we may give Otso back his head." He glanced at the high shelf where the head sat and seemed to notice for the first time the rag I'd draped over it. He turned to glare accusingly at me, the way the head glared at me before I covered it.

I shrugged. "I thought you'd want to keep the dust off it."

"Hmm. *Eh, bien*, fetch it for me, then. And be very, *very* careful, *Bébé*; if you damage it, I will have *your* head."

As I climbed onto the chair, I was trembling, for two very different reasons: I was afraid of dropping the head, of course; as I've said, I was not at all strong. But at the same time I was reluctant to take hold of it; I think I half expected it to squirm in protest, perhaps even bite me.

The thing was heavier than I'd imagined, but somehow I managed to lift it down and carry it to Jacques unscathed. He handed me the cloth, which I used to wipe my sweating palms. In an unsteady voice, I said, "Why do you call him Otso?"

Jacques scowled at me again. He had the wax head in both hands, so there was no way he could strike me; still, I shrank back. "Why do *you* insist on speaking," he said, "when I have told you to keep your *grande gueule* shut?" He turned his attention to the task of attaching the Turk's head to his neck and splicing the thin wires that controlled the various movements. I stood by, like a surgeon's apprentice, ready to hand him each tool when he called for it.

As he performed the delicate surgery, his tongue protruded from the side of his mouth, like that of a child making a drawing. The curses that usually punctuated his work were almost absent. He seemed so absorbed in what he was doing that it surprised me when he muttered, "The original Otso was a companion of mine, back when I was young and stupid and wanted to be a soldier." He paused and gazed into the distance for a moment. "In the Basque language, the name Otso means *wolf*."

"What became of him?"

"What usually becomes of soldiers? He died, of course."

"In battle?"

For a long moment, Jacques made no reply. At last he gave a barely perceptible nod. "*Oui*. In my arms. Bravely, with a smile on his face." He stopped working and rubbed his palms over his eyes as though the close work had strained them. Then he gruffly called out, "*Pinces*."

"Is that pliers?"

"Yes, yes, pliers!" Shoving me out of the way, he snatched them up himself. "*Imbécile*."

When at last the Turk was whole again, Jacques said, "*Et voilà*. Now I will show you how to operate the machine."

Without thinking, I said, "I can do it already. I've been practicing."

He struck me across the cheek with one rough

hand. I staggered backward and the corner of the cabinet rammed into my ribs. "*Petite sotte!* You might have damaged it!"

"But I didn't—"

His hand closed around one of my thin wrists and twisted it. "*Ça suffit!* This is *my* workshop, and *I* make the rules, and the rules are: You will do things only when I tell you to do them, and you will . . . ?" He looked at me expectantly. When I said nothing, he shook me and repeated, "And you will . . . ?"

"I will speak only when you tell me to," I said, in a strained voice. When he released me, I said under my breath, "Just like the Turk."

If he heard this, he ignored it. "*Eh, bien*, now that you understand, let me see what you can do."

I climbed inside the machine, favoring my bruised ribs. I folded down the little chessboard and reached for the pointer, but Jacques again gripped my arm painfully; inflicting pain seemed to be the only way he knew to communicate.

"*Mais écoutes,*" he said. "Do not try force the mechanism. Move it slowly and carefully. Remember that the Turk is sixty-five years old; some of his joints are a little stiff."

I said nothing; I only nodded mechanically, like a clockwork boy.

If Jacques was pleased by my skill, he didn't let on—

unless his way of showing approval was to refrain from hitting me when I clumsily knocked over a piece. In the days that followed, he continued to work on the automaton, tinkering with the gears, fitting brass hinges on the doors and installing them, touching up Otso's wax face—I had come to think of the Turk as Otso, and to see something a little wolf-like in his features.

Apparently satisfied that I could be careful, Jacques put me to work sanding and oiling the maple cabinet, which was worn and discolored by decades of use. But each afternoon I switched from the outside of the cabinet to the inside.

When I entered that felt-lined box, I felt a bit like Varney the Vampire climbing into his coffin. And in truth, being closed up in the cabinet was a good deal like being in a coffin—not that I've ever been in one. It was a little larger, I suppose, but the clockwork mechanism took up a good third of the space; there was barely enough left over for my small frame.

In order to see the miniature chessboard properly, I had to sit in an awkward position, with my knees drawn up and my head tilted forward. For a change, my rounded back actually worked in my favor. Still, after an hour or two, the cramped quarters took their toll on me.

If we kept the front and rear doors of the cabinet open, I got enough illumination from the window, but with the doors closed the interior was almost totally dark; I had to light a wax candle in order to see. I soon understood how Mulhouse had contracted his cough. The Turk's hollow torso was designed to serve as a sort of chimney through which the candle's heat and smoke could escape, but it worked imperfectly at best; if I kept the candle lit for very long, my eyes and throat began to sting.

Jacques wasn't much of a chess player, but he knew enough about the game to be my sparring partner, as it were. Once I got good at working the mechanical arm, I started experimenting with the levers that controlled the head and the eyes and the voice box. I learned that when Jacques made a foolish or illegal move—as he often did—I could get Otso to roll his eyes and shake his head, as though he couldn't believe anyone would be so dense. Even through the layers of felt and maple, I could hear Jacques cursing.

Late one afternoon, as I was preparing to trounce the poor fellow yet again, his game seemed to suddenly improve. He was obviously using a strategy, instead of just plodding along one move at a time. I began to think that maybe he'd been conning me all this time, pretending to be a rank beginner when in fact he knew his way around a chessboard.

I managed to prevail, but only barely, and with more than the usual amount of effort. I blew out the

candle and sat there, waiting. Jacques had made it very clear that I was not to budge until he rapped on the cabinet. After a minute or two, the rear door opened and Jacques peered in. "Why are just *sitting* there?"

"You told me not to move until I got the signal."

"Oh." Grudgingly, he knocked on the cabinet in the same three-three-two pattern Mulhouse had used on the day I arrived. When I emerged, blinking in the daylight, I found Maelzel bent over the board, examining the position of the pieces. So he, not Jacques, had been my opponent for most of the game.

"Very clever," he said, but not to me. He spoke to Jacques instead, as though I weren't there. "The boy is doing well."

Jacques spat out a stream of tobacco juice and gave a brusque nod. "Well enough."

Maelzel looked me over critically. "He looks a bit thin and pale to me."

"He was thin and pale when he came here."

"All the same, we want to keep him healthy. Is he getting enough to eat?"

"He never complains."

"Hmm. And does he complain when you hit him?"

"*Non.* That is—I mean—"

"I know you and your temper, Jacques. Do not strike him too hard. We do not want to damage his organ of Locality." He glanced at the chessboard again. "He is making good progress. We will bring in Mulhouse tomorrow, to show him the Knight's Tour." Maelzel headed for the door.

Ignoring Jacques's rule, I called after him, "I can do the Knight's Tour already."

Now, if you're not an avid chess player, you may not know about the Knight's Tour. It's fairly simple to explain. You see, it's a sort of puzzle, or challenge. You start out with the knight on any square, then move it around the board in its usual pattern. The object is to land on each of the sixty-four squares once, and *only* once. That may sound easy enough, but I assure you it's not. I struggled with it for several days before I found a solution. Of course, I *was* only seven at the time.

Maelzel turned back and, for the first time, spoke to me directly. "From any square on the board?"

"Yes."

"Show me," he said. I began clearing the big board, but he stopped me. "No, no. From *inside* the cabinet."

I shrugged. "All right." I'd never tried a Knight's Tour using the Turk, so I made a few false starts. But on the fourth try, I performed the feat flawlessly—and then I sat, dutifully waiting, until I got the signal to emerge.

Maelzel was smiling with self-satisfaction, like a

man who has gotten more than he bargained for in a business deal. "Who taught you to do that?"

"No one. I taught myself."

He turned to Jacques. "It looks as if the boy will be ready sooner than we thought."

"Ready for what?" I asked.

"Why, to perform in public."

"Where?"

The man's smile faded. "You ask far too many questions. Let me see your head." As he had done at our first meeting, he clamped his fingers on my skull and examined it roughly. "Ah, yes, I see now that your organ of Causality is much larger than normal. I missed that before."

"Causality?" I said.

"The desire to know." He probed the spot that he had identified before as the seat of Cautiousness. "Hmm. Causality and Caution. A curious combination. But I like curiosities. And I like curious people; without them, I would be out of business. Very well. You wish to know where you will be performing, and I shall show you. Come."

CHAPTER

8

THE HUGE OUTER SHOP WAS EMPTY OF people. Ensconced in my smaller workroom, I had little sense of time, only an awareness of dark and light. Clearly it was late in the day and the workers had gone home.

Maelzel led me through a heavy door and into another vast room that held a variety of mechanical exhibits. Scattered among them were half a dozen people. Only when we were almost on top of one did I realize that it was an automaton, so lifelike did it seem. It was a beautiful woman, sitting at a writing desk with a pen in her hand and a sheet of paper before her; on the paper, in graceful, precise handwriting, were the words, "My Dear Friend, I am able to write these lines to you thanks to the cleverness of my creator, Johann Nepomuk Maelzel."

"I never miss an opportunity to advertise," said Maelzel.

"The automaton wrote that itself? *Herself*?"

"Of course. She is also able to write several short poems and draw two different pictures."

"Really? That's incredible."

"Yes, it is, isn't it? But these—" He led me to a pair of figures who stood perhaps eight or nine inches tall; they wore circus garb and were poised on a thin rope stretched between two miniature trees. "—these are my star performers. They do all the same sorts of acrobatics that a human rope dancer does. They are puppets, of course; if you look closely, you may see the silk threads that move their limbs." The threads, which were nearly invisible, descended from the branches that arched over the dancers' heads. "There is no human operator; it is all mechanical." Maelzel plucked the rope, and the figures sprang an inch or two into the air. "They will not be the stars much longer. When the Turk's resurrection is complete, he will steal the show, as he always has."

"Does the audience believe that he runs by clock-work?"

"People believe what they wish to believe. I do not

try to convince them of anything. I merely display the machine and let them make up their own minds."

"No one has guessed the truth yet?"

Maelzel shrugged dismissively. "Many years ago, long before I owned the Turk, a scoundrel named Racknitz published a booklet, complete with illustrations, explaining his theory of how the famous automaton chess player worked."

"Was he correct?"

"For the most part. But it was not proof; it was only a theory. In any case, his book faded into oblivion long ago, and the Turk still survives. In fact, he is in better shape than ever, thanks to a few improvements. You might even say that he is a whole new species of Turk."

"What sort of improvements?"

"Well, for one thing, he now has a voice. Not to mention a new head. When we were still in France, my operator—who is no longer with us, obviously—knocked over the candle and set the felt on fire. It scorched the Turk's torso and melted his face." He gave me a stern, almost threatening glance. "I trust that *you* will not be so clumsy."

I tried to answer, but my throat seemed suddenly constricted and dry—a reaction to the phrase *no longer with us*, and what it implied. I swallowed hard and managed to say, "No." I wanted to ask whether the operator he mentioned was the mysterious Mademoiselle

Bouvier. If she had damaged the Turk, that might be reason enough for Maelzel to get rid of her—though hardly reason enough to do her in. I didn't ask, of course, for I was supposed to know nothing about the matter.

As we turned to leave, a door at the far end of the hall opened, and two figures entered. One was a youngish, stocky man with curly hair that framed an outsized head, half of which seemed to consist of forehead. Though I knew little about phrenology, I guessed that he would make an ideal subject; there was so much territory to explore. He wore an elegant velvet coat, a silk waistcoat, and a flamboyant striped cravat that blossomed all down his shirtfront.

He was pushing a wheelchair, which held a Negro woman so ancient and shriveled that she might have been a mummy. Her eyes were so clouded by cataracts, they resembled pearls. Their sightless gaze was nearly as unnerving as the Turk's. She seemed as inanimate as the Turk, too; only her claw-like right hand, which had long, curved fingernails, moved jerkily from time to time. I couldn't help wondering whether she was actually a living person, or just an especially well-crafted automaton.

Though she seemed incapable of speech, her caretaker certainly wasn't. His voice was as outsized as his head. "Good evening, Herr Maelzel! I hope business is good!"

"Thank you, Mr. Barnum," said Maelzel. And in case you're wondering, yes, it was the same Mr. Barnum who has since earned fame and fortune by introducing to the world the Feejee Mermaid and Tom Thumb and Jenny Lind, the Swedish Nightingale. "Our box office has declined a little of late," Maelzel went on, "but I expect that to change once the Turk is back in action. I see that you are drawing good crowds, sir."

"I should say I am! In the few months that I have had her, Mrs. Heth's fame has spread far and wide! We recently received an offer to appear at Niblo's Garden in New York!"

I approached the figure in the wheelchair, curious as always, but careful to keep out of range of that claw-like hand. "What does she do?" I asked.

"Do? She doesn't need to *do* anything!"

"Then why do people pay to see her?"

Mr. Barnum gave a hearty laugh. "Who is this lad, Herr Maelzel? Does he always ask so many questions?"

"Yes, unfortunately," said Maelzel. "He is no one, only a street urchin who did not have the price of admission. I felt sorry for him."

"Well, whatever your name is—"

"It's Rufus."

"Well, Rufus, you are looking at a genuine piece of American history! Mrs. Heth was the very nursemaid who coddled and swaddled the Father of Our Country!"

"General Washington?"

"Ah, he knows his history, this one!" said Mr. Barnum sarcastically. "Of course, General Washington!"

I'm sure you're thinking the very same thing I was thinking: George Washington was born in 1732, and this was 1835. "But—but she would have to be well over a hundred years old."

"And a good command of mathematics as well! Yes, my boy, Mrs. Heth has attained the almost Biblical age of eight score and one! And yet her memory is as that of the proverbial elephant!" Mr. Barnum seemed to be speaking not to me, but to some imaginary crowd of curiosity-seekers. "Not only can she can relate in astonishing detail events from the earliest years of the life of our first president, she can sing several traditional hymns!"

Right on cue, the old woman opened her toothless mouth and began to sing, in a throaty and tremulous but surprisingly melodious voice:

"Welcome, sweet day of rest

That saw the Lord arise.

Welcome to this reviving breast

And these rejoicing eyes."

Mr. Barnum gently patted her shriveled shoulder and shouted into her ear, "Not now, dear! Save your strength for the paying customers!" He turned to Maelzel. "I actually came in here for a reason, but I've forgotten what it was! I believe Mrs. Heth's memory is better than mine! Oh, yes! I meant to ask whether you plan to open your exhibition in the evenings!"

"No, I am afraid the attendance does not warrant it. As I said, the Turk's return will change that."

"And when will that be, do you think?"

"Two weeks. Perhaps three."

"I haven't seen the machine at work yet, but I understand it's quite astounding!" Mr. Barnum leaned in closer and said in a voice that anyone else would have considered loud, but that I suppose he considered subdued, "I hear its movements are controlled by magnetic force. Is that true?"

Maelzel gave him a rather peevish smile. "Is it true that Mrs. Heth is one hundred and sixty-one years old?"

Barnum let out another hearty laugh. "Ah, I take your meaning, sir! We all have our trade secrets, eh? Be careful of that boy, though!"

Maelzel frowned. "Why do you say that?"

"Well, it's obvious that he is possessed of a keen and inquiring mind! If you let him hang about for long, he'll ferret out all your secrets! Rufus, my lad, we'll be doing an evening performance! Why don't you come and watch? Tell them Phineas T. Barnum said to let you in at no charge whatsoever!"

When he was gone, Maelzel shook his head. "I am

certain he will make a great success in this business. The public must surely realize that Mrs. Heth is a hoax, yet they still pay money to see her."

"I'd like to see her. He said I wouldn't have to pay."

Maelzel snorted scornfully. "*Ach!* You don't suppose he offered out of the kindness of his heart, do you? He wants to interrogate you, to see whether he may learn anything."

"Why would he think I know anything? You told him I was a street urchin."

"Yes, and he told you that woman was George Washington's nurse. *Nein.* We cannot take any chances. For the time being, you will remain well out of sight."

And so I returned to my hidey-hole. As we passed through Maelzel's office, I eyed the half-dozen books that were strewn about. If I was to be confined to a cell, like my father, a book would be welcome company. I was not exactly bored; I could always play chess inside my mind or inside the Turk. But I did long for a little variety. I spotted a volume titled *Elements of Phrenology.* "May I borrow that book?"

Maelzel's plucked eyebrows rose. "You have an interest in phrenology?"

"I have an interest in everything."

He considered a moment, then handed me the book, which was open to a line drawing of a bald man. His scalp was made up of several dozen various-shaped patches, as though, like Dr. Frankenstein's creation, he'd been pieced together from odd scraps. In the margins, Maelzel had scrawled a number of illegible notes. "Be very sure you do not damage this, or drop food on it, or anything of the sort. I paid nearly three dollars for it."

I was tempted to ask how much he had paid for me, but I didn't. Nor did I ask whether it was permissible to scribble in the margins, as he had.

Between putting a new finish on the cabinet and putting the Turk through his paces, I was busy for most of the daylight hours. I had lost track of the days of the week, or even what month it was, but I believe it must have July or August, and the days were long. Each night, before I fell into an exhausted sleep, I managed to read for half an hour or so by the light of the Turk's candle; Jacques didn't seem to mind my using it, as long as I took it out of the cabinet.

When I was inside the Turk, we nearly always left the doors open. Jacques was afraid that, if we used the candle, I might knock it over and cause another conflagration. "Have you thought of getting a Carcel lamp?" I asked. I had learned that, if I was careful, I could break the silence rule now and again without being struck or told to shut my *grande gueule*.

He stared at me, and for a moment I thought I had

overstepped my bounds. But then he returned to his work without making any reply. A trace of puzzlement in his gaze made me suspect that he had never heard of a Carcel lamp, which was a little odd, since it was a French invention. The lamps weren't widely used in America, but for some reason we'd had one in the library of the Parsonage. "They're a lot safer," I ventured. "And they don't give off as much smoke."

Jacques spat a glob of tobacco juice into the box of sawdust at his feet. "*You* will be a lot safer," he grumbled, "if you do not talk so much." But later that day as he was leaving for the Oyster Cellar, he said grumpily, "What did you call that *maudit* lamp? A parcel?"

"Carcel. *Comme les mots francais* car *et* celle."

He blinked at me in surprise. "*Tu parles francais?*"

"*Un peu.*"

"Why have you never told me this?"

"Because," I said. "You told me to keep my *grande gueule* shut."

One corner of his usually grim mouth twitched and turned up, ever so slightly. If I hadn't known better, I might have taken it for the beginning of a smile.

He was gone for at least two hours. When he returned, he was even more ill-tempered than usual; he seemed to have more trouble walking than usual, too, as if he'd pulled a tendon or turned an ankle. He propped his crutch against the worktable and sank heavily onto his stool. "Don't be expecting any supper," he growled, "for I haven't brought any."

"Why? Have I done something wrong?"

"You sent me on a . . . how do you say? A goose chase? No one has heard of such a thing as a *car-celle* lamp. From now on, you obey the rule: no speaking—in English *or* in French—unless I tell you to. *Compris?*"

Late that night, some noise woke me and I opened my eyes to see Jacques sitting at his worktable. By the light of two candles, he was tinkering with some device or other. At first, I thought it must be one of the Turk's body parts. But then he lifted the thing off the table, and I got a better look at it. It was a wooden leg, fashioned of three separate pieces—a thigh, a calf, a foot. They were held together at the knee and the ankle by some sort of spring mechanism that allowed the joints to move.

As I watched, Jacques pulled up his right trouser leg; for the first time, I realized that there was no limb inside it, only a stump that ended well above where his knee should have been. He fitted the artificial leg onto the end of the stump and fastened it in place with a web strap, then pulled down the trouser leg again. When he slid off the stool, the movement hiked up his left trouser leg a little, revealing that the limb inside it was also made of wood.

How curious, I thought; the man who keeps the Turk's machinery in order is half machine himself. Jacques took a few shuffling steps across the floor, testing whatever repairs he'd made. I quickly closed my eyes; it wouldn't do to let him know that I had been spying on him.

CHAPTER

9

A FEW DAYS LATER, MULHOUSE TURNED up at the workshop. In contrast to his fellow Frenchman, he was even more agreeable and easygoing than usual, but also a bit unfocused, the way our old friend Father Barry used to get when he'd had a glass or two of my father's brandy. "I was supposed to teach you the Knight's Tour," said Mulhouse, "but I understand you taught it to yourself. I trust you were a good teacher. And a good student."

"Shall I show you?" I said eagerly.

Mulhouse laughed. "If you can do it to Maelzel's satisfaction that is all that matters. We will work on endgames, instead." He drew a small morocco-bound book from the pocket of his frock coat and opened it to a drawing of a chessboard with six pieces of each color arranged on it. "There are seventeen endgame positions in this book. Your opponent will have the opportunity to choose any one of them, and also to choose which color he will play."

Now, an endgame, as you may know, is just what the name implies: the final series of moves that decides the outcome of the game—although in fact the outcome is often predetermined by the first few moves. "I won't be playing complete games?"

"No, no. Our audience is made up of ordinary folk, not chess aficionados. They would never have the patience to watch a game that took several hours. These endgames seldom last more than fifteen minutes."

I glanced at several of the drawings. "Who gets first move?"

"You do. That is, the Turk does."

"But that's not fair. In all of these positions, whoever makes the first move is bound to win, unless he does something stupid."

"It is not meant to be fair, Rufus. The purpose is not to prove what a good chess player you are, but to prove what a clever machine the Turk is."

I sighed and nodded glumly. I didn't need reminding that, to Maelzel, I was not a boy with an extraordinary skill; I was only another cog in his machine, another pawn in his game—a game whose object was to make as much money as possible.

Using the chess set from Maelzel's office—which was still lacking a rook—we spent several hours going over the various endgames. When dinnertime came and Jacques had hobbled out of the room, I asked Mulhouse, "What happened to his legs?"

"I am not sure. Like the Turk, Jacques keeps his secrets well. But my friends in France—the same friends who say that he murdered a man—told me that his legs were shattered by a cannonball at the Battle of Trocadero."

"He did say he'd been a soldier." I shook my head sadly. "How awful. Do you suppose he made the wooden ones himself?"

"Perhaps. For all his faults, he is very clever with his hands. According to Maelzel, Jacques once worked for the celebrated Madame Tussaud, sculpting wax figures for her museum."

"Really?" I glanced over my shoulder at the Turk, whose dark eyes were fixed on our chessboard as though following the moves. "Perhaps he fashioned Otso's head, then."

Mulhouse laughed. "Otso?"

"Isn't that what you call him?"

"I have always just called him the Turk."

Our next endgame seemed very familiar to me. I stopped and put a hand to my head, which had begun to ache.

"Is something wrong, Rufus?"

"It just struck me: this is identical to a game I played years ago, against my father. It was the first time I ever beat him." A few moves later, I said, "Have you been to the debtors' prison to check on him?"

Mulhouse hesitated before replying, as though confused by the question. Then he smiled faintly. "*Excuse-moi;* I was searching desperately for a way to avoid being checkmated. Your father? Yes, yes, he is well taken care of—for the moment. We shall have to give the keeper more money soon, though. Apparently one cannot actually *buy* a bed for a prisoner; like the boards at the Chess Club, one only rents them."

"I don't have any money; Maelzel still hasn't paid me."

Mulhouse frowned. "I shall have to speak to him about that." For the first time that afternoon, a cough rose in his throat.

"Is your cough improving?"

"*Pardon?* Oh, no, not really. It is just that I have found a way to keep it under control." From the other pocket of his coat he took a small, tapered glass bottle with a label that read GODFREY'S CORDIAL. He withdrew the cork, swallowed a sip of the dark liquid, and gave a slight sigh of satisfaction.

"I remember Godfrey's Cordial," I said. "When I was three or four and feeling badly, Fiona would give me a spoonful of Godfrey's. I never knew adults took it, too."

"The pharmacist recommended it. I have never trusted patent medicines, but this works. Not only does it calm the cough, it gives one a sense of . . . I don't know . . . well-being, I suppose—as if all is right with the world."

"I remember that feeling." I grinned sheepishly. "Sometimes I only pretended to be in pain, in order to get a dose. But then my father found out, and that was the end of that. Fiona meant well; she didn't realize there was laudanum in it." As a four-year-old, I'd had no idea what laudanum was, of course; it was only after I began to read widely that I discovered it was made from opium. "I wonder," I said wistfully, "what's become of poor Fiona. She was always so kind and good."

"Do you know her family name?"

"Grady. I remember because she used to make a joke of it. It means 'illustrious' or 'grand,' I guess, and she'd laugh and say, 'Sure, and am I not the grandest lady you've ivver seen?'"

"I shall try to find out something about her. As I said before, you just have to ask the right person. How is your new nursemaid treating you?"

"Jacques, you mean? He's been in a sour mood toward me lately."

"*Quelle surprise!*"

"Well, even more than usual. I tried to tell him about Carcel lamps, but he thinks I'm making it up. You've seen them, haven't you? "

"The ones with an oil pump that is run by clockwork? In France, yes. In America, no."

"I thought it would be safer than a candle, and less smoky, but he couldn't find one."

"I shall add that to my list of things to find out about." He clapped the book of endgames shut. "Eh, *bien*. I have had quite enough of these infernal exercises. What do you say we play a real game?"

Perhaps he was trying to boost my spirits, or perhaps the Godfrey's Cordial had made him more careless than usual; whatever the reason, I beat him handily.

In the week that followed, Mulhouse came around nearly every day to work on the endgames with me, but he had nothing to report about my father or Fiona, and just as little concerning Carcel lamps or my chances of being paid. One thing he had done was to convince Maelzel that I was ready to make my public debut.

Though I was responsible for operating the Turk, Maelzel was the one running the show. He insisted on rehearsing the act over and over until every detail, no matter how small or insignificant, was exactly the way he wanted it. Perhaps the most crucial moment was at the very beginning, when Maelzel opened the doors of the cabinet to show the audience that there was no dwarf or trained monkey inside, only that impressive array of gears and springs and levers.

You probably assume that I wasn't in the cabinet yet, otherwise the audience would notice me, right? Not at all. You see, the shelf where I perched was on tracks, so that I could slide it forward and back. When Maelzel opened the two doors on the right, I slid all the way to the left. My body was concealed by that maze of machinery, and my legs were hidden by a drawer in the bottom of the cabinet. When he closed those doors and opened the one on the left, I slid forward, behind the first two doors, and crunched myself up so tightly I could scarcely breathe.

Though Maelzel demanded perfection, he also knew that, no matter how diligently we practiced, occasionally something was bound to go wrong, and he had made provisions for that. On the rear wall was a brass disk with numbers engraved on it. If I had a problem, I could turn it, like the combination lock on a safe, to a specific number that indicated what the trouble was. Let's say I dropped one of the miniature chess pieces; I'd turn the dial to the number 6. If the candle went out, it was a number 4. If my shirtsleeve got caught in the gears—well, I just had to tear it loose.

Obviously, I kept as quiet as I could, but if I couldn't

help making a noise—ripping my shirtsleeve, for example, or sneezing—I could cover it up by turning a small crank that produced a loud ratcheting sound. Of course the audience thought it just was the machinery at work.

Following a week of intensive practice in the workshop, we wheeled the Turk into the main hall; each evening, after the exhibit closed, we spent several hours rehearsing every move we would make during an actual performance. Initially, the Turk would be concealed behind a heavy curtain. "Once you are inside," said Maelzel, "I will roll the machine over to this spot. I will stretch a rope across *here*, to keep the audience from getting too close. There will be a table *here*, where your opponent will sit."

"He won't play on the Turk's chessboard?"

Maelzel shook his head emphatically. "That would be far too risky. He might hear you, or he might damage the mechanism somehow. No, he will have a board of his own. I will go back and forth between the players, making your moves on his board, and his moves on yours. When the game is over, I will roll the Turk behind the curtain again and give you the all-clear signal."

I have always considered myself a careful person, but after half a dozen practices I felt pretty confident. Not Maelzel. When we had chalked up twenty run-throughs, I began to wonder whether he'd *ever* consider us ready for a public performance.

To make sure I had no idle time, Jacques put me to work sanding the chessmen and finishing them with a special gritty lacquer that made them easier for Otso's fingers to grasp. One morning, while we were busy with that task, Maelzel strode into the workshop and said matter-of-factly, "I have placed a placard out front, announcing that on Tuesday next the famous Turk will again take on all challengers." Then he strode out.

"What day is today?" I asked, forgetting Jacques's rule once again.

"Friday," he said. For a time, we sanded in silence. Then Jacques glanced at me with his usual scowl. "You do not seem worried."

I shrugged. "There's not much to worry about. I won't even be playing complete games, just endgames that are designed to let me win."

"I did not mean about winning or losing."

"What, then?"

"It is the small mistakes you should worry about. The ones that tell the audience there is a person inside the machine."

"I'll be careful."

He gave a skeptical grunt. "*Alors, Bébé*; you had better be."

"Why do you call me that?"

"You are asking too many questions again."

"Sorry. But why?"

Jacques gave an exasperated sigh. "*Bébé* was a famous hunchbacked dwarf. The king of Poland bought the boy from his parents and gave him to the queen as a birthday present. I saw his skeleton once, at the Musée de l'Homme. It's about three feet tall. And he was fully grown."

"What happened to him?"

"He did something stupid; I forget what. The king had him beaten. He died not long after that."

"The king?"

"No," said Jacques. "The hunchback."

CHAPTER

10

AFTER JACQUES'S WARNING, I DID BEGIN to worry; despite the long days of work and rehearsal that wore out my weak body, I had trouble falling asleep at night. To occupy my mind, I sat up reading the phrenology text by candlelight until the book fell from my hands.

Though phrenology has lately fallen out of favor, for several decades it was considered a serious science. As you may know, it's based on the premise that our personalities are controlled by specific areas in the brain. Let's say that, like me, you have an insatiable curiosity; the part of the brain devoted to curiosity—or Causality, as it's called—will be larger than normal, and that part of your skull will protrude a little, to make room.

I spent a lot of time feeling my skull to see where

the bumps were. There's no bump specifically for Chess, but there is one for Ability to Pattern, and mine seemed pretty sizable. Of course, so did the bump for Matrimony, and I didn't have the slightest desire to get married.

One odd thing about the system is that it deals mostly with desirable traits, such as Hope and Spirituality and Harmony. There don't seem to be many bumps for the despicable parts of human nature. There's one for Acquisitiveness and one for Combativeness, but nothing for Murderousness or Ill-Temperedness. I suppose the theory is that, if you're nasty, it's not because you have *too much* of a thing, such as Ill Temper; it's because you're *lacking* something, such as Agreeableness. So those areas are sort of sunken in.

I would have liked to poke around a bit on Jacques's skull; the organ of Agreeableness must have been severely shriveled. And Maelzel's organ of Acquisitiveness was undoubtedly huge. But I suspected they would not be very willing subjects. Otso, on the other hand, wasn't likely to mind very much.

For the past two weeks or so, the Turk had been exiled to the exhibition hall, which certainly suited me; I no longer woke in the night to find his eyes glaring at me or his voice speaking to me. In the evenings, Maelzel often left me there alone with him, so I could practice manipulating the chess pieces. And sometimes

I did practice, but other times I wandered through the hall, examining the other exhibits. Even more fascinating to me than the automata were the dioramas, especially the one that depicted the 1812 burning of Moscow.

I never got to see the display all lit up, with music playing and fake flames fluttering from the windows and miniature people in motion, fleeing the conflagration. But even without light or music or movement, the scene was eerily life-like. Really, I think that seeing it in the dim light from the Argand oil lamp overhead gave it even more semblance of reality. Since I couldn't see the brushstrokes or the marks of the carving knife or the ends of wires sticking out, the figures seemed organic, like some new species specially bred to be small in size. It was easy to imagine that the tiny townfolk themselves, and not Maelzel's craftsmen, had built those little buildings and wagons and raised those little horses, including the rearing white steed on which Napoleon sat brandishing his sword.

I was tempted to remove the Little Corporal's bicorne hat and feel his skull to see whether he had a bump indicating an excess of Ambition, but I would have needed smaller fingers. I returned to where the Turk sat staring at me, waiting for me to animate him. "You'd like to be phrenologized, wouldn't you, Otso?" He didn't say yes, but he didn't say no, either.

Part of me dreaded touching the head, but a larger part of me was curious to see what I would find. I carefully removed the turban and set it aside. The only hair Otso possessed was his drooping mustache, which was made of actual human hair, pressed into the wax. Since the top of his head was entirely covered by the turban, he had no need for tresses. "This won't hurt a bit," I said, as much for my own benefit as for his.

Gingerly, I placed the tips of my fingers against his skull. The wax felt warmer than I expected, and more yielding to the touch—almost like human skin. My hands trembled slightly as I moved them about, searching for telltale bumps. "Let me see. Ah. Obviously you have high Self-Esteem. And . . . a Love of Home. A strong capacity for Friendship. And for Fun. You actually seem to be quite a likable fellow, Otso. Except . . ." My fingers found a protuberance just above the ear. "Sorry, I'm not quite sure what that represents." I concentrated on my mental picture of the phrenology chart. "Oh. Now I remember. Destructiveness." I wanted to stop, to take my fingers away, but they had become adhered to the wax. I felt Otso's head move slightly under my hands, as though he were trying to shake me off, but I couldn't seem to let go.

"What do you think you are doing?" demanded a hoarse voice that might have been the Turk's. Then I heard the sound of heavy feet shuffling across the floor of the hall. My hands unstuck themselves, and I managed to cram the turban back on Otso's head a moment before a rough hand seized my arm. "I asked what you are doing!"

"I—ah—it seemed to me the Turk's head was wobbling a little. I was just checking, that's all."

"That is *my* job!" shouted Jacques. "If you think there is a problem, you ask *me*!" He cuffed me alongside the head, right where my organ of Secretiveness lay. "You are never to place your hands on the Turk's head, *compris*? The heat from them could soften the wax!" His anger spent, he growled, "Now, get inside, *Bébé*, and do what you are paid to do."

There was no use pointing out that I hadn't, in fact, been paid at all. A few days before, when Maelzel seemed in an unusually good mood, I had found the courage to mention it to him, but he only said what he always said: "First, we shall see how well you perform."

Tuesday arrived at last, and with it my chance to prove myself. First on the program was the Mechanical Trumpeter, who played several marches, accompanied by his creator on the piano. Then came the Slack Rope Dancers and, for the grand finale, the first appearance in over three months by the Celebrated Chess-Playing Turk.

The show began at two. Before Maelzel opened the hall to the public, I secreted myself behind the curtain, next to the Turk, until it was time to climb into the cabinet; any noise I made was masked by the audience's enthusiastic applause for the Slack Rope Dancers. After a few minutes, the cabinet lurched, throwing me off balance; I nearly fell out the rear door before I caught hold of the platform and righted myself.

I could see nothing at all, inside the machine or outside it, but we had rehearsed so many times that I knew exactly what was going on. Maelzel was rolling me and Otso to a spot about ten feet from the audience, who stood behind a velvet rope. For exactly a minute and a half, he delivered his spiel about how the Turk had withstood the finest players of Europe and America and excited universal admiration.

When I heard his key turning in the lock, I slid my seat carefully backward and closed my eyes so the light wouldn't blind me. Through the open doors, I heard his voice: "As you may see for yourselves, ladies and gentlemen, this side of the cabinet is entirely empty except for a few levers and dials that are necessary for the proper functioning of the machine. And now—" As soon as the doors swung shut, I slid forward into my fetal position. The left-hand door opened. "—that there is nothing behind this door but the Turk's intricate and ingenious clockwork mechanism. Once I have wound that up, we may begin."

While he inserted a crank and noisily wound the

mainspring, I opened a small cavity in the Turk's abdomen and lit the candle, then pulled the folding chessboard down onto my knees. For the next several minutes, I knew, Maelzel would be conferring with someone from the audience, someone who was confident that he could defeat a mere machine. All I could do was sit and wait.

Though the inside of the cabinet was cramped, it didn't feel claustrophobic, as you might expect. It felt . . . How can I explain it? It felt like a sanctuary, like pulling the bedclothes over your head, like the den you make for yourself beneath an overturned armchair. It felt like playing hide-and-seek and knowing that, if you stay perfectly still and quiet, the seeker will never discover your secret hiding place, no matter how hard he tries.

At last I heard the brass dial being turned; it stopped on 14, indicating that my opponent had chosen endgame number 14. Then Maelzel began setting up the board. As he put down each chess piece, it lifted the little metal ring beneath it, and I stuck a corresponding peg into my little board.

The last piece Maelzel set down would indicate which color my opponent had picked. Mulhouse had pointed out that, since White had one more piece than Black, nine out of ten players would choose White, not noticing that Black actually had the stronger position.

Sure enough, the last piece in place was the White king. Maelzel released the mainspring; the clockwork began clicking and whirring. I put the mechanical arm into action and threatened White's queen with my knight.

I checkmated the poor fellow in just seven moves. I assume it was a fellow; in my experience, women don't seem to care much for chess—except, of course, for the ill-fated Mademoiselle Bouvier. Anxious to avoid a similar fate, I checked the candle to make sure it couldn't possibly fall over and catch the felt on fire.

A second player challenged us, with the same swift result, and then Maelzel wheeled the automaton back behind the curtain. I snuffed out the candle and sat in the dark, replaying the two endgames in my mind, until I heard the series of raps that meant the coast was clear. But I found myself curiously reluctant to climb out of the cabinet. Partly it was because I wanted to savor that delicious sense of sanctuary a little longer. But there was more to it than that.

When I was inside that felt-lined box, I inhabited a small, well-ordered world, like the one in which I grew up. And when I played those two endgames, it gave me an unaccustomed, almost heady feeling of . . . well, of power, I suppose. After months of being nothing more than a pawn in someone else's game, I was actually in control of something, however inconsequential and artificial. Instead of being shuffled about or cast aside at the whim of others, or at the whim of Fate, I was the one calling the shots, dictating the moves—for half an hour or so, anyway. Is it any wonder I wanted to put off returning to the real world for as long as possible?

Finally, Maelzel yanked open the rear door of the cabinet and pulled me out. "What are you doing in there? Sleeping?"

"No. I—ah—I dropped one of the pieces, and I was searching for it."

"In the dark?"

"The smoke from the candle was choking me."

"Well, you had better get used to it. If someone asks to play a full game, you could be in there a long while."

"Aren't we only doing endgames?"

"During regular hours, yes. But if you continue to play as you did today, I may welcome more serious challengers after the hall closes."

"So, I did well?"

He shrugged. "Well enough."

"You'll pay me, then?"

He gave an exasperated sigh. "If you do not stop pestering me about it, I shall pay you right enough, but you will not like the currency." He waved an arm toward the spot where the spectators had stood, now empty. "Did you see the pitiful size of our audience?"

"I couldn't see anything. There was a lot of applause."

"*Ja, ja*, they were enthusiastic. But take my word for it, I did not make enough profit even to cover the rent; the devil knows how I shall manage to pay my workmen."

Any lingering feelings I might have had of power or control had vanished. I was back to being a helpless pawn once again.

CHAPTER

II

ALL THAT WEEK, I DID MY CHORES IN
the workshop even more cheerfully than usual,
knowing that, when the afternoon came, I
would have my moment in the sun—or rather in the
dark. For a short while, I would be transformed from
servant to master, from pawn to queen. I was like some
perverse species of prisoner who felt free only when he
was locked inside a tiny cell. It made me think of poor
Ezra's attempt to escape the House of Refuge by cramming himself into a packing crate.

As I swept up sawdust and shavings and dumped
them into the bin in the earth closet, I hummed the
Mechanical Trumpeter's march. I noticed Jacques eye-
ing me suspiciously, as though wondering whether I

was right in the head. "If you like work so much," he growled, "I can always give you more."

"No, thank you," I said. "I'm just trying to do as I was taught: accept my situation with good grace."

"Hmm. And I suppose you think I do not."

"Well . . . no."

"Of *course* I do not! Nor would you, if you had lost all the things I have lost!"

I was tempted to tell him that I'd had my share of losses—my mother and my surrogate mother, Fiona, and my home and my pleasant, privileged life—but I didn't. I might have pointed out that my father was in debtors' prison with no hope of gaining his freedom, but I didn't. No doubt it would have only earned me another blow.

Jacques pounded at his chisel for a time and then said, a bit more civilly, "If you always accept things as they are, *Bébé*, then nothing changes." That reminded me of Ezra, too. *It don't mean you have to just give up,* he'd told me. *Sometimes you got to fight back.*

"But some things *can't* be changed," I said.

"No. Some can only be mourned and regretted."

"Or accepted."

He turned on his stool and, to my surprise, hiked up the legs of his trousers to reveal his wooden limbs. "When they took off my legs, I could have accepted it and been a beggar on some street corner in Paris, surviving on people's pity. Instead, I got *these*. When the Turk burned, we might have let him die. But we resurrected him and made him better than ever."

I stared at him, openmouthed. This sudden spate of speech contained more words than he usually uttered in an entire week. Seeming surprised himself by the outburst, he went back to his work.

At the risk of inviting his curses, I said, "Was it the Battle of Trocadero?"

"Who told you that?"

"Mulhouse."

"Mulhouse knows nothing about it," he said contemptuously. "The only battles he ever fought were on a chessboard." He chiseled away for a few moments, then went on. "*Oui.* It was at Trocadero. An artillery shell. Otso put tourniquets on the stumps and carried me to safety. I owe him my life . . . such as it is."

And I owed my situation—such as it was—to Otso's namesake. If it hadn't been for the Turk, I'd have been the one begging on a street corner. Of course, I might have had better luck getting money from random passersby than from Maelzel.

Now that he knew I could handle the job, he added an extra show each evening. I continued to play my part well but, if Maelzel could be believed, we were still not drawing big crowds. After Saturday afternoon's performance, he gave me a very different sort of task—refilling the lamps beneath the Moscow diorama. This surprised me; normally he didn't trust anyone but Jacques to maintain his machines.

As I was taking out the last lamp, the door that led to the adjoining exhibition hall opened. I expected to see Mr. Barnum again. Instead, a stranger entered, a slender fellow with a gloomy expression and a pale complexion that was accentuated by his dark hair and mustache and black clothing; his only resemblance to the boisterous showman was in his forehead, which was every bit as massive as Mr. Barnum's. *Another prime phrenology subject,* I thought. If I'd had to guess his occupation, I would have said undertaker. But as it turned out, he was a poet, and apparently one of some repute, for when he introduced himself, Maelzel clearly recognized the name.

I am sure you recognize it, too; in recent years, his works—"The Tell-Tale Heart," "The Pit and the Pendulum," "The Gold-Bug," "The Raven"—have made Edgar Allan Poe a household name. I am sorry to say that the man was less admirable than his stories. In fact I found him downright unpleasant. He gazed about the hall with a rather disdainful expression, as though he were used to more elegant surroundings. The Southern flavor of his speech added to that air of haughtiness. But seen close up, he looked a little shabby. The cloth of his frock coat was threadbare and shiny at the elbows; I suspect he had rubbed soot onto some of the worst spots.

"How did you make your way in here, Mr. Poe?" asked Maelzel, a bit peevishly.

"Mr. Barnum let me in. I thought I might write something for the *Inquirer* about your . . . *show*." The way he said it, the word sounded slightly unsavory.

Maelzel didn't seem to notice. In fact, his manner suddenly became much more cordial. "The *Inquirer*, eh? Yes, yes, of course. I shall be happy to show you around and answer any questions." He glared at me as though I were the intruder. "Please get your broom and finish sweeping, now." He shook his head and smiled wearily. "It is so difficult to find a boy who is willing to work; they would rather stand about gaping at the exhibits."

I knew he was passing me off as a common chore boy so that Poe wouldn't suspect my real role. I drifted off in search of a broom. When I found one, I drifted back within earshot. "The truth is, Mr. Maelzel," Poe was saying, "I'm mainly interested in the chess-playing automaton. I've heard that it's quite extraordinary." He glanced around in search of the Turk.

"I like to think so," said Maelzel, with unaccustomed modesty.

Poe was not quite so modest. "I consider myself a fairly accomplished chess player. I would like to play a game against your . . . machine; it would add a great deal of interest to my newspaper piece."

"That may easily be arranged. If you will come back tomorrow, just before we close, I shall have everything prepared."

"Oh. I was hoping you could oblige me now."

"My apologies. In this afternoon's performance, the Turk's joints were squeaking a little; we need to lubricate them before he plays again. I would like him to be in top form when you take him on."

"I see. Well. I'll return tomorrow afternoon, then."

"Excellent. I should warn you, sir, the Turk is . . . what do you Americans say? A *crack* player?" Though Maelzel wasn't exactly praising me, it was the closest he was likely to come, and I felt a small swell of pride. "You may want to practice your chess moves in the meantime."

"Thank you. But I hardly think that'll be necessary."

When Poe was gone, I said, "I didn't notice the Turk squeaking."

"No, no, of course not. It was only an excuse to put him off. If I had let him play now, how would we have gotten you inside the machine without his noticing?" Maelzel rubbed his hands together in anticipation. "A newspaper article about the exhibition could do us much good. Now, here is the plan: After the two o'clock performance tomorrow, you remain inside the cabinet, you understand? I announce to the audience that the Turk will be playing a complete game, and anyone who wishes may stay and watch; it is always more impressive if there are people standing about oohing and ahhing when the machine makes a clever move. *But,*" he said sternly, "remember this: You must be especially careful when you play Mr. Poe. He is not your ordinary *dummkopf*, who wants only to be entertained. I do not know how skilled he is at chess, but I have read his work, and he is a shrewd and intelligent fellow; if you make the slightest blunder he will notice."

After several weeks of concentrating strictly on endgames, I would have liked to play a few complete games, just to get back in practice, but Maelzel was too busy and Jacques didn't offer much of a challenge. I hoped Mulhouse might come around, but it didn't seem likely. We'd seen no sign of him for weeks.

"What do you suppose has become of him?" I asked Jacques. I'd been breaking the rule of silence quite a lot lately, and I usually got away with it.

"I have no idea. And I care even less."

"You don't like him?"

"He is not . . . what is the word? *Fiable.*"

"Reliable?"

"*Oui.* He is not reliable. When he ran the Turk, he often failed to show up. And once he nearly gave away the secret."

"On purpose?"

"No. We were at a hall in Baltimore. It was a very hot day. The moment the audience left, Mulhouse burst from the cabinet, gasping for air. There were two boys outside, looking through the window; they saw it all, and they told the newspaper."

"Did the paper report it?"

Jacques nodded. "But Maelzel said it was all a . . . *comment dit-on*? A *stunt*. He said he had put the boys up to it, just to get publicity. Everyone believed him."

"Really?"

He shrugged. "People believe what they want to believe. A machine that runs by itself is a curiosity; one that is run by a person is just a trick."

Though Mulhouse's blunder had done no real damage, it might well have turned Maelzel against him. What if my friend had met the same fate—whatever it was—as the Turk's other operators? And what if the same fate awaited me, when I had outlived my usefulness? I said before that I felt I'd stumbled into water that was over my head; now I began to suspect that the situation was even worse, that I was mired in a deadly morass from which there was no escape. My only hope was to make myself indispensable—and make sure I did nothing to incur Maelzel's displeasure.

I missed Mulhouse and his kindness, but I didn't really need him as a sparring partner; I could always play against myself. I did just that all the next morning, and Jacques didn't object. In fact, several times I caught him surreptitiously watching my moves when he was supposed to be repairing the male rope dancer, who had broken an arm.

The men who challenged me that afternoon, whoever they were, didn't offer much of a challenge. After the performance, instead of wheeling us behind the curtain, Maelzel left the Turk in place. I knew he was inviting the real chess lovers to stay for the main event—Otso the Turk vs. Poe the Poet.

Poe claimed to be a strong player but, like many of the men I had played at the Chess Club, he wasn't quite as strong as he thought he was. Oh, he was competent, even clever, but certainly not in the same league as Mulhouse. His style was nothing like Mulhouse's, either. I thought I was slow and cautious, but compared to Poe I was a jackrabbit. I began to worry less about my ability to beat him than about my ability to sit there, cramped up and breathing in candle smoke, for two or three hours.

An hour into the game, I was already feeling light-headed, and my poor stooped shoulders were aching. I felt a cough welling up in my irritated throat, and it was all I could do to suppress it. I could have masked it by cranking the noisemaker, but I was afraid the sound might make Poe suspicious. I swallowed hard and soldiered on. Hoping to speed up the game, I took only a few seconds to consider each move, which put me at a disadvantage. Nevertheless, I managed to back Poe into a corner.

I would have checkmated him in three more moves, but then something odd happened: Several of the metal disks dropped suddenly, indicating that the pieces on those squares had fallen over or been removed. At the same time, I felt the cabinet tremble, as though the hall were in the grip of a mild earthquake.

Ordinarily, I couldn't hear anything at all from outside the machine, but now I became aware of a faint rumbling, as though dozens of feet were pounding across the floor. Barely audible over the rumble was a sound that might have been a scream, and a voice shouting a single word over and over. By putting one ear up against the wall of the cabinet, I could just make out what it was.

"Fire! Fire!"

CHAPTER

12

AS I'VE SAID, MAELZEL WAS FANATICAL about anticipating and preparing for anything that could conceivably go wrong. But he'd never told me what to do in case of a fire, or if he had, I'd forgotten it. All I could remember was how many times and how emphatically he'd said, "No matter what happens, do *not* leave the cabinet until I give you the all-clear signal." Once he'd added, "If some frustrated chess player should pull out a pistol and shoot me dead, what will you do?"

"I'll stay in the cabinet," I had dutifully replied.

But it wasn't Maelzel's death I had to worry about; it was my own. And Otso's, of course. If the other exhibits were going up in flames, I wasn't sure I could count on Maelzel to save us. The rear door opened from the inside, so I could let myself out, but I held off, hoping desperately that Maelzel would send me a sign. When several minutes passed and he neither spun the dial nor knocked on the cabinet nor wheeled it off, I began to panic.

Though I certainly had no desire to be burned alive, I believe I was more worried about the Turk's welfare than my own. If he went up in smoke, so would my career as his operator, and along with it my best hope of freeing my father. And yet I had to be cautious; I couldn't just come bursting out of the cabinet, the way Mulhouse had once done. Though at this point the spectators were surely more concerned with saving themselves than with learning the Turk's secret, I couldn't risk being seen.

I took a deep breath to calm myself, then blew out the candle and eased the door open a crack, hoping to get some sense of how immediate the danger was. Instantly, the door slammed shut again, pinching my fingers. Startled, I gave it another push, but it wouldn't budge; something was blocking it. A fallen beam? A dead body?

I'd always tried to follow my father's advice and accept with good grace whatever befell me. But I wasn't sure that advice applied to my current situation. I could hardly be expected to sit there and wait stoically for the flames to consume Otso and me; I was going to have to *do* something.

I flopped down flat on my back and cocked one leg in the air, meaning to kick the big chessboard loose and squirm out through the hole. But just as I was about to deliver the blow, the cabinet began to move. I cried out in alarm, fearing that the floor was collapsing beneath us. Then I realized that someone was pushing us, presumably to safety. We stopped rolling, and there was a moment of stillness in which I sat motionless, waiting to see what would happen next.

The rear door swung open and a voice said, "You may come out now."

I started to emerge from the cabinet, then abruptly stopped myself. What if this was some sort of perverse experiment conducted by Maelzel to test me? Instead, I slid forward into my fetal position and stayed there, barely able to breathe. A long moment passed, and then someone rapped on the cabinet: three, three, two. With a sigh of relief, I unfolded myself and crawled through the opening. The hall was bright, but not with flames, only with ordinary daylight. Squinting, I peered upward to see who my savior was. "Monsieur Mulhouse!"

"Are you all right, Rufus?"

"I will be, once my heart leaves my throat and goes back in my chest."

Laughing, he helped me to my feet. "As you see, there was no fire, just some audience member playing a trick—probably hoping to flush you out. I spotted the culprit and went after him, but in the confusion he made his escape."

"What did he look like?"

"A strongly built man, perhaps thirty years of age, with curly hair."

"That sounds like Mr. Barnum."

"I doubt it could be him. He's taken his exhibition to New York."

"Well, whoever it was, his trick nearly worked."

"I know. I am sorry I had to hold the door shut. I knew there was no danger, but you did not."

"Where's Maelzel?"

"Outside, reassuring everyone. I thought you could use some reassurance, too."

"Thank you." I was more reassured than he knew. I nearly told him how, when he disappeared for such a long while, I began imagining that he had suffered some dire and mysterious fate. But now that he was here, safe and sound, my fears seemed a bit fanciful and foolish, so I didn't speak of them. I only glanced about the empty hall and said, "Well, Mr. Poe will have plenty to write about."

Mulhouse smiled wryly. "I am sure he was grateful for the interruption. A few moves more, and you would have checkmated him."

"If I didn't suffocate first. You haven't by any chance found a Carcel lamp, have you?"

He winced and shook his head. "I am sorry. It completely slipped my mind. I did make inquires about your friend Fionnula. "

"Fiona."

"Yes. No luck yet."

"And my father?"

He patted me on the shoulder. "We will talk later. You need to go now, in case anyone should slip past Maelzel."

I was in no hurry to return to the workshop and Jacques's sullen company. I wandered about the large outer workroom for a while, examining the multifarious projects spread out on the tables. They made up a fascinating exhibit of curiosities all by themselves: miniature body parts, human and animal; tiny trees of every species; piles of birdshot-sized boulders and toothpick-sized boards; articles of clothing too small even for fairies.

When neither Mulhouse nor Maelzel appeared, I pushed open the door to the exhibition hall a few inches, curious to know what they were up to. The door was masked by the same curtain that concealed the Turk, so I couldn't see much, but I could hear voices. At first, I couldn't make out the words; gradually they increased in volume and in vehemence.

"I am not a rich man, Mulhouse. I cannot keep supporting your laudanum habit forever. If the Chess

Club has fired you, then you will have to find something else."

"What do you suggest? I have no skills whatsoever, aside from playing chess."

"Then take a position as a crossing sweeper; that takes no skill. In any case, it is not my problem."

"I would not need laudanum if I had not ruined my lungs sitting inside your machine, which would serve equally well as a smokehouse."

Maelzel gave a scornful laugh. "Oh, well, if you did not use laudanum, then your only vices would be liquor and gambling. You may as well admit it, Mulhouse: No matter much money you have, you will always find some means of throwing it away."

"And no matter how much *you* have, you will not part with any of it. I think you owe me something, just for keeping the Turk's secret all these years."

"I paid you a fair wage for most of those years! You cannot expect me to go on paying you for all eternity!"

"You want me to go on keeping the secret, do you not?"

There was a pause, then Maelzel said, in a voice so low I could barely hear, "That sounds suspiciously like a threat, Monsieur Mulhouse."

"It is not. It is merely a possibility."

"It had better not be. I hope I do not have to remind you what became of Mademoiselle Bouvier."

"What *did* become of her, exactly? I have never been certain."

"Surely you do not expect me to give you all the details. There is one way to find out, however."

"And what is that?"

"Sell the Turk's secret, as she did, and you will come to the same unenviable end."

"Now, that *does* sound like a threat."

"Good. I meant it to."

There was a silence, then Mulhouse's voice again. "So, you are not willing to give me any support at all?"

"I would be happy to write a letter of recommendation. I am even prepared to lie a little, and say how reliable you are."

That seemed to be the end of the discussion. Hearing footsteps headed my way, I closed the door softly and retreated to the inner workshop.

In the wake of the quarrel, Monsieur Mulhouse, who had only just reappeared, vanished from my life again. I had not only lost the nearest thing I had to a friend, I had also lost the sole link to my father. I knew that Maelzel would never take me to visit him nor let me go on my own, and there was no use in asking Jacques.

I told myself that Mulhouse would be back, and I tried my best not to let those same foolish fears worm their way back into my head. But the fact was, this time I had far more cause for concern; this time Maelzel had actually threatened him. Though the nature of the threat wasn't completely clear, what else could "an unenviable end" mean, except murder? Mulhouse had said that he would put nothing past Maelzel. And even if Maelzel himself wasn't capable of killing anyone, I had little doubt that Jacques was.

In the week that followed, my prospects of getting paid began to look brighter. The *Inquirer* printed a lively account of the duel between man and machine and how it had been left undecided when participants and spectators fled in panic. "We may be thankful," wrote the reporter, "that the alleged fire was nothing more than some puerile jokester's idea of an amusing prank. The Turk, for all its astounding skill, is only made of wax, and wax and fire do not make a good mix."

There's nothing like a good scare to get people's attention. After the piece appeared, our audience doubled, and it went on growing. I had discovered a hole in the fabric of the curtain large enough to peer through, and I saw the phenomenon for myself. Maelzel would never admit we were doing well, of course; he preferred to pretend that we were just scraping by. But the boost in business put him in an uncharacteristically good mood; he even called me by my name occasionally, instead of just addressing me as "boy." If

I ever hoped to pry some money out of him, there would be no better time.

I knew it was no use just asking him nicely. Financial negotiations are like a chess game—to win, you have to be in control of the board. Well, now that the Turk was drawing record crowds, I was in a good position to make my move. After all, how long would people keep coming if Otso just sat there, looking impressive and making clockwork sounds? He needed someone to bring him to life. He needed me.

I pointed this out to Maelzel, though not in those words. I foolishly expected him to react as he had when I beat him at chess; though he wouldn't be happy, he'd see that he was defeated and would grudgingly concede. He did no such thing. Instead, he responded the same way he had when Mulhouse asked him for money. "Are you threatening me, boy?"

"No, of course not. I'm just saying that if I'm making a profit for you, then I deserve to be paid."

"And if I don't pay you?"

I didn't reply.

"And if I *don't* pay you?" he demanded.

As I've said, I'd experienced enough pain not to fear being knocked about a bit. But we all fear the unknown, and I couldn't help thinking of how, when the Turk's previous operators had crossed Maelzel, they had mysteriously disappeared. I couldn't imagine that he'd do me in just to avoid paying me, but I couldn't dismiss the possibility, either. It took some courage to say what I said next: "Then— then I don't work, I suppose."

To my surprise, he didn't strike me, or even shout. Though his expression was grim, he simply nodded and said, "Very well." But I sensed that there was more to come. Sure enough, he bent down and poked a blunt finger in my chest. "However, I should tell you that if you do not work, you do not eat." He unlocked the door to the workroom and pushed me roughly inside. "Jacques, you are not to bring this ungrateful whelp any more food until further notice. *Verstehst du?*"

Jacques stared at him for a moment. "What about water?"

"Yes, yes, water is all right. We do not want to kill him, only to let him go hungry for a while, until he feels more cooperative."

CHAPTER

13

THE FIRST SEVERAL DAYS OF MY ENFORCED fast were the hardest and the longest. I got through them by thinking of my father in his prison cell; unless Mulhouse had given the keeper more money, Father was probably back to subsisting on bread and water. It gave me a sort of sense of shared misery, which is always better than misery endured alone.

I couldn't really believe that Maelzel would keep the punishment up for long; after all, each day that the Turk sat idle was a day of lost profits. But, as interested as he was in money, he was apparently more interested in teaching me a lesson.

He'd gone back to his old trick of refusing to speak to me directly, as though it were beneath his dignity.

Each day he asked Jacques whether I was ready to go back to work, and each day Jacques gave him my reply, which was always the same. I was determined to beat him at this game, just as I did at chess. After examining my skull so closely, he may have thought he knew me. But I had one trait in abundance that didn't appear on the phrenology chart—stubbornness.

After a few days the hunger pangs blessedly faded; the problem now was that I could feel myself growing weaker, and I'd never been very strong to begin with. I had trouble focusing on even the least demanding task. At first, when I stopped sweeping or sanding and sat staring vacantly, Jacques cursed at me and gave me a swat. After a while, he saw that this tactic wasn't working; I was just too listless to care.

Jacques actually seemed a little concerned. "You should let him have his way, *Bébé*. He will see you starve before he will give in."

"And you?" I said.

Jacques scowled and spat tobacco juice into the box of sawdust at his feet. "I must do what he tells me."

"Why?" My cautiousness must have been fading, too; instead of letting the matter drop, I pressed him for an answer. "*Why* must you?"

He turned on me, thrusting out his carving knife in such a threatening fashion that I shrank back. "The devil take you and your infernal questions!"

Once again it was obvious that, if I was going to survive, I'd have to take matters into my own hands. I had no idea how I might manage to feed myself, unless I ate sawdust. But that night, when I heard the familiar *chunk, chunk* of the night soil men clearing out the contents of the earth closet, a plan began to form. I crept into the little privy room and quietly lifted the lid of the toilet. The small door that gave access to the earth closet from the outside stood open; the men's shovel blades appeared, scooped, withdrew, appeared, scooped, withdrew.

Groping about in the dark of the workshop, I located a stick of wood several feet in length. When the men finished their task and were closing the access door, I thrust the tip of the stick into the opening, just enough to keep them from latching the door. They gave it few halfhearted tries and then I heard a voice say, "Let 'em fix it theirselves. 'Tis not our job."

I waited ten minutes or so, to make sure that they were gone and that Jacques was sleeping soundly. Then I dredged several double handfuls of shavings and sawdust from the bin, dumped them into the toilet, and spread them out to make a clean, dry layer. I might be desperate, but I wasn't quite desperate enough to crawl through night soil.

My small size, which was such an advantage in operating the Turk, also served me well in my escape. It was a fairly easy matter to slip down the toilet hole and crawl out through the access door. For a moment I just stood there, relishing the fresh air and open space after so many weeks of being shut up in that gloomy, dusty workshop. Then I drew a deep breath and began walking.

There was no point in going to a tavern; I didn't have enough money to buy a crust of bread. No, I had another strategy in mind. I'm sorry to say that it wasn't entirely honest, and I hope you won't be inspired to follow my example—unless, of course, you happen to be starving to death.

The Parsonage was probably no more than a mile from Masonic Hall, but in my weak condition it seemed like the distance between Marathon and Athens; I feared that, like the Greek messenger in the legend, I might collapse and die when I reached my goal.

Obviously I didn't, or I wouldn't be telling you all this, would I? It was a struggle, though, and when I entered the yard of my old home, I had to sit and rest for a long while before I could continue with my plan.

As I sat there in the shadow of the house, which was dark and silent, I saw a female figure approaching on the far side of the street. When she passed beneath a streetlamp, I got a better look at her—a thin woman dressed in the sort of plain cotton dress and coal-scuttle bonnet so common among servants and working girls.

But, as you know, those girls tend to favor bright calico or gingham. As nearly as I could tell in the uncertain light, this woman's garb was black as a widow's weeds.

Anxious to avoid being seen, I shrank back against the wood-shingled wall of the Parsonage. The woman in black walked past the house, then turned back and stood gazing at it for the longest time, the way a visitor to Venice will stare at the Doge's Palace, as if imagining what it would be like to live there. Or perhaps, I thought, she was *remembering* what it was like, for the figure put me in mind of my old nursemaid, Fiona. I was tempted to call out to her, but I didn't want to give myself away. In any case, just then she came out of her reverie and began walking back the way she had come.

When she was out of sight, I crept up to the back steps of the Parsonage, located a familiar stone about the size and shape of a cow pile, and lifted one edge of it. The key still lay beneath it, just as it had all the years I lived there. I retrieved it and quietly let myself in through the rear door.

The darkness inside didn't deter me in the least. I knew every square inch of the place, as well as I knew the squares on a chessboard, and I made my moves the same way I did in chess—cautiously but with confidence. I went first to the pantry, where I found a flour sack and put into it as much bread and cheese and fruit as it would hold. Then I slipped into the parlor. The Carcel lamp still sat exactly where we had always kept it—on the marble-topped walnut table. And the center section of the sideboard still held a bottle of colza oil. I added them to my bag of booty. After a moment's thought, I snatched up a sheaf of paper from the small writing desk and crammed that in the sack, too.

I'd never stolen anything before in my life, and yet for some reason I had no qualms about it, maybe because I felt that all this—the Parsonage and its contents and the privileged life I'd led there—had been stolen from me. I was just reclaiming some small part of it.

So far I'd been both clever and lucky. No one stirred in the upstairs bedrooms; there was nothing to suggest that my presence was known. I was well aware that I ought to leave at once, while my luck held, and yet I couldn't bring myself to. Standing in that parlor, I was overcome by powerful feelings, but they weren't painful ones of nostalgia and regret, as you might expect. What I felt was more like the sense of well-being and relief you experience when you wake from a miserable dream and find yourself in safe, familiar surroundings again.

On that marble-topped table, my father and I had

played hundreds of games of chess. On that fainting couch, I had lain covered in quilts and lulled by laudanum and listened to Fiona's soft Irish lilt as she read to me, in her halting, unschooled fashion, from *Tales of the Arabian Nights*. For a moment I convinced myself that all I'd suffered these past four months or so had been nothing but a fever dream; if I stretched out on the fainting couch, in a little while I would wake and everything would be the way it was when I was nine or ten.

Then the bottle of colza oil fell from my flour sack, bounced off my foot, and rolled across the floor as loudly, it seemed, as the rumble of thunder. I didn't wait to find out whether I'd disturbed anyone's sleep. I snatched up the oil and scurried out the way I'd come in, pausing just long enough to lock the door and shove the key back in its hiding place. No point in letting the new owners know that they'd been raided. If Maelzel continued to hold out, I might be back.

As I was making my getaway, I spotted the woman in black again; she hadn't left, she'd only walked up the street a little way, out of the streetlamp's circle of light, and was again gazing at the Parsonage in that same rapt fashion. I took a few steps toward her and called softly, "Fiona?"

The woman gave a start and looked my way. "Who's there?" she asked, in a voice that trembled.

"It's me—Rufus."

Though it was too dark to see her face, I was certain she was staring at me. Perhaps she didn't recognize me or hear me identify myself, or perhaps it wasn't Fiona after all. Whatever the reason, when I started toward her again she turned and hurried away; probably she took me for some street urchin bent on robbing her.

I nearly called out to her again, but just then a lamp was lit upstairs in the Parsonage, in the very room Fiona once occupied. Fearful of being discovered, I slipped away into the dark. When I'd put some distance between myself and the Parsonage, I sat down on a horse block and had a few bites of bread and cheese, hoping to regain a little strength. I had one more task to perform before I could return to the workshop.

I pounded on the door of the debtors' wing at the Arch Street prison for a full minute before the night keeper slid open the little hatch and peered out. Since my head was well below the opening, I waved a hand to make sure he saw me. "What d'you want?" he asked groggily.

"I'm Reverend Goodspeed's son, remember? I brought him some food."

"Couldn't you come at a more reasonable hour?"

"I'm sorry. It's the only time I could get away."

A key snicked and the door swung open. "Let's have it, then."

"I was hoping I could see him." When the man hesitated, I went into the piteous act that had always worked so well on Fiona and my father. "Please, sir; I just want to let him know I'm all right."

The keeper scratched his scraggly fringe of hair. "Well, I reckon 'twon't hurt. No doubt he's awake, anyways. He sits up till all hours sometimes, scribbling in that notebook of his."

I expected my father to greet me joyfully, as he always had. Instead, he seemed unaccountably distressed by my presence. "Ah, Rufus; I wish you hadn't come. I told the daytime keeper not to admit you; I never imagined you'd visit so late."

"I— I thought you'd be glad to see me, Father."

"Oh, I am, my boy. Of course I am. It's just that there's been so much illness here of late, and I didn't want you exposed to it. It's gotten so bad that they've actually let some of the prisoners go, lest they be infected." He laughed weakly. "Not us debtors, though; I suppose we're too desperate and dangerous a lot. They did move some of us to the Walnut Street jail, but I chose to stay. Someone has to take care of the sick." He nodded toward two still forms lying on straw mattresses along one wall.

"Haven't they brought in a doctor?"

"Oh, yes. He examined one patient, announced that it was cholera, and departed as quickly as he could.

You mustn't stay, either; if you come down with the disease, it'll certainly be the death of you."

"What about you?"

"Don't worry about me. I'm as healthy as a horse."

That may have been true at one time, but the weeks he'd spent cooped up within these walls had taken their toll. The sanguine flush had faded from his cheeks, and his ample belly had shrunk.

I glanced about the cell, which was lit by the stub of a candle. "Where's your bed, Father?" He didn't reply. "Did they take it away?"

He shrugged. "It doesn't matter. I can make do with a blanket."

"But why? Didn't Mulhouse come and give the keeper more money?"

"Mulhouse?"

"The man who brought me here last time."

My father shook his head. "As far as I know, he has never returned." He made a shooing motion with one hand. "You must go now, Rufus, please. We can't risk your being infected."

He wouldn't let me embrace him, and he took the food I'd brought only because I vowed not to leave until he did. I'd meant to divide my ill-gotten gains evenly with him, but now that I saw how badly off he was, I pressed most of the food on him, keeping only a chunk of cheese and a few apples for myself.

He readily accepted the writing paper, but declined the Carcel lamp.

"It wouldn't survive more than a few days around here." He gestured at the guttering candle. "Anyway, the keeper gives me all his candle stubs. He used to lend me a pipeful of tobacco from time to time, but not since the contagion began. Well, you can't blame him. Go, now. You may come back in a few weeks, when the cholera has run its course."

It had occurred to me that Jacques might pay a midnight visit to the privy while I was gone. To my relief, the earth closet contained nothing but the layer of sawdust and shavings I had spread there. As I pulled myself up through the toilet hole, I could hear Jacques thrashing about and crying, "*Mes jambes! Mon Dieu, mes jambes!*" My legs; my God, my legs.

I made a wide detour around his bed and found my own. My stomach, which had been shriveling up for several days, had been revived by the bread and cheese and was demanding more. I ignored it and shoved my sack of food beneath the sack of shavings that was my mattress. There was no telling how long it might have to last me.

IN THE DAYS THAT FOLLOWED, EACH TIME Jacques left me alone in the workshop, I sneaked a little sustenance from my hidden hoard, just enough to keep me going. Maelzel continued to check on me daily, to see whether I'd changed my mind. He was clearly baffled and frustrated, so much so that he condescended to speak directly to me. "I know you are hungry, boy. All you have to do is agree to come back to work, and we will feed you."

"But will you pay me?"

"I *would* have, but now you have made me angry. I cannot allow my workers to dictate terms to me."

"I'm not trying to. I'm only trying to collect what I've earned."

He shook his head in disgust. "You know, I gave

you credit for more intelligence than this. You think you are being very clever, but in fact you are being very stupid." He stormed out of the workroom and slammed the door behind him.

"He is right," growled Jacques. "You are being stupid."

"I don't think he's being very smart, either. Every day the Turk sits idle, he's losing money—a lot more than he'd lose by paying me."

"He does care for money. But he cares more about getting his own way, about showing who is *le patron*— the boss."

Well, as I have said, I was used to getting my own way, too.

Though Jacques scoffed at my stubborn stance, he didn't try very hard to talk me out of it. I believe that, underneath the contempt and the cursing, he grudgingly respected me for it. That evening, when he returned from the Oyster Cellar, he tossed me something wrapped in greasy paper. "If you tell Maelzel," he said, "I will give you some new bumps to phrenologize."

I unwrapped the object. It was a roasted potato, still warm.

Mulhouse had warned me once that, in business matters at least, Maelzel could be ruthless. I had thought that starving me was ample proof of that. But I soon learned that the man was capable of much worse.

The following afternoon, after yet another Turk-less performance, he burst into the workshop with a fierce scowl on his face. "People are clamoring to see the celebrated mechanical chess player! I assured them that his absence is only temporary, that he is undergoing minor repairs, but I do not know how long I can continue to put them off before they lose interest!"

I tried to make myself inconspicuous; it did no good. He turned on me, snatched the mallet and chisel with which I had been practicing my carving skills, and flung them to the floor. "I do not know how you have survived this long, boy, but I promise you, if you continue to defy me, you will not survive much longer!" He seized the front of my shirt and nearly lifted me off the floor. "Now! Will you or will you not return to work?"

"I will," I replied shakily. With a smug smile, he released me. It took me a moment to find the breath to add what I had meant to add: "If you pay me."

Maelzel roared something in German and, drawing back his arm, delivered a sweeping blow that nearly knocked my head from my shoulders. As I lay curled up in the sawdust and shavings, he kicked me in the small of the back with one of his shiny imported shoes, then did it again, and again, each kick more savage than the last. I feared that he would break my frail frame beyond repair.

Then, abruptly, the attack ceased. I rolled onto my back and wiped the tears and blood from my face. To my surprise, it was not Maelzel who stood over me now; it was Jacques. But he was not threatening me; he was turned away from me, facing Maelzel and gripping a piece of oak the size of the Turk's arm. "That is enough, Mr. Maelzel," he said, in a voice that was restrained and yet carried an unmistakable warning.

Maelzel glared at him. "You are forgetting your place, Jacques."

"*Non*, you are forgetting yours. You may be his boss, but you do not own him, body and soul." Something in the way he said it made me suspect that he was talking as much about himself as about me.

They continued to eye each other like two chess fanatics, each trying to convince the other to concede. But, like any good player, Maelzel knew when he was beaten; he also knew that losing one game did not mean the match was over. He shrugged and gave a strained smile. "Perhaps you are right." He straightened his frock coat and his mussed hair. "So. You think I should pay him, then?"

Jacques nodded. Maelzel reached inside his coat, drew out a leather wallet, and unfolded it. "And just how much would you say he is worth?"

"That is up to you."

"No, no, you have taken it upon yourself to defend him, to speak for him. Tell me how much he should get."

"All right, then. Five dollars."

Maelzel raised his eyebrows. "You drive a hard bargain, Monsieur Jouy. Perhaps you chose the wrong career; you should have been a lawyer." He pulled several banknotes from the wallet and held them out. "Go ahead. Take it." When Jacques hesitated, Maelzel grabbed his free hand and stuffed the bills into it. "There. I expect the boy to be inside the machine, ready to perform, by half past one tomorrow."

"Am I to feed him in the meantime?"

The German gave a harsh laugh. "He has plenty of money, now. Let him buy his own meals."

When Maelzel was gone, I raised myself painfully from the floor and brushed the sawdust from my clothing. Jacques thrust the banknotes at me, spat into his crude cuspidor, and went back to his workbench. As I bent over the washbasin, cleaning the blood from my face, I said, "Thank you for standing up for me."

"I did not do it for you. I did it for myself."

I turned to him with water dripping from my hair. "I don't understand."

"Shut your face and get back to work!" he snapped. "Do you understand *that*?"

"*Oui*." I set about the never-ending task of sweeping

the floor. No matter how carefully I plied the broom, I always stirred up great quantities of dust that got me coughing. "Do you mind if I open the window a little? I could use a breath of air. I mean, if we're not working on the Turk, it wouldn't hurt for someone to see in, would it?"

I took his silence to mean that he didn't object. When I pulled up the sash, to my surprise I spotted a dark-clothed figure on the far side of the street, gazing at the Masonic Hall in the same spellbound way she had stared at the Parsonage. I still couldn't make out her face, thanks to a lacy veil that hung down the front of her black bonnet.

How strange that she should turn up twice in such a short space of time, and in two such different places. It was almost as if she had followed me here. But that made no sense— unless perhaps it was Fiona after all. But in the light of day, this woman didn't resemble Fiona as much as I'd thought. Though she was about the same height, she didn't have Fiona's sturdy build; she looked rather frail, in fact. Of course, if the last several months had been as hard on Fiona as they were on my father and me, she might not be as sturdy as she once was.

But the encounters might be pure coincidence, too. There were always a few unfortunate, distracted men and women who wandered the streets of the city like lost souls, with no apparent purpose or destination. She might merely be one of those.

As I peered through the narrow opening at the dark, slender figure, thoughts of another mysterious woman entered my mind. I turned to Jacques. Though I knew I was treading on dangerous ground, my avid curiosity couldn't be denied. "Did you—did you know Mademoiselle Bouvier?"

He turned to glare at me. "Who told you about her?" he demanded.

Immediately, I wished that, as he'd so often suggested, I'd kept my *grande gueule* shut. "I—I—"

"*Ça fait rien,*" said Jacques. "I know. It was Mulhouse."

"Well, he mentioned her name once, in passing. I was just curious about her. I mean, there aren't many women who play chess well."

Jacques snorted contemptuously. "Nor did she. Maelzel should never have hired her."

I wanted to ask what became of her, but that ground *did* seem too treacherous to tread on. "What did she look like?" I asked.

Jacques's scowl grew even more fierce. "Why do you want to know?"

"I just thought that perhaps—" I turned and glanced out the window again. The woman in black was gone. "Never mind," I said. "Forget that I asked."

"*Non*, I will not." He shook his chisel at me. "But I advise *you* to forget that you ever heard of Mademoiselle Bouvier."

"I will," I promised. Wincing from the pain in my back where Maelzel had kicked me, I pulled the sash closed and went back to work.

Though I now had money, I was forbidden to leave the workshop during daylight, so I still had to rely on Jacques to feed me. That evening, he brought me another roasted potato and a good-sized piece of fried fish. When I offered to pay him, he waved the money away. "Keep it. Those are left over from my meal."

I had stretched my aching body out on the sack of shavings. As I struggled to sit up, Jacques said, "Your back hurts, eh?"

"That's nothing new. It's been hurting most of my life."

"You have been that way since birth?"

I nodded, very carefully. "I guess I didn't want to be born. The doctor had to yank me out with forceps."

"Did they never put *un appareil*—a brace—on you?"

"No. Nobody ever even mentioned it."

Jacques gave a disgusted grunt. "American physicians are still the Dark Ages. In France, they have been using them for years."

"What are they like?"

"*Très simple*." He tore a piece from the roll of brown wrapping paper that he used for sketching designs and made a quick but well-rendered drawing of something that looked a lot like an instrument of torture. "You see? You put these clamps over your shoulders and buckle this belt around your waist."

"Interesting. Where could I get one of these?"

"*Qui sait?*" He gave me a sour glance. "Perhaps the same place you get those *maudit* lamps you mentioned."

"They're called Carcel lamps. And in case you thought I was making it up—" Groaning with the effort, I pulled the flour sack from beneath my mattress and fished out the lamp I'd reclaimed from the Parsonage. "*Voilà.*"

"Where did you get that?" Jacques demanded.

"I—ah—I asked Mulhouse to find one for me." Which was true, if a bit misleading.

Jacques examined the lamp. "*Ah, oui.* I have seen these before. The clockwork mechanism pumps oil into the wick, *non?*"

"That's right."

"What sort of oil?"

"Colza. It's pressed from the seeds of the *Brassica rapa* plant." Just one of the many arcane facts I'd learned in my years of voracious reading. "It's thicker than paraffin oil and a lot less smoky."

"You are going to try it inside the Turk?"

"It'll be easier on my lungs than a candle—and much safer, too."

I didn't bother to tell Maelzel about the lamp; he might have forbidden it, out of spite. The next day, I slipped into the exhibition hall an hour before the performance and placed the lamp inside the Turk's hollow torso. When Maelzel arrived at one-thirty, I was sitting innocently on a stool, reading *Elements of Phrenology*.

"Ah, so you have seen the error of your ways. I trust there will be no more displays of disobedience." He said this with an air of self-satisfaction, just as though he, and not I, had won our contest of wills.

I wasn't about to contradict him. "No," I said.

"*Sehr gut.* Now, I have some new instructions for you. There is no need for you to comment. Just listen, and do as you are told. *Verstehst du?*" When I nodded, wincing a bit from the pain in my back, he went on. "I have decided that it would be best if the Turk loses occasionally."

"You want me to *lose?*" I said, incredulously.

"What I *want*," he snapped, "is for you to be *silent!*" I nodded again, and he calmed down. "What you must realize is that people have a secret mistrust of machines, a fear that machines will somehow replace them. And that is happening already, *nicht wahr?* The cotton gin, the spinning jenny, the power loom. So, as fascinated as they are by the Turk's ability, they want to see him defeated by a human being. Besides, if the Turk always wins, then there is no feeling of suspense, no wondering whether man or machine will prevail. It is a foregone conclusion, and people do not want foregone conclusions; they want to be kept guessing.

"We have been challenged to another complete game, and this time the challenger is a woman, a Mrs. Fisher. You must agree, it would be very ungentlemanly of the Turk not to let a member of the fair sex win." When I didn't reply, he gave a wry smile. "All right, you may speak now."

"I'm not sure Turks are noted for being gentlemanly."

"Perhaps not. All the same, you will see to it that the lady wins. And make it look as though it is *her* doing, not yours, will you?"

"I'll try." I didn't particularly mind the idea of deliberately losing. It actually took more skill to lose convincingly than it did to win. When I played against my father, even after I could trounce him without much effort I still threw a game occasionally, just to keep him happy. And if that was all it took to keep Maelzel happy, I was willing to humor him.

CHAPTER 15

FOLDING MYSELF UP INSIDE THE CABINET was even more painful than usual after the drubbing Maelzel had given me. On the bright side, the Carcel lamp proved to be a big improvment over the candle. It gave off far more light and far less fumes. It was also quite sturdy and stable, and I knew from childhood experience that, even if I did manage to knock it over, I wasn't going to immolate myself or the Turk; the flame would simply go out.

Otso and I made short work of the two audience members who played endgames against us. After a short interval, Maelzel set the board up for my game against Mrs. Fisher—whoever she was. I didn't know what to expect; I'd never played against a woman. If she wasn't a strong player, it would be nearly impossible for me to lose without making it obvious that I was doing it on purpose.

Early on, she did something that suggested she was a rank beginner: She made an illegal move with her knight, moving him two spaces forward and then two to the side, instead of two and one. I shook the Turk's head, picked up the offending piece, and returned it to its previous spot.

But a few moves later, she made the same mistake with her other knight, and I concluded that it wasn't a mistake at all; it was a test, to see how the Turk would react. Maelzel could have corrected her, of course, but he obviously preferred to let the machine handle it, to demonstrate how clever it was. This time I drummed the Turk's fingers impatiently and replaced the knight more forcefully than before.

It soon became clear that she was no beginner; in fact, if I didn't pay attention I might conceivably lose *without* meaning to. But ultimately she made a genuine mistake—the same one that I've seen hundreds of others make. You may already know what castling is; if not, I'll just say that it's a move in which the rook and the king swap places. Cautious player that I am, I usually castle early on. That way my king isn't right in the thick of things, but tucked safely away in a well-protected corner.

Some see castling as a defensive move, a wasted

play; they'd rather take the offensive. Mrs. Fisher was one of those. The trouble was, she couldn't move all her pieces freely, because some were needed to protect her king. All I had to do was keep threatening the Black monarch and I could pick off his subjects one by one.

Out of old habit, I started to do just that. And then I remembered that, oh, yes, I was supposed to *lose*. I was going to have to hold back, to make some inconspicuous error of my own, to give Mrs. Fisher the advantage. But for some reason I couldn't bring myself to do it.

As I've said, prior to the game I had no real qualms about throwing it. But from inside the Turk, things looked different. It wasn't that I'd changed my mind and was suddenly determined to win. It was more like the machine had a mind of its own, as if a drive to win had been built into it, as if that were its purpose, in the same way that a loom's purpose is to weave cloth, or a reaper's to cut down grain.

Normally, when I operated the Turk, I experienced that heady and unaccustomed sense of being in control. Now I had the disturbing feeling that I wasn't really deciding the moves at all, that the Turk had somehow taken over.

I'd always thought that his gaze held a sort of challenge, as though he considered everyone a potential foe. And when I'd examined his waxy skull, I'd felt a distinct bump in the area that denoted Destructiveness. Perhaps I was a bit light-headed from the pain in my back and from so many days without food. Or perhaps in such close confines the colza oil fumes had some kind of hallucinatory effect. Whatever the reason, I had the peculiar notion that the Turk saw poor Mrs. Fisher as the enemy and was bent on destroying her.

When I reached for my bishop, meaning to subtly sacrifice it to her queen, the Turk's arm suddenly became stiff and unresponsive. I struggled with it and finally got his hand poised over the bishop, but then I couldn't manage to grasp the piece properly. It must have fallen from the wooden fingers and rolled across the board, for several of the metal disks dropped, which meant that I'd toppled some of the other pieces.

Once Maelzel had replaced all the chessmen, I tried again. Again the mechanical arm resisted my attempts to put the bishop in harm's way. I was sweating profusely now, and could barely keep hold of the mechanism that controlled the fingers. For the first time since we'd begun performing, Maelzel opened the rear door of the cabinet in the middle of a game. I heard him say loudly to the audience, "I shall just be a moment." He stuck his arm inside, as though to adjust the clockwork, but his hand seized my sleeve instead. "What the devil is the matter with you, boy?" he whispered.

"It's the machine!" I protested softly. "It's not working properly. We'd better concede the game."

He slammed the door shut. After a minute or two, the cabinet began to move. He was wheeling us to our hiding place behind the curtain. He rapped the all-clear signal and I climbed out, stiff and sore and sweating.

"Are you trying to sabotage me?" demanded Maelzel. "Is this your way of getting revenge?"

"No! The arm was giving me trouble, that's all!"

"It was working well enough before. What did you do to it?"

"Nothing, I swear."

"Ja, well, we shall see. I will have Jacques examine it." While he was gone, I slid into the cabinet and tried the mechanism again, to make sure I hadn't just been imagining things. The arm moved smoothly and effortlessly. "Oh, Lud!" I breathed. Maelzel was sure to think that I'd faked the problem, just to get even with him.

Jacques arrived with his tool kit and set about testing the Turk's arm while I watched anxiously. Finally he turned away, scratching his beard thoughtfully. "The boy is right. Perhaps one of the wires is twisted or bent."

Malezel cast me a disgusted glance, as though he'd been hoping to catch me in a lie. "Have it fixed by tomorrow. I told Mrs. Fisher she could have a rematch."

He left us alone with the Turk. But instead of

tinkering with the machine, Jacques turned to me and growled, "*Eh bien*. What is your game?"

"My game?"

"There is nothing wrong with the arm."

I spread my hands helplessly. "I know; it's working all right now. But during the chess match it wouldn't let me move one of the pieces."

"Which piece?"

"I tried to let Mrs. Fisher win by giving her one of my bishops. But it was almost like . . ." I gave a sheepish grin. ". . . like Otso didn't want to lose."

Jacques neither scoffed at me nor struck me. He merely frowned and scratched his beard again. Finally, he said, "You play this woman again tomorrow?"

"I guess so."

"Who is she, this Madame Fisher?"

"I have no idea. I never even saw her. One thing I do know—Maelzel will still want me to let her win."

"Then you had better find some way of doing so."

"What if the Turk doesn't cooperate?"

Jacques shrugged. "You beat Maelzel in a contest of wills. Surely you will not let a machine tell you what to do."

"How can it tell me *anything*? It's just a bunch of gears and levers." There was no reply. "Isn't it?" When Jacques continued to ignore me, I heaved a sigh. "I know, I know. I ask too many questions."

All through the endgames the following afternoon, the Turk performed flawlessly. But then I came face-to-face—metaphorically speaking—with Mrs. Fisher again. I tried to give her an advantage by neglecting to castle my king. But as soon as I did, I felt something change. I don't know whether it was something in me—maybe deep inside I just hated losing—or in the machine. Each time I tried to make a deliberately stupid move, the Turk's arm resisted. I knew that if I tried to force it, I'd end up knocking over half the pieces again.

I put the brass dial on 3, to indicate that I needed more time. Then I slid my seat to a more comfortable position, took a deep breath, and said in a soft, reasonable voice, "Look. I can't pretend again that the arm isn't working right. Maelzel won't believe me. If I don't finish the game and let this Mrs. Fisher win, Maelzel's going to give me another beating, and this time he'll pick someplace where Jacques won't interfere." I wasn't quite sure who I was talking to—myself or the machine. Either one seemed a little odd, but I didn't know what else to do.

"Sometimes it's okay to lose a battle in order to win the war," I went on. "And anyway, Mrs. Fisher isn't the enemy, Maelzel is. So. I'm going to let Mrs. Fisher take my knight, now."

I wiped the sweat from my hands, took hold of the

pointer, gently lifted the knight, and moved it into the path of the Black bishop.

When I emerged from the cabinet half an hour later, Maelzel didn't exactly look pleased, but neither did he look enraged. "For once you were smart and did as you were told. Just remember who the boss is, boy, and we will get along."

"Did Mrs. Fisher enjoy winning?"

"Very much. In fact she gave us a . . . what do you call it?"

"A bonus?"

"*Ja*. A bonus." He tossed a half-dollar coin to me. "That is your share."

"Who is she?"

"Frau Fisher? Who knows? Who cares? She will boast to her friends, and they will all try to duplicate her success."

"And should I let them?"

"Not unless I say so. The Turk has a reputation to uphold, after all."

When I returned to the workshop, Jacques said, "Well? Did Otso let you lose?"

I grinned wearily. "*Oui*. Though I did have to coax him a little."

Now that I was in Maelzel's good graces—or as good as his graces ever got—I decided to push my a luck a little. The following day, I asked whether I could leave the workshop on my own. "I'll go late at night, when nobody will see me."

"For what reason?"

"To take some money to my father."

"He is still in debtors' prison, is he?"

"Yes. He needs a bed, and better food."

Maelzel contemplated this for a moment, then shook his head. "I am afraid not. If you go wandering the streets alone, the night watch will pick you up, and you will be put in the House of Refuge again."

That possibility had never occurred to me. I'd been incredibly lucky to avoid the watchmen on the night I raided the Parsonage. "You could come with me," I suggested.

He gave a contemptuous snort. "I am not your servant, boy."

"I don't suppose . . ."

"What?"

"I don't suppose you could ask Mulhouse to take me?"

He scowled at the very mention of the man's name. "*Nein*. I do not even know where he is, and I do not really care to know."

I could hardly ask Jacques and his mechanical legs to trudge all the way to the prison with me. I did, however, ask him to send the money by messenger.

"Yes, yes, all right!" he snapped. "Now pay attention to what you are doing!"

"What *am* I doing?" He had me sewing together wide strips of leather, but I had no idea what for.

"Making a back brace, *évidemment*."

I stared at him, dumbfounded.

"Close your *grande gueule*," he said. "And hold still." With a cloth tailor's tape, he briskly measured the length of my curved spine, the width of my shoulders, and the girth of my waist, and jotted down the dimensions—which would have been excellent for constructing a scarecrow. There was no point in asking why he would want to build me a back brace. He would only have made some disagreeable reply, or else ignored me.

CHAPTER 16

WE COULDN'T LET MAELZEL KNOW about the back brace, of course. He would have accused us of neglecting our other tasks. But in truth, there weren't many other tasks; the automata were all performing splendidly and, I gathered, attracting record crowds. Jacques kept a cloth handy and, when Maelzel happened to pay us a visit, he spread it over the curious device.

Though Jacques's personality left a lot to be desired, no one could fault his skill as a craftsman. It took us only a few days to finish the brace, and when he strapped it on me, it fit perfectly. I couldn't help laughing, imagining how I must look—like some bizarre meld of human and machine.

It was more than just a metal frame with straps and padding; Jacques had made it flexible and had attached to it a small metal box full of gears and springs. When turned, one tooth at a time, the mechanism straightened the frame by slow degrees, pulling backward on the clamps that fit over my shoulders. Ever since I arrived here, I'd been little more than a clockwork boy, expected to function smoothly and without complaint. Now I was actually being equipped with gears.

"If this is to do any good," said Jacques, "you must wear it constantly."

"Even when I sleep?"

He nodded. "Take it off only when you operate the Turk."

"What if Maelzel sees it?"

Jacques shrugged. "There is nothing he can do about it now."

Though I suspected he wouldn't want my thanks, I tried anyway. "Merci bien."

He gave a dismissive grunt. "You will not be so grateful when you have worn that for a few days."

My back had always pained me a certain amount, especially when I sat bent over a book or over the chessboard too long. Now, with the brace pulling at it, my spine ached continually. I could more or less ignore the pain during the day, when I was busy in the workshop, but it was difficult to sleep at night, especially since I could lie with relative comfort in only one position—on my stomach.

The brace had one unexpected benefit, though; I found that I could suddenly breathe more easily. My lungs had always been weak, and I know now that it was partly due to my slumped posture. What's more, my stomach felt less cramped and queasy; my appetite improved so dramatically that, instead of *Bébé*, Jacques began calling me *Porcelet*—piglet.

Every few days, just when the pain began to subside a little, he turned the gears a notch, tightening the frame and testing my endurance. The only respite I got was the time I spent operating the Turk. Ironically, the straighter my back became, the harder it was to fold myself up inside the cabinet.

It was nearly a week before Maelzel visited the workshop and saw me decked out in my corset of leather and metal. He didn't seem to mind that we'd been using his time to work on a project of our own. In fact, he behaved less like a boss than like a fellow craftsman, openly admiring Jacques's handiwork and minutely examining the mechanics of it. He ignored my presence completely; I felt more than ever like one of his automata.

"So," he said, "you turn the gears and it straightens the frame, eh?"

"*Oui*," said Jacques. "You use this handle."

Maelzel took the brass crank from him and inserted it in the side of the little gearbox. "Very neatly done," he said. And then he abruptly turned the handle—not just one notch, but a half a dozen at least. My spine felt as though it were being shattered. I let out a howl of pain and protest.

"Oh, dear," said Maelzel, calmly. "I must have over-done it."

Jacques lurched toward me and pushed the lever that released the gears. I slumped forward, gasping. Though Maelzel made an apology of sorts, I knew very well that it wasn't genuine, that he'd done the deed deliberately. It was his way of reminding me that, though I'd defied him once and won, he could still bend me to his will—quite literally.

As he was leaving, he turned back to say, "I hope you made the boy pay for the materials you used."

"The device was my idea," said Jacques, "not his. And I was just doing what I always do—repairing the machinery."

Though I'd done what I could to help out my father, I still worried about him. He'd said I could return in a couple of weeks, when there was no risk of my catching the cholera. Two weeks had passed, and I still had no one to accompany me to the prison; I'd have to risk it alone.

I waited until the night soil men came to clean out our earth closet, then repeated my trick of jamming the access door and spreading a thick layer of sawdust to crawl on. It was difficult to disentangle myself from the torture rack, but I couldn't ask Jacques for help, and I certainly couldn't squeeze through the toilet hole while wearing it. With a bit of painful squirming, I managed to escape from the brace, and then from the building.

As I made my stealthy way down Market Street, I spied only one night watchman, and he paid no attention to me; he was busy chasing off the vagrants who made beds out of the benches in the public market. When I neared Arch Street Prison, I heard faint footfalls behind me; I slipped into a dark doorway and looked back the way I had come, expecting to see either a watchman or a thief. Instead, I saw the Woman in Black.

She'd stopped walking and was just standing on the street corner, glancing this way and that, as though searching for someone. I had the distinct feeling that the person she was looking for was me. I couldn't imagine why. But neither could I dismiss this as just another coincidence.

I stayed in the shadows until she gave up and disappeared down 13th Street. Whoever she was, she must be either very brave or very foolish to wander about the streets alone at this hour. But in truth she probably had little to fear. Any ruffian who crossed her path would assume she was demented, and wouldn't bother her.

The night keeper at the prison recognized me at once. "You're Reverend Goodspeed's son," he said. "I reckon you've come for his effects."

"His effects?"

"There ain't much, I'm afraid. He sold most everything at one time or another, even his spectacles and his pocket watch." The keeper handed me a small parcel wrapped in paper. "That's all I saw that might be worth saving. 'Tis that notebook he was always writing in."

I couldn't seem to make any sense of the man's words. Why would he be giving me my father's notebook? "Can't I see him?"

"See him?" echoed the keeper, sounding as baffled as I was. Then he put a hand to his head, as though he'd been struck. "Oh, thunderation. Nobody's told you, have they?"

"Told me what?"

"I'm dreadful sorry to have to be the one." He placed a heavy hand on my shoulder. "The Reverend has been in the ground for nearly a week now, son. The contagion took him."

I don't know how I made it back to Masonic Hall, or whether I encountered anyone on the way. I must have somehow avoided both the night watch and the night prowlers. A whole gang of thieves might have set upon me, and I would scarcely have known or cared, I was so dazed and distracted.

As bad as my situation had been these past months, I'd always held in my heart the belief that somehow I'd release my father from his debt and from his stone cell and find Fiona, and we'd reclaim that idyllic life we had lost, or something like it—perhaps not at the Parsonage, but somewhere quiet and comfortable and safe.

That hope had abandoned me, now, just as my father had, and my mother and Fiona and even Mulhouse. There was no one in the world I could trust, no one who cared about me or valued me for myself, only people who cared about my freakish skill at chess and the money they could make from it.

I'm not sure why I went back to the workshop at all. I'd only taken the job in order to earn the money to free my father. Well, he was free now—in the words of his favorite poem, "free from every anxious thought, from worldly hope and fear."

I suppose I returned simply because I had nowhere else to go. Despite all I'd suffered at the hands of Maelzel and Jacques, I was better off there than in the House of Refuge, winding bobbins and being tormented by the big boys.

That thought didn't occur to me at the time, though, at least not consciously. I didn't think about much at all, not even chess. I just lay on my sack of shavings, staring senselessly at the fly-specked ceiling. I didn't bother to strap on the back brace; I just couldn't see the point of it, or of anything else.

When the sun came up and Jacques tried to rouse me, I didn't respond. He shook my arm a few times, then gave up and just let me lie there. As performance time approached, and I'd still made no move or sound, he left the room and returned with Maelzel. After bending over and glaring at me for moment, the German said, "The boy looks well enough to me—at least as well as he ever looks. I expect he is only feigning illness, in order to avoid working." He prodded me in the ribs with one shiny shoe. "Get up, boy. I am not paying you good money to lie there and daydream."

I cared no more about money than I did about back braces or food or chess. I didn't even care whether or not he beat me. Since I seemed to feel nothing, I doubted that I'd even notice the blows. But you know, they say that, even in a mesmeric trance, people never lose themselves entirely. There's some essential part of us that won't give up control, that keeps us from, say, murdering someone just because the mesmerist commands us to.

And the truth was, underneath all that apathy, that

near-paralysis of my emotions, I *did* feel something. Not sadness; that would come later. And not self-pity or despair; I'd never felt those, not even when things looked their worst. No, it was the same feeling that allowed me to cope with all the troubles that had befallen me so far. What I felt was stubbornness.

Though the thought of a beating didn't bother me, the thought of being *beaten*—in the non-physical sense—did. I could have defied Maelzel just by lying there and refusing to work, of course. But that would have put me in the same league with those infuriating chess players who spend an hour mulling over a single move—reasoning, I suppose, that if they don't play, they can't lose. If I wanted to prove my worth—to Maelzel, to the world, to myself—I couldn't do it lying on my back and staring into space; I needed to get back in the game.

Unlike the church deacons who had condemned my father without ever reading his book, I'd struggled through all four hundred pages of *The Development of Species*. It seemed to me that the basic idea behind all those words was really pretty simple: *In nature, it's the strongest and healthiest members of a species that survive and pass their traits on to the next generation.*

I'd always taken that to mean *physically* the strongest. But I've come to realize that there are different sorts of strength. Sometimes it's the Davids who survive, not the Goliaths, the puny humans who flourish and the great mammoths who die out. My father had always regarded me as weak and sickly, like my mother, and fated to die young. But he was only seeing my frail, bent body, and not my spirit.

"Well?" snapped Maelzel. "Are you going to get up, or do I have to beat you again?"

Slowly, like someone waking, I turned my head toward him and met his glowering gaze. "You won't beat me," I murmured.

The man laughed, but it sounded slightly strained, a bit uncertain. "I shall do to you whatever I like."

"Maybe," I said. "But you won't beat me."

He continued to stare at me a moment, with a puzzled frown, then abruptly turned away. "We open the doors of the hall in fifteen minutes. You had better be in your place."

IT PROMISED TO BE A LONG AFTERNOON, one that would leave my body stiff and sore. The Turk had again been challenged to a complete game, and I could tell from the very outset that my challenger knew what he was doing. I opened with the old reliable King's Gambit, in which you give Black the opportunity to take one of your pawns. A mediocre opponent will jump at the chance—but if he does, he no longer controls the center of the board. This fellow—I assumed it was a fellow—didn't fall for it; he trotted out his knight instead.

When I was younger, I had often tried the King's Gambit on my father; he had invariably replied with that same countergambit. In my dazed, disoriented state, I began to imagine that my unseen opponent was, in fact, my father. Could the night keeper be mistaken? Maybe he hadn't been hauled off to the graveyard at all; maybe he'd just been released.

The more I dwelt on it, the more real the possibility seemed. It should have comforted me; instead, it made me angry. Why hadn't he come to find me, or at least left a note, telling me he was all right? Why had he let me suffer under the delusion that he was dead?

As you might guess, I'm not normally given to fits of anger. Anyone who examined my skull would find that my organ of Agreeableness is well developed, and my Combativeness is as flat as yesterday's champagne. And in fact the anger didn't seem to be coming from inside me, but from some other source. It was as though I were in a hypnotic trance, with the mesmerist telling me that I was playing chess against my worst enemy and that I must crush him.

Clearly, I wasn't in my right mind. I didn't play in my usual methodical, careful fashion. Instead of analyzing every move and its ramifications, I played totally by instinct, making outrageous sacrifices and apparent blunders. Anyone watching the game must have thought that the machine's clockwork had slipped a few gears; Maelzel must have been ready to tear out his hennaed hair, wondering what the devil I was up to. Each time my opponent took more than half a minute to consider his next move, I drummed the Turk's wooden fingers on the board and rolled his dark eyes.

There was, of course, method in my madness. Though Black captured almost half of my pieces, with the other half I constructed a prison from which there was no escape. Eventually it dawned on my opponent that he was doomed; no matter how impatiently I shook my head or drummed my fingers, he made no more moves. Then the metal ring beneath his king dropped, and I knew he'd conceded.

Slowly I became aware of a faint fluttering sound from outside the cabinet—similar to the pounding of feet I'd heard weeks earlier, when the cry of "Fire!" had cleared the hall, but without the accompanying vibrations. It took me a few moments to realize that what I was hearing was applause.

When I emerged from the cabinet, Maelzel said nothing, only stared at me again as though wondering what had gotten into me. I didn't speak, either; I returned to the workshop, struggled into my back brace, and set about sweeping up. After watching me curiously for a moment, Jacques said, "Those shavings have proven useful, *n'est-ce pas?*"

"What do you mean?"

"You know what I mean." He jerked his head in the direction of the earth closet. "I heard you leave last night."

"Why didn't you stop me?"

He shrugged. "I thought perhaps you had a good reason."

"I did. I went to see my father." I hoped he wouldn't ask about my father's health; I didn't want to have to answer. I needn't have worried; Jacques seldom kept a conversation going any longer than absolutely necessary.

But, to my surprise, he did say something more. "That was an interesting game, *Porcelet*."

"The one this afternoon? You saw it?"

He nodded. "I was not sure you were in any shape to perform."

"I wasn't; at least not the way I usually do."

Jacques made an unfamiliar sound that might have been a laugh. "*C'est ça.* Your tactics were daring and *dangereuse*—the sort Mulhouse might use."

"Or Otso," I said.

He gave me a fierce glance. "What do you mean?"

"I just meant, if he were a person, and not a machine."

For several minutes, Jacques worked in silence, planing off long ribbons of wood from a piece of ash. Then he said quietly, "The real Otso was like that. Daring and dangerous. But he was also generous. And loyal." He shook his head and gave a sad half smile. "And he could drink more *sagardo* than any man I have ever met, before or since."

"*Sagardo?*"

"Fermented cider."

"It sounds good."

He snorted derisively. "It tastes like *pisse*."

In the weeks that followed, I gradually went back to my old, cautious style of playing. But from time to time I still felt the urge to make a totally outrageous move, and often I obeyed the urge. Sometimes it put me in a real predicament, one that took all my skill to work my way out of. It did keep things interesting, though. And Maelzel grudgingly admitted that audiences loved this sort of derring-do far more than they did a plodding, predictable game.

Even more gradually, I began to recover from the shock of my father's death. The night keeper had told me where he was buried—in the graveyard next to the church whose pulpit he had once occupied every Sunday. The same deacons who had scorned him when he was alive had welcomed him back into the fold now that he couldn't stir up any more controversy.

At first I couldn't bear the thought of visiting his grave; it would be like giving up on him, admitting that he was gone. But I have never liked lying, even to myself, and it began to seem cowardly to me, to keep avoiding the hard truth. I have never been superstitious, either, but I have to admit that the prospect of wandering alone about a churchyard at night was a bit daunting.

I'd said nothing to either Maelzel or Jacques about my father's fate. Again, it would have seemed a betrayal of some kind. Besides, I knew how Maelzel's mind worked: He would conclude that, since I no longer had an urgent need for money, he could withhold my wages again. But the fact was, I *did* need the money—not because it could buy things, but because it meant that my skill and my services were worth something.

Jacques hadn't told our boss about my nighttime forays, at least as far as I knew. Maybe, I thought, I could trust him in this, too. As we sat at the workbench, tinkering with the innards of the mechanical woman—I had taken to calling her Fiona— I said, cautiously, "Would you ever consider letting me out during the daytime?"

As usual, Jacques took his time in replying. At last, he muttered, "*Peut-être.* If it was a matter of life or death."

"It is."

"Which one? Life? Or death?"

My reply was almost as slow in coming as his. "Death."

He grunted. "*Votre père?*"

"*Oui.* He died of cholera."

"How long have you known?"

"Since that night I sneaked out."

"Hmm. You want to visit his grave, I suppose."

"*Oui.*"

There was another long silent spell, then he growled, "We can do it only when Maelzel is gone."

"We?" I said.

"*Oui,*" he said.

I couldn't help snickering. "We both sound like *porcelets*. Wee, wee, wee."

Jacques bent his head so that his nose nearly touched the table. He might have just been taking a closer look at Fiona's gears, but I had the feeling he was also hiding a grudging smile.

Our opportunity came a few days later. On Sundays and Mondays, when the exhibition was closed, Maelzel often went away on business—he seldom said what sort, or where. I suspect now that he had a lady friend in the country, but that thought never occurred to me at the time.

Aside from the small hours of the morning, the best time to wander the city unseen was on Sunday afternoon. All respectable people, even the constables, were home having Sunday dinner with family and friends, leaving the streets to those of us who had no family and no friends.

We must have made a curious sight, Jacques and I: A bear-like man shuffling along with the aid of a crutch, and a puny boy who appeared to have gotten stuck inside a bizarre sort of birdcage. But the few people we passed—street urchins, mostly—paid us little attention; no doubt they'd seen far stranger things.

As we approached my father's old church, I sighted a black-clad figure moving about among the stones in the graveyard. "Oh, Lud," I murmured. "It's her again."

"Who?" asked Jacques.

"The Woman in Black. I seem to see her everywhere I turn. You don't know her, do you?"

Jacques, who had grown nearsighted from all the close work, squinted in her direction, then shook his head. "*Non.*" When we passed through the wrought-iron gate and into the graveyard, the woman spotted us. Abruptly, she turned and hurried off, her long skirts brushing against the lichen-covered gravestones. "Does she ever speak?" asked Jacques.

"Not so far."

"Ah. Perhaps she is *un fantôme.*"

"A ghost?" I shivered. "You think there are such things?"

"*Mais oui.*"

"But she looks perfectly real. Besides, ghosts stay in one place. They don't follow you around, do they?"

He gazed off in the direction the Woman in Black had gone. "Perhaps they do, sometimes."

It was easy enough to find my father's grave; it was the most freshly dug. Though I knew that the live people in graveyards sometimes talk to the deceased, I didn't think Father would approve, so I only knelt by the dirt mound for a while and wept silently. When I rejoined Jacques, he said, "Is your mother's grave here, too?"

"No. Her parents insisted on burying her in the Raybold family plot, but I'm not sure where that is. We never visited the Raybolds; they didn't like Father very much. I think they blamed him for her death. They said that he should have known she was too fragile to bear children."

"She died giving birth to you?"

"No, but it wasn't long afterward, I think. Father didn't like talking about it."

Most of the way back to Masonic Hall, Jacques was his usual taciturn self; the effort of plodding along on his mechanical legs made him even more sullen than usual. He made certain that, when we let ourselves into the workshop, no one was around to observe us, not even the spectral Woman in Black.

"Do we really need to be so careful?" I said. "I mean, why would anyone suspect me of being the Turk's operator? Wouldn't they just think I was an ordinary chore boy or apprentice?"

"They might have seen you perform at the Chess Club."

"Oh. I suppose you're right. But I can't stay shut up in this room forever. I know! I could wear a disguise!"

Jacques gave a derisive laugh. "You would still be four feet tall and hunchbacked."

"I'm getting less hunched all the time. I think the brace is helping, don't you?"

He grunted noncommittally. "Now, if we take the show to another city, where no one knows you . . ."

"Do you think that's likely?"

"We have talked about it. Eventually, people will stop coming, and it will be time to move on."

"To where?"

He scowled at me. "How do I know? You ask too many questions."

CHAPTER

18

J ACQUES WAS RIGHT; EACH AFTERNOON, I peered at the audience through the tiny hole in the curtain, and after another week or so of big crowds, I noticed the attendance starting to dwindle. As we were putting away the chess pieces after a performance, I casually asked Maelzel, "Are we taking the exhibition to another city?"

He glared at me. "Who told you that?"

"No one. I just wondered. I—I read somewhere that you've already been to New York and Boston." Actually, that information had come from Mulhouse, but I knew better than to bring up his name.

Maelzel scratched his head thoughtfully. "I may decide to move, yes." He seemed to be waiting for a reaction from me. When I said nothing, he went on. "I suppose now you will give me some wretched story about how you could not possibly leave your father all alone."

"No."

He raised his plucked eyebrows. "No?"

"I need the job. If you travel, I'll come along."

"*Sehr gut*. I could have forced you to come, of course, but it is easier this way." He drew a piece of paper from his waistcoat pocket and unfolded it. "As it happens, I just received a letter from Mr. Poe; you remember him?"

I nodded. "The man who yelled 'Fire!' because he was losing."

Maelzel gave a sharp laugh. "Well, he did not do the actual yelling, but he may have hired someone to do it for him. It would not surprise me; he has a devious air about him." Maelzel tapped the letter. "He is in Richmond now, editing a magazine. According to him, it is a thriving metropolis, and its people have money to spend. He feels the exhibition would be a huge success."

"He could just be luring us there to get another look at the Turk."

"That does not worry me, as long as we are careful." He folded the letter and tucked it away. "It is tempting, particularly with cold weather coming. I would far rather spend the winter in Virginia than in Pennsylvania."

The prospect of leaving Philadelphia didn't bother me much. It may seem strange that I was so willing to leave the city where I grew up, where everything was familiar to me. But the truth was, I had no great love for the City of Brotherly Love. It hadn't been kind to me. I had felt at home only in the Parsonage. Ever since our eviction, I'd been like a stranger in a strange land. Now, the only place I felt I really belonged was inside that claustophobic cabinet.

By the beginning of November, we were playing to audiences of only fifteen or twenty, which Maelzel used as an excuse to lower wages—not only mine, but those of all his employees. When they complained, he fired most of them, keeping on only two men to disassemble the automata and dioramas and pack them into wooden crates.

These men weren't permitted to handle the Turk. Jacques and I pulled poor Otso apart at the waist and placed his torso gingerly in a box filled with shavings. His lower body didn't require such care; it was made of solid wood. We removed the clockwork and the mechanical arm from the cabinet and laid them in a nest of crumpled newspapers; the cabinet went into a padded crate all its own.

As I was removing the maple doors and wrapping them in cloth, I noticed a spot in one corner of the cabinet's interior where the felt lining bulged just slightly, as though some tiny object were lodged beneath it. Carefully I lifted the edge of the felt and coaxed the object from its hiding place. It was an earring, a single pearl dangling from a silver hook. When I held it closer to the window and examined it, I saw that the silver was tarnished with some dark brown substance—a substance that I was very familiar with. As a young child, I was subject to frequent nosebleeds, and no matter how diligently Fiona laundered my handkerchiefs, most of them remained spotted with dried blood.

"What do you have there?" demanded Jacques.

"Oh, nothing." I shoved the earring into my trouser pocket. "A chip of dried glue from the cabinet, that's all." I didn't think it wise to mention the earring or ask who it had belonged to. The answer was obvious. It would have been downright foolish to ask why it was caked with dried blood.

Our boxes were loaded, along with at least fifty others, onto a huge freight wagon pulled by six draft horses. Maelzel's two remaining craftsmen rode in the wagon bed, to keep an eye on the crates and their contents, some of which were irreplaceable.

I wouldn't have wanted their job. I had overheard the draymen talking about the main highway that ran south from Philadelphia. They called it the King's

Road, but it sounded more like the road to perdition—except that the latter is said to be paved with good intentions, whereas the former was paved with nothing but a few planks laid down in the boggiest spots. And the freight wagon had no suspension at all to even out the bumps; I only hope that Maelzel paid those poor wretches well for their services—though I doubt it.

In good weather, stagecoaches traveled the King's Road daily, carrying mail and a few hardy passengers who paid a fare of five cents a mile for the privilege of having their teeth jarred loose. It wouldn't have surprised me if Maelzel had expected Jacques and me to walk all the way to Richmond, to save the cost of the stage. Instead, he did something wholly unexpected: He bought a covered wagonette and two horses to haul it. At first I was astonished, but I should have known Maelzel wouldn't do something so extravagant without a reason. He had heard there was a shortage of good vehicles in Richmond, and when we arrived there he sold the rig—for fifty dollars more than he'd paid for it.

I could spend an entire chapter recounting the many miseries and mishaps that befell us on that journey, which took us six days but seemed more like sixty. They would make for a pretty tedious tale, though. It can be amusing, in a perverse way, to hear about a person's trials and tribulations—after all, they've made up the bulk of my story so far—provided they're interesting ones. But there's nothing very interesting about prying a wagon out of the mud, especially after the fourth or fifth time, or being assailed by bedbugs at some shabby inn twenty miles from nowhere.

The things that befell me when we reached Richmond are a lot more compelling. There's even a beautiful young lady involved. What could be more compelling than that?

When he described Richmond as a thriving metropolis, Mr. Poe wasn't using poetic license. It was only a tenth as large as Philadelphia, but what it lacked in size it made up for in rambunctiousness. Up until then I'd led a very quiet life—I don't mean *uneventful,* of course, for in that sense it had been anything but quiet lately. I mean *quiet* as in *not noisy.* For me, entering Richmond was like being caught in a sudden, violent thunderstorm.

If you've ever been in Philadelphia on Independence Day, you know what a racket there is: bands playing and people cheering and fireworks exploding. Well, Richmond was like that every day. No one was celebrating; it was just business as usual. Pathways called "rolling roads" converged on the city from all directions, like strands of a spiderweb, and a constant parade of wagons rumbled along them, hauling hogsheads of tobacco from distant plantations to the docks at Rocketts Landing.

From the broad James River came the rhythmic splash of a dozen paddle wheels, some of them attached to flour mills and some to steamboats, and every so often a steam whistle let loose a startling shriek. From the ironworks came a constant clanging, and through the open windows of the tobacco factories floated the sound of Negro workers singing "Heaven Bell A-Ring" and "I Can't Stay Behind." From the street in front of Bell Tavern came the shout of an auctioneer selling slaves. From Haymarket Pleasure Gardens came the squeals of delighted children and their terrified mothers riding the Flying Gigs.

In the daytime, mockingbirds chattered insanely in the trees; in the evening, the croaking of bullfrogs competed with the wails of repentant sinners at camp meetings in the fields outside of town. And underneath it all, like the harpsichord part in a Bach cantata, was the monotonous music made by the river itself as it tumbled over the rocky stretch known as The Falls.

It was a great relief to settle into the relative silence of the exhibition hall at the Virginia Museum. Our new headquarters wasn't nearly as spacious or as modern as the one we'd left behind. Twenty years earlier, the museum had been the pride of the city, with its natural science exhibits and its plaster reproductions of classical statuary like the Apollo Belvedere and the Venus de' Medici, but there just weren't enough people in Richmond to support such a grand enterprise. It now felt more like a mausoleum than a museum. To free up the main hall, the exhibits had been crammed into two small side rooms. The stuffed badgers and foxes had grown smelly and mangy, and the plaster statues were losing bits of themselves, like decaying corpses.

The main hall couldn't possibly have held all of Maelzel's automata and dioramas. He'd arranged to loan many of the pieces to an exhibition in Washington, D.C.; those crates had been dropped off in the capital city, along with one of the two remaining craftsmen. The Conflagration of Moscow, which had so entranced me with its lifelike miniatures, was no longer part of the show. It had been sold to some collector of curiosities. According to Jacques, Maelzel planned to create a whole new incarnation of the Conflagration, one that would be even more detailed and lifelike.

There was no room in the Mausoleum for an office or a workshop; naturally, Jacques and I couldn't use it as our lodgings, either. Maelzel grudgingly put us and his craftsman—a bony, humorless fellow named Mr. Moody—in a cheap boardinghouse nearby; he himself took a room at the more sumptuous Eagle Hotel.

Mr. Moody got a room to himself; I had to bunk with Jacques. I wasn't about to share a bed with him; he was still having his violent nightmares and might well strangle me. I made a pile of blankets in one corner of the room and slept on that. It wasn't comfortable, but then I don't think I would been comfortable on even the most plush featherbed, for I was still strapped into that infernal back brace most of the day and all of the night.

One of the few amenities in our room was an ancient looking glass in a scarred wooden frame. Some of the mirror's tin and quicksilver backing had flaked away, so my reflection looked pitted and decayed, like those plaster statues in the Mausoleum. But when I examined my profile in the glass, my back definitely looked straighter than it had been before the brace; I was determined to endure it until my stoop was gone altogether.

Naturally, when I walked from the boardinghouse to the Mausoleum, clad in my torture device, I drew curious stares from passersby—the rude ones, anyway. The polite ones looked pointedly away, or else gave me a sympathetic smile filled with pity. I wasn't bothered by any of it; I had been stared at and pitied for most of my life. Besides, there was a real advantage to being seen in the back brace; no one would ever imagine that such a sad case was capable of operating the Turk.

It was, in fact, getting more difficult and painful to fold myself up inside that cabinet. It wasn't due only to my straightening spine; I was bigger than I had been six months before—not a lot, but enough to make a difference. I had put on a good ten pounds and grown an inch or more in height. My wrists had begun to protrude from my jacket sleeves, and my ankles showed below my trouser cuffs.

I had no other clothing, only the stuff on my back. Aside from the Carcel lamp and my father's note-book, it was all that remained to me of my former life. Purchased by my father before his financial ruin, the items were well made and had held up admirably, considering all I had been through. I kept them as clean as I could; every week or so, I washed my linen and my trousers and brushed the dust out of my jacket. Still, it was clear that, sooner rather than later, I'd have to spend some of my hard-won wages on a new outfit.

Though I was perhaps in better health than I'd been in my life, I was still as weak as apple water. Once we had the Turk unpacked and reanimated, I tried to lend a hand with the other exhibits, but was more hindrance than help. Finally Maelzel drew me aside and thrust a sheaf of handbills at me. "Here. Normally, I hire some local lad to stick these up, but I am already paying you, so you may as well make yourself useful."

"You mean— You mean, I can go out there by myself?"

"No one knows you here, so it should be safe—as long as you keep your mouth shut. If someone should engage you in conversation, be very careful. People are always trying to pry the Turk's secret out of me, and when they find you work for me, they may question you, too. Do not be rude or secretive; that will just make them more suspicious. And do not try to mislead them; you are not clever enough. Just tell them you are only a chore boy and you know nothing. And listen—" He stuck a thick finger in my face. "Under no circumstances are you to discuss chess with *anyone*, or let anyone know that you play. Do you understand? Above all, make certain you steer clear of Mr. Poe; I do not want him interrogating you. I do not trust the man."

CHAPTER 19

Jacques provided me with a pot of glue, and I set about papering the town with the handbills, which read:

. MAELZEL'S .
✳
EXHIBITION
VIRGINIA MUSEUM

PERFORMANCES EACH TUESDAY
THROUGH SATURDAY

Doors open at half-past 7 o'clock.
Performance to commence at 8 precisely.

. Part First .

THE AUTOMATON TRUMPETER
The mechanical musician plays his instrument with a distinctness and precision unattainable by the best living performers. The pieces were written expressly for him by the first composers.

THE MECHANICAL THEATRE,
purposely introduced for the gratification of Juvenile Visitors. Figures include the Amusing Little Bass Fiddler, the French Oyster Woman, the Chinese Dancer, and the Little Troubadour playing on several instruments.

. Part Second .

THE ORIGINAL AND CELEBRATED AUTOMATON CHESS PLAYER

Invented by VON KEMPELEN,
Improved by J. MAELZEL

The Chess Player has withstood the finest players of Europe and America, and excites universal admiration. He moves his head, eyes, lips, and hands with the greatest facility and distinctly pronounces the word Échec when necessary.

Actually, at the moment, Otso was pronouncing the word *Échec* more like "Aw, shucks." His vocal mechanism had gotten jarred in transit, and Jacques was impatiently and profanely trying to put it right. I was just as glad not to be in the same room with them.

As odd as it may seem, being outdoors for any length of time was a new experience for me. I had been confined to the workshop for many months, of course, and in the House of Refuge before that. But even when I lived at the Parsonage, my world was a very limited one, made up of three tiny kingdoms—my bedroom, the parlor, and the library—in which I was absolute monarch. I went abroad only as far as the Chess Club—oh, and once each Christmas season, Fiona would bundle me up like an Esquimau and trundle me in a Bath chair down Chestnut Street to see the holiday decorations.

My father spent half his life in the outdoors, tramping through bogs and wild woodlands, collecting specimens. I begged him to take me along—just once, even—but he refused; it would be too hard on my frail constitution, he said. I know he meant well, but I think now that the fresh air would have done me far more good than harm.

Once I got used to all the noise and activity, I actually enjoyed walking around Richmond, pasting my handbills up on walls and fences and streetlamp posts.

For all its industry, the city still had a sort of frontier feel to it. The thoroughfares were unpaved and, except for a short stretch along Main Street, there were not even any sidewalks. Gaslights had not yet made their way that far south; the streetlamps were still fired with whale oil.

Though the women's fashions seemed much the same as those in Philadelphia, the men had a more rough and ready, Davy-Crockettish look about them; most wore their hair long and many, as Jacques did, tied it back in a horse's tail. I'd expected everyone to speak in the same Southern drawl Mr. Poe used; instead I heard an astonishing array of accents—from a Scots burr to the untutored speech of plantation slaves—and a Babel of languages, some familiar to me, some unintelligible.

With all the clamor and conversation going on around me, I didn't notice the figure standing right at my elbow until she spoke, in a soft, sweet voice. "Are you one of Mr. Maelzel's automata, sir?"

I nearly dropped my glue pot. I did, in fact, drop the brush, which stuck to one of the straps on my back brace. She put a hand to her mouth to stifle a giggle. "I'm sorry. Perhaps that was rude of me. It's just that . . . well, you do look a bit mechanical, with your . . ." Blushing, she made a slight, ladylike gesture to indicate the back brace.

I felt myself reddening, too, as though I'd been out in the sun too long. And perhaps I had, but that wasn't the reason for the flush on my face. I tried to think of a sensible reply, but even if I had, I don't believe I could have gotten it out; like Otso, I seemed to have lost control of my vocal mechanism.

I've often found myself speechless in the presence of some wonder of nature or some masterful work of art, but I don't recall ever being struck dumb, before or since, by a woman's beauty. Well, I say a woman, but really she could not have been much older than I was—perhaps fourteen or fifteen. Trying to describe her would be like trying to describe a sunset, or the aurora borealis. Have you ever seen a reproduction of the Venus de' Medici? Let me just say that, if someone clothed that statue in a dress and bonnet, the two would have looked like sisters. Their hair was even done up in a similar style and they had the same pale, flawless complexion. But the flesh and blood sister had an advantage over the marble one, thanks to her large violet eyes, her raven hair, and her red lips.

"May I see one of those?" she asked. I placed a poster carefully in her gloved hand. After perusing it for a moment, she glanced at me. "Can the mechanical chess player really speak?"

I got my voice box to say something that sounded like "Yes."

From the delighted look on her face, anyone would have thought I had said something devastatingly witty. "Oh!" she cried. "And you can speak, too!"

"Yes," I said again. My vocabulary was not even as good as the Turk's.

"How does it work?" she asked.

"My voice?"

She tittered again, very charmingly. "No, you goose. The chess player's voice. Is Mr. Maelzel a ventriloquist?"

When Maelzel warned me that people might quiz me about the Turk, I hadn't taken him very seriously. But it seemed he was right. "I don't know, Miss," I lied. "I'm just a chore boy." Though Maelzel was no ventriloquist, he was putting words in my mouth.

She handed the poster back to me. "Well, I suppose I'd better let you get back to your chores. I'm sorry I startled you." She removed one of her gloves and, with delicate fingers, pried the glue brush off me and stuck it in the pot. "There. I hope you'll be able to get the glue off your . . ." She gestured discreetly at my torture device again.

"It's a back brace," I said.

"It looks as though it would hurt. Does it hurt?"

I was not used to being asked so many questions. Usually I was the one doing the asking. "Not much."

"Back in Baltimore, I had a friend who wore a leg

brace; she said it hurt all the time." We stood there, awkwardly silent, for a minute or two, then she said, "May I stick up one of your handbills? It looks like fun."

"It's messy."

"I don't care." She tucked her gloves—which I now noticed looked rather threadbare— into her crocheted handbag, took a poster from me, and slathered the back of it with glue.

"Not so much, or I'll run out before I'm done."

"I'm sorry." She held up the handbill. "Where shall I stick it?"

"I just put them wherever there are other bills. That way I reckon no one will yell at me." Suddenly I was managing to string whole sentences together. Though the girl had the Venus de' Medici's beauty, there was nothing cold or aloof about her; like the sunbaked dirt under our feet, she exuded warmth. After only ten minutes in her presence, I was feeling surprisingly at ease. Like being outdoors, it was something of a new experience for me. Growing up sequestered and sheltered as I did, I'd had very little contact with women—except for Fiona, of course—and even less with girls my own age.

There were a few females in the congregation who clearly had their eye on my father. But, though he accepted their covered dishes and cut flowers gratefully, he gave them no encouragement at all; I believe that

Lily, my mother, was the only woman he could imagine sharing his life with. The ladies generally lost interest anyway, once they met dear Reverend Goodspeed's son, the invalid, hunchbacked chess fanatic.

One of the more persistent parishoners was a widow with a daughter just my age. Instead of being repelled by my condition, the girl actually seemed fascinated by it, in the way that people were fascinated by the mammoth bones in Peale's Museum, or by Mr. Barnum's oddities. I wasn't a person to her, only a curiosity. As soon as I determined that she couldn't play chess, I ignored her.

The beautiful young lady I met in Richmond seemed to care nothing one way or the other about my deformity. Once we'd discussed the back brace briefly, that seemed to be the end of it. From then on, she treated me as though I were any ordinary boy—which is exactly how I'd always wished to be treated.

It had never occurred to me that pasting up handbills might be considered a form of amusement. But for some reason, my new acqaintance took great delight in it. "There's something a little naughty about it, I think," she said. "Sort of like defacing property, except that it's legal."

"Do you think you might come to the exhibition? It's even more fun than posting handbills."

She laughed. "That's hard to imagine." Then she lowered her gaze, and her face took on a more somber expression. "I would like to come, but I'll have to ask my mother. I'm not sure . . . Well, to be honest, I'm not sure we can afford it. Once we've paid for our room and board, there's not much left for 'frivolities,' as Mama calls them."

"What if . . . what if I could get you in for free?"

Her face brightened. "You'd do that for me? I mean, it's not as if we're friends or anything. You scarcely know me."

"Well, if you tell me your name and I tell you mine, then we'll know each other."

"Virginia."

"That's your name?"

"Yes."

"You're *from* Virginia, and your *name* is Virginia?"

"Well, I'm from Maryland, actually. We've only been here a few months. And your name is . . . ?"

"Kentucky." When her eyes went wide, I laughed. "No, I'm teasing. My name's Rufus."

She held out one small white hand and we shook in a businesslike fashion. "It's very nice to meet you, Rufus." When she tried to withdraw her hand, we discovered that the dabs of glue on both our palms had stuck them firmly together.

"Oh, Lud!" I groaned. "I'm sorry! I told you it was messy!"

But Virginia didn't seem dismayed in the least; in fact, she was laughing as giddily as a five-year-old—and at the same time covering her mouth with her free hand, as well-bred young women are expected to do. I would come to learn that this was typical of her—this odd, appealing mixture of the childlike and the womanly. Still hiccuping with laughter, she said, "Oh, dear, what will people think? We've known each other such a short time, and already we're holding hands."

I didn't find the situation quite so amusing; I was puzzling over how we were going to get our hands apart. The glue was made from animal hides, and once you stuck things together with it, it wasn't easy to unstick them. The usual method was to soak them in boiling water, which didn't really seem like a very good option.

We tried forcing our palms apart, but I was afraid that, if we pulled too hard, it would peel the skin right off. "There's a horse trough. Maybe if we soaked our hands in that for a few minutes."

As we sat on the edge of the trough with our hands submerged in the tepid water, Virginia said cheerfully, "You know, if it doesn't work, we can always pose as Siamese twins, like Chang and Eng. Perhaps we could do a world tour."

The longer we sat there, the more persuaded I was that it mightn't be so bad, being attached to this young woman for a good long while. When the glue began to dissolve, I felt a sharp twinge of regret, not so different from the twinges of pain that went through my spine every now and again.

Virginia stood and rolled down her sleeve to cover her slightly plump, pale forearm. "Well, that was entertaining. But I should be getting back to the boardinghouse, Rufus; Mama will think I've been abducted and transported to Trinidad or somewhere."

I nodded glumly. "I hope you'll be able to come to the exhibition."

"So do I. If not, we'll surely bump into each other somewhere else. It's a small city." She glanced at the glue on her palm and smiled impishly. "I think it's best if we don't shake hands in farewell."

"You're probably right. And don't worry; if you can't soak that off, you can always use a chisel."

As she strolled off, she was laughing again. I hadn't made anyone laugh, or done much of it myself, for what seemed like a very long time.

Maelzel opened the exhibition to the public on the following Tuesday. Otso still sounded a lot like an adolescent boy whose voice is changing, but otherwise he was in fine fettle. Though the hall was arranged differently, our routine remained much the same. We stored the Turk in one of the small rooms of the Mausoleum, alongside the plaster Venus; over the doorway we draped the same heavy curtain we'd used in Philadelphia. My tiny peephole was in a different spot, but if I stood on a crate I could still get a glimpse of the audience.

As I perched on the box, scanning the crowd, hoping to see one face in particular, one of the slats cracked; my foot crashed through the top of the box. Luckily, the automaton trumpeter was in the middle of a rousing cavalry march, so no one could possibly have heard my fall.

I withdrew my leg carefully and painfully—the splintered wood had badly scraped my shin—and climbed into the Turk's cabinet. According to Maelzel's orders, I was to be in place when he opened the doors to the exhibition hall, but that would have meant I'd be cramped up, half suffocating, for nearly an hour before I even got to perform. Lately, I'd been postponing the ordeal as long as possible.

It was a good thing for, after several quick endgames, someone challenged the Turk to a complete game, and it promised to be a long, dragged-out affair. Every experienced player has a distinctive style, and it didn't take me long to realize that I had faced this opponent and his maddeningly slow responses before. "Oh, Lud," I muttered. "It's Mr. Pokey Poe."

I was tempted to let him win, just to get the agony

over with, but I couldn't bring myself to do it. Though I made my own moves almost instantly, in an effort to speed things up, it didn't help much. After half an hour or so, I noticed that I was having trouble seeing the board. At first, I blamed the sweat that was running into my eyes; then I glanced at the Carcel lamp and saw that the flame was rapidly shrinking. I wound up the mechanism that ran the oil pump, but it made no difference. I'd forgotten to fill the reservoir with fuel.

CHAPTER 20

HAD TWO CHOICES, NEITHER OF THEM very satisfactory. I could turn the brass dial to the number 4, indicating that my light had gone out. But I'd never told Maelzel about the Carcel lamp, and this didn't seem like a good time to spring it on him. My other option was to play in the dark.

I'd played blindfolded many times, of course, but that was different; there, I had just called out my moves, and someone had made them for me and told me what my opponent's response was. Here, I'd have to do everything by touch.

The lamp guttered and then went out altogether. I now had only the faint light that seeped through the airholes in the bottom of the cabinet. I took a deep breath and, with my kerchief, wiped the sweat from my own hands and from the pointer that controlled the Turk's arm.

I could picture the board in my mind easily enough, but moving the miniature chessmen was trickier. I had to grope about gingerly with my left hand, locate the proper piece, then guide it to its new position without dislodging any other pieces. All the while, of course, I was manipulating the Turk's arm and fingers with my right hand. I could usually anticipate what piece Poe would move, and where, but the only way I could confirm it was to feel the metal rings on the bottom of the big board. Fortunately—or not—he always gave me plenty of time to do that.

At first, the process was awkward; the prospect of dropping a piece and never finding it again made me sweat even more than usual. But after half a dozen moves, I became less tentative and relied more on instinct. At times, it was almost as if Otso were controlling his own hand. If so, he was a good player. Despite all Mr. Poe's considering and analyzing, we defeated him in seventeen moves. I moved the levers that made Otso say *"Échec et mat."* Or was it "I shook a mop"?

As Maelzel wheeled us behind the curtain, I murmured to myself, "Good work." Then I added, "You, too, Otso." It was the only praise either of us was likely to get.

"What happened back here?" Maelzel demanded as soon as I was out of the cabinet.

"What do you mean?"

"I mean the noise, of course! What was the noise?"

I shrugged innocently. "Maybe one of the crates fell over."

He regarded me suspiciously for a moment and then let it drop. "Can you guess who your opponent was just now?"

"Mr. Poe. He didn't yell 'Fire' this time, did he?"

"No. But he certainly examined the Turk thoroughly—or as thoroughly as he could from ten feet away. I even noticed him jotting down notes on a pad."

"Maybe he'll write a piece about us for his magazine."

Maelzel snorted derisively. "The *Southern Literary Messenger*? Not likely. They print poetry and philosophical essays."

As he started off, I called after him, "Um, you didn't happen to notice a young woman in the audience who looked like the Venus de' Medici, did you?"

He gave me a skeptical glance. "No. And I feel sure a young woman with no clothing on would have drawn my attention."

"I didn't mean—" I protested, but he was gone.

Several of the exhibits had been damaged on the bumpy ride from Philadelphia and, since there were now only four sets of hands, we spent nearly every hour of the daytime working on them. What's more, Maelzel decided that, while the machines were disassembled, he might as well make a few improvements. He fitted Fiona, the lovely lady automaton, with a metal disk, like those found in music boxes, that enabled her to write out a short sentence in French, complete with accent marks and cedillas. Then he equipped the mechanical trumpeter with a larger bellows that increased the volume of his playing considerably.

Maelzel was not the sort of creator imagined by the Deists, who fashions a sort of clockwork universe and winds it up, then sits back and watches it go and never interferes. He was more like my father's idea of the creator: constantly tinkering with his creations, looking for ways to make them run more smoothly and perform more cleverly—the kind who makes it possible for new species to develop. If only Maelzel had been as concerned about the condition of his employees as he was about his machines. He often kept us at our tasks until half an hour before the doors opened.

I have to admit that my thoughts were not always on my work; in fact, more often than not, they were on Virginia. My distractedness earned me a good many curses from Jacques, and the occasional swat.

As silly as it may sound, every chance I got I slipped into the small exhibition room where the statues were displayed and gazed longingly into the face of the

Venus de' Medici. The plaster woman was no substitute for her flesh and blood sister; still, after working alongside Jacques and Mr. Moody for days on end, it was nice to see a friendly face, even if its nose was flaking a little.

Jacques had never been very good company in our off hours, either. But to my surprise, that began to change. The other boarders had been complaining about his nocturnal ravings and thrashings. Though he didn't ordinarily indulge much in strong spirits—just a pint of ale with his meals—the only way he'd found to keep his nightmares under control was to drink himself into a stupor before he retired.

I've known perfectly affable people who turned nasty under the influence of alcohol. It had the opposite effect on Jacques. For an hour or so each evening, before he passed out, he became almost pleasant, or at least not entirely unpleasant.

The bourbon, which he swigged straight from the bottle, seemed to loosen his tongue, too. Every so often, he got carried away and uttered eight or ten sentences, one right after the other. Usually he seemed to be recalling some incident from his youth, but it was hard to be sure. Not only did he ramble a lot and slur his words, he sometimes spoke in a regional dialect of French that I couldn't quite follow. I nodded a good deal as if I understood, all the while playing mental games of chess or plotting how I might make good on my promise to sneak Virginia into the exhibition hall—presuming I ever saw her again.

When we finally had all the exhibits working properly, I was allowed an afternoon off, which I planned to spend looking for a new suit of clothing. Well, I say *new*, but of course I couldn't afford to pay a tailor, and ready-made clothes weren't common at the time. Pawnbrokers were, though. I'd never visited one, but I understood that, when pawned items went unclaimed long enough, the broker put them out for sale.

During my handbill hanging, I'd noticed the three gilded globes, the universal sign of pawnbrokers, in a poor section of the city known as Screamersville. Like you, I wondered how it came by this curious name. According to some, the residents had a habit of sitting on their rickety porches and shouting the latest gossip to each other. Others swore that, in the graveyard on certain nights of the year, souls in torment could be heard screaming. Though I doubted that story, I was glad enough to be going there in the light of day.

The pawnbroker was conveniently located next to a grog shop, so that a working man without the price of a drink could get a little ready cash by hocking his vest or his tools or his wife's petticoats; with any luck, he would redeem them on the next payday.

Clearly, not everyone was so lucky. The front of the

pawnshop was like a miniature version of Peale's Museum, except that the curiosities on display were more mundane—vases and ewers, fiddles and flutes, prayer books and hymnals, blankets and pillows, rings and brooches, tarnished silverware and chipped china. A table in one corner held dozens of items of clothing, neatly folded. But before I could examine them, my eye was caught by something even more interesting—a barleycorn chess set with red and white men carved from whalebone. I fingered one of the pawns covetously.

"Be careful with that, then," said a voice, in a heavy Irish brogue. I looked around to see a scruffy, bald-headed fellow leaning across the counter that bisected the shop. He didn't seem to be scolding me; in fact, he was grinning mischievously. "You don't want to become a pawnbreaker, do you, now?" He gave a cackle of laughter. "You get it? Pawn*breaker*?"

I smiled wanly. "Very clever."

"Ah, puns are me specialty. You might even call me a *pun*broker."

I did my best to laugh along with him.

"Do you play chess, then, my lad?"

"Oh, yes," I replied eagerly. Then I remembered Maelzel's warning. "That is—No. Actually, I don't know the first thing about the game." Again, I felt like a ventriloquist's dummy mouthing Maelzel's words. "I just meant I'd *like* to play."

"Oh, well, I can give you some instruction, if you like. I was the chess champion of Skibbereen, you know, back on the auld sod."

"Um, no. Thank you. I need to get back to work. I just wanted to buy a suit of clothes."

The man shrugged. "Suit yourself." He laughed again. "*Suit* yourself?"

"I get it," I assured him, and gave my attention to the array of jackets and trousers.

A few moments later, the bell over the door jangled softly and someone entered. "Ah, and it's you, Miss Clemm," said the pawnbroker. "What can I do for you this fine day?"

"I wondered how much you could give me on this cameo."

The voice sent a tingling sensation, almost like a pang of pain, up my crooked spine. I turned, hardly hoping to see the Venus of Richmond, but there she stood.

CHAPTER
21

ONCE AGAIN, MY THROAT SEEMED FAR too tight and dry to let any words out. She mightn't have noticed me at all if the Irishman hadn't spoken up. "I believe the young gentleman is after trying to get your attention, Miss Clemm."

She turned toward me with a puzzled expression that, to my great gratification, turned into one of delight. "Rufus! I told you we'd bump into each other again, didn't I? How have you been?"

I cleared my throat. "Um, busy. Very busy."

"With the Original and Celebrated Automaton Chess Player?"

"No, no. They don't let me near the Turk. Just sweeping and dusting and that sort of thing."

She brushed one sleeve of my jacket with her worn white glove. "You do look a little dusty."

"Well, I'm going to buy a new suit of clothes, if I can find something suitable." I winced as the punbroker let out another cackle.

"Oh, good; I'll be your fashion adviser!" said Virginia. "I've always loved dressing up dolls. You can be my life-sized doll."

"What about the cameo, then?" asked the Irishman.

"We can discuss that later." She tucked the pin in her handbag and began searching through a pile of clothing that, judging by its size, had belonged to a boy of nine or ten—which meant it was probably just right for me. Though I had grown a little lately, I was still a runt. Virginia selected a dark blue sack coat and held it up in front me. "Oh, you'd look *very* dashing in that. Can you take off your brace and try this on?"

I felt myself reddening with embarrassment. "That's easier said than done. I'm like a turtle climbing out of its shell."

"Here, I'll help you," she said cheefully, and proceeded to unbuckle the straps. When I was free of the torture device, I stood there like a plaster statue, trying to keep my back as straight as possible while Venus—I mean Virginia—helped me out of my old jacket and into the new one. "Yes, that looks perfect, don't you agree, Mr. Tindle?" She held up a calico shirt with blue stripes. "Mama would love this; she fancies bright colors. Oh, and here are some trousers to match the coat." She giggled. "You'll have to put those on yourself."

If I was red before, I must have gone positively crimson. "In here," said the pawnbroker, and ushered me into a small enclosed booth. One wall of the booth held a door leading to the outside; the front opened onto the counter. "This is for me customers who don't wish to be seen hocking their valuables—but 'tis also me dressing room."

When I emerged, Virginia clapped her hands. "A perfect fit!"

"How much?" I asked the Irishman.

"Well, being as you're a friend of the young lady, I'll let you have them for a dollar."

Virginia moved up next to me and took my arm. "Now, Mr. Tindle," she said, in a voice that managed to be both sweet and reproachful, "you mustn't try to take advantage of Rufus just because he's new here. He may not have noticed the ink stain on the trousers, but I did." She leaned close to me and said, in a stage whisper, "I wouldn't give him more than fifty cents for the lot."

The pawnbroker sighed. "If all me customers were

like you, Miss Clemm, I'd be out of business in a week. Seventy-five cents, then."

I started to hand over the money, but Virginia put her gloved hand on mine. "I think you meant *sixty-five*, didn't you Mr. Tindle?"

Mr. Tindle smiled wryly and shook his bald head. "We shall have to change your name to Miss *Clam*, for it's that hard to pry anything out of you."

"I don't mind—provided I may call you Mr. *Swindle*."

The pawnbroker looked to me helplessly. "Can you believe it? Not only does she out-haggle me, she out-puns me as well!"

After helping me into my turtle shell, Virginia took my arm again and we strolled back toward the center of the city. "I think," she said, "that we should take the thirty-five cents you saved and squander it on something completely frivolous and decadent."

"What did you have in mind?"

Her eyes bright with excitement, she said in hushed, dramatic tones, "The Flying Gigs!" At that point, I had no idea what she was talking about. Before I could ask, she went on. "I've always wanted to ride on it, but I can't do it alone, and Mama refuses to try it; she insists that it would send her into conniptions. I know you wouldn't be afraid in the least."

"How do you know that? You only just met me."

She shrugged and smiled slyly. "Woman's intuition."

"Well," I said, in my usual cautious fashion, "I could try it, I suppose."

"Oh, good! It's at the Haymarket Gardens."

The Gardens was an extensive pleasure park that sat on a series of terraces overlooking the river. On our way there, we passed a site that was the furthest thing from a pleasure park—the gallows that stood in a field behind the State Penitentiary. Virginia paused before the wooden structure, and I felt her shudder and draw nearer to me. "I hate this place."

"Why stop here, then?"

"I don't know. There's something compelling about it, as there is about the scene of some great battle. I think that, in places where some dreadful event has happened, there's a sort of . . . presence that lingers."

"Like—Like a ghost, you mean?"

"Not exactly. Just a feeling, as if the spot were charged with electricity." Her delicate fingers gripped my arm so hard it hurt and she said, in a low voice, "Do you know that, only a few years ago, they hanged three Spanish pirates from this gallows? But here's the most interesting part: After they took the bodies down, they tried to bring them back to life by giving them electric shocks!"

"Oh, Lud!" It was my turn to shudder. "Did it work?"

"Yes!" she whispered. "There's one of them now!"

When I jerked my head around—not an easy thing to do while wearing a back brace—she broke into giggles. "I'm only teasing, Rufus!"

"I knew that," I muttered.

"I'm sorry if I sound morbid," she said as we walked on. "I just find stories like that so fascinating. I won't tell you about the boy who was killed on the Flying Gigs."

"You're just trying to scare me again."

"No, really. My cousin says that, years ago, a little boy tumbled out of the Gigs and the carriage ran over him. Don't worry, I'm sure it's perfectly safe, as long as you hold on tight."

"I'm not worried," I lied. As I've said, I was taught that we should accept gracefully whatever befalls us, but that doesn't mean we should go around *inviting* things to befall us.

When we entered the Haymarket Gardens, the first thing I saw was a small group of spectators gathered around a stone table at which two men sat playing chess. I was drawn to the spot as irresistibly as Virginia was to the gallows. I felt something like the electrical charge she had mentioned running through me; it made my fingertips tingle. One of the men had his fingers poised over his bishop—a really bad choice. It was all I could not to reach out and make the right move for him. Unfortunately, I couldn't control human players the way I did the Turk. The man moved his bishop—and three plays later met his doom. "*Échec et mat,*" I murmured under my breath.

"What did you say?" asked Virginia, over the sound of the spectators' applause.

I mentally scolded myself for forgetting Maelzel's instructions to show no knowledge of the game. "Oh, nothing. I was just wondering why it's over when there are still lots of pieces on the board."

She laughed. "You don't know much about chess, do you?"

"I know those are called pieces, and that's called a board."

"It's a good thing you're not operating the Original and Celebrated Automaton Chess Player."

Though her comment took me aback, I tried not to show it. "What makes you think someone operates him?"

"*Him*? You think of him as a person?"

"In a way, yes. I call him Otso."

"*Otso*? What sort of name is *Otso*?"

"Basque. It means *wolf*."

"Where did you learn that?"

I shrugged. "I read a lot."

She gave me an amused glance. "What a curiosity. A chore boy who reads."

"I wasn't always a chore boy."

"Oh? What were you?"

"You certainly ask a lot of questions," I said with a sigh.

"That's what Mama always tells me. I'm sorry. I guess I'm just naturally curious."

"Don't apologize; I'm the same way. People always say I ask too many questions, too."

"Well, if you're so curious, surely you must have wondered what makes Otto work?"

"His name's Otso, actually."

"I like Otto better. It sounds like a real name." She yanked at my arm so hard, it almost knocked me off my feet. "Oh, look! There's the Flying Gigs! And they're loading it up! Let's hurry!"

The ride consisted of four carriages, each about half the size of a real horse-drawn gig; their wheels ran on a wooden track that descended the hill toward the river. There were six passengers aboard already. A boy in a cloth cap and rumpled corduroy suit helped us into the rearmost carriage. We were barely settled in our seats when the whole thing began to move—slowly at first, but as the grade grew steeper we quickly picked up speed, until we were traveling faster than a toboggan on an icy hillside.

Beside me, Virginia let out a shriek; though my wide eyes were fixed on the track ahead, I forced myself to look her way. She hadn't swooned and wasn't having conniptions; in fact, her face was the very picture of delight. Mine, I imagine, was more like one of the fearful faces in Michelangelo's *The Last Judgment*.

Ahead of us lay the river; we were traveling so fast that I was convinced we would take flight and plunge into the water. At the last possible moment, the tracks made a sweeping curve and headed back up the hillside. Our momentum carried us uphill quite a distance before we slowed to halt; as we started to drift backward, some sort cable caught hold of us and dragged us back to our starting point.

"Oh, my!" Virginia exclaimed breathlessly as we stepped—in my case a bit shakily—from the car. "That was even more thrilling than I expected! Can we go again?"

"Umm . . ." I fingered the dimes and half dimes in my pocket. "I suppose we could."

She laid a hand on my arm. "Oh, I'm sorry. I don't mean to make you spend all your money, Rufus."

My hesitation was due more to a lack of courage than a lack of money, but of course I couldn't say so. "No, no, I've got more than enough." I dug the coins from my pocket and the courage from somewhere, and we flirted with death one more time. "If my heart stops," I said, "just have them give me an electric shock, the way they did with those Spanish pirates."

She laughed; no doubt she thought I was joking.

Obviously I survived, and didn't even require the electric shock. As I unsteadily led her away from the Flying Gigs, I asked whether she had a watch.

"I used to." She smiled ruefully. "Unfortunately, Mr. Tindle has it now. You know, when you're out with a young lady, it's not good manners to worry about the time."

"Sorry. It's just that, if I'm not back by five o'clock, Maelzel will have my head."

"I'm sure it's nowhere near that late. Oh, look!" She dragged me toward a booth where two men were engaged in a curious enterprise. One was a tall, gangly fellow dressed all in black, like a clergyman or a physician. His eyes were closed and his huge hands were clamped onto the head of a smaller man seated in a straight-backed chair. It looked almost as if he were trying to crush the smaller man's skull, but of course he wasn't. His true purpose was made clear by the sign that stood next to the booth:

PROFESSOR PALMER

· LICENSED PHRENOLOGIST ·

DETAILED READINGS
10 CENTS

"I've always wanted to have my head examined!" whispered Virginia.

"Maybe you should rephrase that," I suggested.

She giggled. "You know what I mean!"

I fished around in my pocket again and came up with two half dimes—plus Mademoiselle Bouvier's pearl earring. For a moment I stood staring at the blood-tarnished jewelry, a graphic reminder of how ruthless Maelzel could be when crossed and of the fate that awaited me if I should let slip any information about the Turk. I would even be risking his wrath if I returned late to the Mausoleum. I glanced about, hoping to spot someone who could tell me the time.

"Is that for me?" asked Virginia.

"What?"

"The earring."

"Oh. No. Just—just something I found." I crammed it back into my pocket and thrust my ten cents at Professor Palmer.

"Oh, I didn't expect you to pay!" Virginia protested.

"I don't mind." The truth was, if it made her think well of me I would have given her my last penny or ridden on the most terrifying ride ever devised.

The Professor probed Virginia's bonnetless head so gently that he barely disturbed her raven hair, which she wore in a simple style, without the elaborate curls favored by more vain young women. "Your organ of

Spirituality is highly developed," said the Professor, "as is that of Kindness. I also perceive that you are quite modest." The Professor smiled at the crowd that had gathered—more to admire Virginia's beauty, I suspect, than the Professor's ability. "There is no organ of Modesty, I hasten to add. That diagnosis was due solely to the fact that the young lady is blushing so deeply." His long fingers explored a bit more. "You have a very pronounced protrusion in the Matrimony area; I predict that you will marry at an unusually young age. Ah, I see that you are also very Agreeable—perhaps too much so. I do hope you'll be cautious, my dear, and not accept the first marriage proposal that comes along, just to be agreeable."

There was laughter and applause from the audience. As Virginia made her way through the crowd, a grinning young dandy doffed his hat and bowed to her. "Will you marry me, Miss? I wanted to be the first to ask."

She gave him a sweet smile. "I'm flattered, sir. But I'm afraid you're too late. The truth is, I'm already betrothed."

The fellow clutched his chest in mock dismay. "Ah, my heart is broken!"

When Virginia took my arm, I received a dozen envious looks. "That was great fun!" she said. "This whole afternoon has been delightful, in fact. Thank you."

I didn't reply at once. I was still mulling over what she had said a few moments earlier. Finally, I got the nerve to ask, "Was that true? The part about you being betrothed?"

"Well, not *betrothed*, exactly. I did promise my cousin that I'd marry him when I came of age. But I expect he'll have lost interest in me by that time. He's a good deal older and more worldly than I am."

Though it was foolish of me, of course, it gave me a great sense of relief to know that she wasn't actually, formally engaged. And though I wasn't bold enough to say so, I couldn't imagine anyone losing interest in her, not even if they had to wait twenty years.

Ordinarily I looked forward to the evening performance, to crawling into my little lair where, for an hour or two, I had some control over things, where no one could order me about or curse at me for being stupid and clumsy and lazy. But I must admit that having Virginia's soft arm in mine was more satisfying than gripping the Turk's mechanical one. I wished the afternoon could go on forever.

It ended abruptly when the bell at the State Capitol tolled. "Oh, Lud!" I groaned. "It's five o'clock! I have to go!" Reluctantly I withdrew my arm from hers. "Will you come to the exhibition? I'll find some way of getting you in."

"Never mind that now! Just go! I don't want you to

get in trouble!" She made a shooing motion with her hands, then hurried off, as if fearing that her presence would make me linger. I gazed wistfully after her, but only for a moment; then I turned and broke into a run, or as close to it as my spindly legs could manage.

The Mausoleum had no earth closet through which I could creep in undetected. But there was a side door that opened into one of the small exhibit rooms, and the curator often left it unlocked, even though Maelzel had repeatedly lectured him about the danger of someone sneaking in to get a look at the Turk.

Luckily for me, the curator was terribly absentminded. I slipped through the door, very conscientiously locked it behind me, and sank down, panting, on a crate. I barely had time to catch my breath before I heard Maelzel shout, "This place needs sweeping! Where the devil is that useless boy?"

I sprang from behind the curtain like an actor taking a bow. "Here I am. I was just checking the Turk, to make sure he's working right."

"The Turk is fine; it is your *own* working you need to worry about."

The day before, with Mr. Moody's grudging help, I had rehung the curtain so that my little peephole was once again at eye level. When the audience began to drift in, I scanned them eagerly, selfishly hoping that Virginia would pawn her cameo after all and squander some of the money on yet another frivolous and decadent bit of entertainment. But if she was in the crowd, I couldn't spy her.

I did, however, catch sight of another familiar figure— a small, slender woman dressed all in black.

CHAPTER
22

SEEING THE WOMAN IN BLACK STARTLED
me so that I gave an involuntary gasp—and
then silently cursed my own stupidity. The
audience mustn't suspect that I was behind that curtain.
But, I told myself, it was a noisy crowd; neither they
nor Maelzel could possibly have heard me. All the
same, I climbed out of my torture device and into
the cabinet, just in case he should check up on me.

Once my heart was beating at a normal rate, I tried
to think rationally about the situation. Maybe I'd over-
reacted. It was hard to make out details through that
little peephole; all I'd really seen was someone in a
dark dress and bonnet. There must be any number
of widows and generally gloomy-minded women in
Richmond who dressed that way. There was no reason

to think that this was the same ghost-like figure who had haunted me back in Philadelphia. After all, why should she suddenly turn up in Richmond? Unless, of course, she was deliberately following me. But why on earth should I be pursued by someone completely unknown to me?

I shook my head briskly, sending a jolt of pain down my spine. I couldn't afford to dwell on such things right now; I needed to focus on the task at hand. For the first time in months, I felt ill at ease inside my coffin-like box;. I hoped that, once Otto—I had decided that should be his name, since Virginia preferred it—once Otto and I had dazzled the audience with our endgames, they'd be content to let us go. But no; just when it seemed we were done, I heard the brass dial turn and glanced at it. Number Six. We'd been challenged to a complete game.

After only half a dozen moves, I realized we'd faced this opponent before. When one of the Black knights moved, it mistakenly went two spaces ahead and two to the left. I'd played only one person who made that particular error; at the time, I'd thought it was a test, to see how the Turk would respond. Now I got the distinct feeling that it was a signal—my challenger's way of identifying herself. I say *her*self, because I was almost certain it was Mrs. Fisher, the woman I'd allowed to win back in Philadelphia.

But if she was identifying herself, then she must know, or at least suspect, that there was a a person inside the machine to identify herself *to*. I'd have to be careful—as careful as I'd been with Poe—not to give myself away. I took longer than usual to make my next move; I needed time to think.

If my opponent was indeed Mrs. Fisher, did that mean she was following us around? Not necessarily. After all, Richmond was a major crossroads; nearly everyone heading south passed through the city. Our paths could easily have crossed purely by chance.

I might have chalked the whole thing up to coincidence . . . except that I had just glimpsed another mysterious female figure from Philadelphia. Instead, I found myself thinking the very thing you're thinking right now: Maybe Mrs. Fisher and the Woman in Black were one and the same person.

It was a long time before I would learn the truth of the matter. When the game was over—no, I didn't let her win—I asked about my opponent. But as I've said, Maelzel paid far more attention to his creations than he did to actual people. "I did not ask her name. She may have been same person you played in Philadelphia . . . or perhaps not. I do not recall that woman. This one was . . . well, ordinary looking—neither tall nor short, neither fat nor thin. Her clothing was ordinary, too; it may have been dark, but I am not certain it was black. I was concentrating on the game, not on her. Anyway, what does it matter?"

"I was just curious. Not many female players are that skilled. I thought maybe . . ."

"What?"

"Umm . . . nothing." I reached into my pocket and fingered the pearl earring. The hook had been jabbing my skin, reminding me of a certain female player who had been skilled enough to operate the Turk before she disappeared. What if Mademoiselle Bouvier hadn't met an untimely end after all? What if she had mysteriously *re*appeared, and was using an alias? In truth, it didn't seem very likely. Unless she was equally skilled at disguising herself, Maelzel would surely recognize her; he couldn't be *that* unobservant. In any case, I didn't dare mention her name. I was supposed to know nothing about her.

Each evening after that, I peered through my peephole but I spied neither the Woman in Black nor the Venus of Richmond. On my next free afternoon, I shuffled around the city for as long as my pitiful body would stand it, without encountering either of them. I retired to a bench in Haymarket Gardens, hoping Virginia might return to the scene of our outing.

I sat close enough to the stone chess table to follow the progress of the games, but not so near that anyone would suspect me of being a chess fanatic. Still, there were times when I could barely keep from shouting, as I'd once shouted at my father, "No, you mustn't move *that* piece!" When the bell in the tower struck half past four, I got wearily to my feet and, sighing, headed back to the Mausoleum.

Despite Maelzel's disapproval, the curator insisted on keeping his shabby exhibits open to the public several afternoons a week. Maelzel, in turn, insisted on draping his automata and dioramas with sheets, so that the three or four people who came to view the museum's curiosities couldn't get a free look at ours in the bargain.

I made a quick visit to the room that contained the statues; if I couldn't see Virginia, I could at least pass the time of day with her less lively sister, the Venus de' Medici. And who should I find standing before the plaster Venus but the flesh and blood one? I was treated to the same delighted smile I'd gotten at the pawnshop. "Rufus! I thought I might catch you here! I hope you didn't get in trouble the other day, when I made you late."

"Not at all." Glancing furtively about, I whispered, "I sneaked in the side door."

She giggled. "Good for you!" Leaning close she said, in a conspiratorial tone, "You don't suppose I could do the same thing, do you? I'd so like to see your exhibition, and we haven't a dime to spare. I get to tour the museum only because my cousin knows the curator."

I hesitated for a long moment. My offer to get her into the hall for free had been a foolish one, an attempt to impress her. I hadn't been thinking about the possible consequences. If I were caught sneaking someone in, there'd be the devil to pay. But as reluctant as I was to run afoul of Maelzel, I was even more reluctant to disappoint Virginia. "I reckon I can manage it. Why don't you come to the side door at about a quarter past seven, and I'll let you in."

"Oh, good!" She clapped her hands together. "We'll be partners in crime! How exciting! Can we have a secret knock?"

Her little-girlish enthusiasm made me laugh. "How about three raps, then three more, then two more?"— the very code, you will recall, that Maelzel used.

"Like this?" She rapped her gloved knuckles on the glass display case containing the stuffed fox.

"Exactly."

"Three, three, two. Three, three, two," she repeated to herself. "All right, then, I'll see you at a quarter past seven, *mon capitaine*." She gave me a naval salute.

"You have to leave?" I asked in dismay.

"No, *you* do. You got away with being late last time, but don't press your luck. Oh, you needn't look so glum; I'd have to go soon, anyway—the museum closes at five."

As usual, Maelzel found some menial task for me to do—in this case, greasing the gears inside Fiona, the artistic automaton. I'm sure it was his way of showing me that my skill at chess didn't make me special; as far as he was concerned, I was little better than a chore boy. His attitude didn't bother me much; I was used to it. What did bother me was letting Virginia think I was good for nothing but sweeping floors. If she came back, of course, she'd see my brilliant chess moves; unfortunately, she'd never know it was me making them.

"I wish I could tell her," I whispered to the lovely mechanical lady. "But if Maelzel found out, he'd have a conniption, wouldn't he?" I put a hand on Fiona's wooden head and gave it a solemn nod. "What about you? Do you know it's me inside the Turk? Or do you think he's run by clockwork, the same as you?" She didn't reply. "I'll bet you wish you and Otto could go to Haymarket Gardens and ride the Flying Gigs, don't you?" She nodded quite emphatically, with a little help from me. "You could have Professor Palmer phrenologize you, too. I'm sorry you're both stuck here, and can only come to life for an hour each evening. I know how it feels. I'll tell you what: I could read your skull for you. Would you like that?" Not surprisingly, she nodded. I placed my other hand on her head and felt about with my fingers. Her skull was disappointingly even and smooth; it gave no hint of what her character might be.

When seven o'clock came I was at the side door, waiting for the secret knock. To tell the truth, I half expected Virginia not to show. It wouldn't be the first time someone had abandoned me. A girl so charming and beautiful surely had far better things to do; perhaps her worldly cousin would escort her to the opera or the theater or a society ball.

At seven-thirty, I heard Maelzel open the entrance to the main hall; there still was no sign of Virginia. With a sigh, I turned away from the door. Just as I did, there came a light rapping sound: three, three, two. I rushed back, unlocked the door, and flung it open, nearly knocking poor Virginia off her feet.

"I'm sorry!" I whispered.

She gave me a wan smile. "It's all right."

"Did I hurt you?"

"No, no," she said, "I'm fine." But I sensed that something was wrong; she no longer seemed so enthusiastic about our escapade.

"You're sure?"

She nodded, avoiding my gaze. "Where should I go?"

"Well, the customers are already coming in—a lot of them, it sounds like. You should be able to slip in without anybody noticing." I led her to the door that opened into the exhibition hall, unlocked it, and pushed it open a few inches. A few feet away, a dozen young men and women were grouped around the miniature carousel, oohing and aahing over its lifelike horses and riders. I guided Virginia through the doorway and she merged with the others just as though she belonged.

At that moment, I heard someone moving about in the adjoining room, the one where Otto sat waiting to go on. I weaved my way through the museum's exhibits, fearing that some audience member was snooping about, trying to discover the Turk's secret. Instead, I found Maelzel crouched beside the cabinet, staring at the empty interior.

When I entered, he sprang up with an agility I didn't know he possessed and seized the front of my new striped shirt. "Where have you been?" he demanded in a harsh whisper, his scowling face only inches from mine.

I said the first thing that came into my mind. "I—I had to use the privy!"

"You are supposed to be in *there!*" He shoved me toward the Turk.

"I'm sorry! I couldn't help it!" I protested as I climbed into the cabinet.

"*Ja, ja,* now shut up and listen. We have another challenger; he claims to be chess champion of the entire South, for what that is worth. He has brought a group of fellow chess fanatics with him. If the Turk defeats him, it will get us a good deal of publicity, so be sure you play your best."

"I always play my best," I said, a bit indignantly. As he locked the cabinet door, I murmured, "Except when I'm ordered not to."

I don't mean to sound snide or conceited, but if my opponent really was the chess champion of the entire South, all I can say is, the South had better stick to raising cotton and tobacco. I have to admit that, despite my promise to Maelzel, I didn't play my best. I didn't want to humiliate the poor fellow, after all, so I dragged the game out longer than it actually deserved.

It wasn't easy. Each time I tried to make a stupid move, I felt Otto's arm stiffen and resist, as if he wanted me to go ahead and massacre the man. When the game ended, I heard the faint patter of applause, like rain on a rooftop. I imagined Virginia's delicate, white-gloved hands clapping in delight, and I ached to tell her that it wasn't Otto's cleverness she was applauding, or Maelzel's; it was mine.

I blew out the Carcel lamp and sat in the dark, replaying the game in my mind and wishing I'd had a stronger challenger, until Maelzel wheeled me behind the curtain and signaled that it was safe for me to emerge. As I stood, wincing at the pain in my crooked back, I heard a noise from the adjoining room: a soft thud, like something falling to the floor. I knew from Maelzel's expression that he'd heard it, too. Fiercely, silently, he jerked his head sideways, indicating that I should investigate.

I crept between the statues and glass cases, meaning to take the intruder, if there was one, by surprise. To my relief, I found no one lurking in the shadows, only a stuffed snowy owl lying on the floor, with one wing all askew. The big bird had been listing dangerously of late and had finally toppled from its perch, a victim of decay and gravity.

Or so I thought. But just then a breeze caught the back door, which had apparently been ajar, and flung it open with a bang that nearly stopped my heart. "Oh, Lud," I breathed. I was positive that, after letting Virginia enter, I had closed and locked it. How on earth could it have come open again?

There was only one possible explanation: Someone had been in the room. Someone was spying on us.

23

I RUSHED TO THE DOORWAY AND STUCK my head out, hoping to catch sight of the fleeing culprit. That hope was immediately dashed. Dozens of audience members were milling about before the main entrance, doubtless discussing the downfall of their champion chess player. Any one of them might have been the intruder.

In the feeble glow of the gaslights, I caught a glimpse of two dark-clad figures on the fringes of the crowd, one female, one male. The former might have been the mysterious Woman in Black—or not. The other resembled Mr. Poe—more or less. I also spotted a stocky, curly-haired fellow who could conceivably have been the fire-alarmist from several months before— or not. Shaking my head helplessly, I pulled the door shut, locked it, and glanced around the room. How long had the spy been hiding here, waiting for us open the Turk's cabinet? And how had he—or she—gotten into the room without my noticing?

Though I was sure that I'd secured the outer door earlier, I wasn't quite so certain about the inner door. When I ushered Virginia into the main hall, had I locked that door after her? Or had been I so distracted by the noise in the Turk's room that I'd forgotten? I checked the door in question. It was locked now, but of course if the spy had entered through it, he could have fastened it behind him.

I took a deep breath to calm myself and then rejoined Maelzel. Naturally I said nothing to him about unlocking either door. That would have been asking for trouble. "It was just the stuffed owl," I said, "falling off its perch."

I should have known he wouldn't let me off that easily. "*Nein, nein*, someone was in here, I am certain of it! You said that you went outside to use the privy. How long were you gone?"

"Only a few minutes."

"Even *one* minute is enough time for someone to get inside! When you returned, did you lock the door?"

"Of course."

"How can you be sure?"

"Well, it's locked now. I don't suppose it locked itself."

"Do not be smart with me, boy, or you will regret it!" He thrust his face close to mine again. "And if you have given away the Turk's secret, you will regret it far, far more, I promise you."

The weeks that followed were anxious ones for me. If the intruder had seen me pop from the cabinet like a malformed jack-in-the-box, he would surely tell his tale to the newspaper. And the *Enquirer* would jump at the chance to print such a story. After all, people had been trying for decades to determine how the Turk operated; the news would create a sensation. It would also create no end of trouble for me; I knew all too well whose thin shoulders the blame would fall on.

But I had a second, almost equal reason to feel anxious: After Virginia's visit to the exhibition, she had disappeared as suddenly and completely as Monsieur Mulhouse or Mademoiselle Bouvier. I spent nearly every free hour sitting on my bench at Haymarket Gardens, willing the chess players to make intelligent moves and willing Virginia to appear—without the slightest success on either score. Even when it rained, I kept my vigil, taking shelter under the portico of the Dancing House.

One damp, chilly afternoon, as I sat gazing dully at the traffic on the river, a ragged boy with a smudged face approached me. "Are you Rufus?" he asked.

Taken aback, I merely nodded. The lad handed me

a small, square envelope; before I could ask who had sent him, he dashed off. I pried open the letter as carefully as I could, considering how my fingers trembled. If it was from the Venus of Richmond—and who else was even aware of my existence?—I didn't want to mangle it.

The note was a brief one, with no salutation or signature. The writing was elegant but slightly shaky, rather like that produced by Fiona—the automaton, I mean—when she needed a little grease:

> *The girl has betrayed you.*
> *You will find her at Mrs. Yarrington's boardinghouse, Twelfth and Bank streets.*

For a long time I simply sat and stared at the message. Who could possibly have sent it? There was no doubt who "the girl" was; I knew only one. But how had she "betrayed" me—aside from acting like a friend at first and then completely ignoring me?

Though I didn't want Virginia to think I was spying on her or pursuing her, I couldn't have stayed away from that boardinghouse any more than I could from the chess table in the Gardens. I didn't go there looking for proof that she'd betrayed me, as the letter claimed; she was so sweet and childlike, I couldn't imagine her deliberately deceiving or hurting anyone. I only wanted to see her, to reassure myself that she was well.

It may be hard to believe that I was still so naive and trusting, considering all the hard knocks I'd taken since I left the Parsonage. But when you grow up with kindness and fairness around you, you're inclined to believe that the whole world is that way, even when you see so much evidence to the contrary.

Of course, if I'd been totally trusting, I would have just knocked on the door of the boardinghouse and asked to see Miss Clemm. Instead, I crossed the street, sat down on the low stone wall that surrounded the Capitol grounds, propped my back brace against the iron fence, and watched and waited.

In such a situation, most people would be bored, but I kept myself entertained by playing mental chess. As I was about to trounce myself for the third time, the front door of the boardinghouse opened and a man stepped onto the porch. Though I was half a block away, I recognized him at once, from his black hair and mustache and his great expanse of forehead. He seemed to be waiting for someone, too, and was clearly one of the majority who are bored by it. After fidgeting and pacing the porch for several minutes, he called, "Sissy? Are you coming or not?" Apparently he got no reply, for a moment later he shouted irritably, "Sissy!"

The door swung open again and a young woman

hurried out, fumbling with her bonnet strings. There was no mistaking her, either—unfortunately. I should have fled the scene at once and spared myself the pain of seeing them together, but I was literally unable to move; I was like an automaton whose clockwork has run down. The only part of me that could feel anything at all was my heart, and I wished it, too, had been numb.

Virginia took Poe's arm, just as she had done with me, and smiled sweetly at him, just as she had at me. She spoke so softly that I couldn't hear her words; whatever they were, they put Poe in a better humor. He leaned over and kissed her brow and then they set off walking, in my direction but across the street from me. I hated for her to see me sitting there, looking as forlorn as an abandoned puppy, but I just couldn't manage to stir.

Though her attention seemed entirely on Poe, I saw her glance my way. She was close enough now that I could make out every detail of her face. Her already fair skin lost every trace of color; she went as pale as the plaster Venus. I heard Poe ask, "What is it, my dear? What's wrong?"

She forced a smile. "It's nothing, Eddy. I felt a little chill, that's all." She drew her shawl more tightly around her. "Perhaps someone walked over my grave."

I felt far more than just a chill; I felt as though the

cold stone of the wall had sucked all the warmth out of me. When they were out of sight, I finally forced myself to my feet and shuffled creakily, mechanically across the street to the boardinghouse. I twisted the handle of the bell several times before the door was opened by a short, plump woman—Mrs. Yarrington, no doubt. She seemed startled by my appearance; perhaps she'd never seen a back brace before—or perhaps I just looked as miserable as I felt. "May I help you?"

"Is this where Mr. Poe lives?"

"Yes, it is, but I'm afraid you've just missed him. He and Mrs. Poe have gone out to dinner."

I blinked at her, bewildered. "Miss Clemm, you mean?"

"Well, she *was* Miss Clemm, before they married. Do you know the young lady?"

I might have said yes an hour earlier, before I discovered that I didn't know her at all. I simply shook my head.

Leaning closer to me, Mrs. Yarrington said confidentially, "She claims to be eighteen, but I don't believe a word of it. She can't be a day over fourteen—far too young to be married off, in my opinion. Well, it's none of my business, I suppose, as long as they pay their rent on time. Do you have a message for Mr. Poe?"

"No," I said glumly. I was certain that we would hear from him soon enough. As I crossed the street again, I turned and looked up at the windows on the second floor, wondering which room was hers. I noticed that the curtain on the window farthest to the left was pulled back; someone was watching me. At first I thought it must be Virginia's mother. Then the figure moved a little and caught the light. Virginia had mentioned that her mother liked bright colors, but the dress this woman wore would have fit in perfectly at a funeral.

Though I was weary and disheartened, I wasn't dead, which meant that my prominent Organ of Causality—otherwise known as curiosity—was still functioning. I suspect that Mrs. Yarrington had been watching me, too, for my second ring of the doorbell barely died away before she opened the door again. "Was there something else you wanted?"

"Yes, I nearly forgot. I do have a message for Mrs. Fisher."

Mrs. Yarrington gazed at me rather oddly, and I thought I had guessed wrong. But I hadn't. "Mrs. Fisher has specifically asked not to be disturbed." She held out one plump hand. "You may leave the message with me, and I'll see that she gets it."

"It's not a written message. Just tell her . . . tell her Rufus wants to talk to her."

I still wasn't sure that Mrs. Fisher and the Woman in Black were one and the same; maybe they both liked dark clothing. Nor was I sure that Mrs. Fisher actually knew who I was; after all, when she played me at chess, I was inside a box. But the boy who delivered the note had known my name, and I was almost certain the note came from her.

One other thing I was almost certain of, though it was a hard thing to admit: Virginia hadn't befriended me because she was so sweet and kind, or because I was such charming company. She'd been doing just what Maelzel had warned me about—trying to pry the Turk's secret out of me. But she hadn't been content with that. There seemed little doubt now that she was the mysterious intruder who had spied on us. After the Turk's performance, she had simply crept back into the storage room, where she observed me climbing from the cabinet.

If she had tricked me only in order to satisfy her own curiosity, there might have been little harm done. But even the biggest fool in Richmond—and I probably qualified for the title—could guess the truth. She'd been put up to it by Poe. And Poe was in a position to do us a great deal of harm. If she let him know that I was running the Turk, and he let the world know, my life would be worth no more than that of Monsieur Mulhouse or Mademoiselle Bouvier.

CHAPTER

24

I HAD TO ASSUME THAT VIRGINIA WOULD tell her cousin—or was he actually her husband, as Mrs. Yarrington claimed?—everything. But if she did, he was very slow to make use of it. It had been two weeks already since the spying incident. Another week went by and still the *Enquirer* printed no sensational revelation about the Turk, only the usual letters from readers with pet theories about the automaton, theories that ranged from the utterly mundane to the wildly fantastic. I began to think that perhaps Poe wouldn't expose us after all—which just goes to show how big a fool I really was, in case there was any doubt.

I heard nothing from the mysterious Mrs. Fisher, either. I considered lying in wait for her outside the boardinghouse, but I didn't want to risk encountering Virginia or Poe. I wanted nothing more to do with either of them. The fact is, I was put off on people altogether; they were far too unreliable and unpredictable. It was a lot easier to deal with the Turk and the plaster Venus and the clockwork Fiona. I knew just where I stood with them. They never lied to me, they never made a fool of me or hit me or cursed me, and they didn't want anything from me—except when Otto wanted me to let him win.

I couldn't avoid people altogether, of course, but I did my best. I worked diligently and silently all day long—which certainly suited Maelzel and Jacques— and in the evening I retreated to our room, where I read Philidor or played mental chess.

Jacques was still drinking himself into a stupor each night; when he reached his talkative stage, I had a little trouble concentrating on my book or my game. Most of the time I ignored him, but every so often my curiosity got the best of me. During one of his rambling, almost unintelligible monologues, I heard him mention the name *Madame Tussaud*. As you may recall, Mulhouse told me that Jacques had once worked for her, crafting wax figures for her famous museum, and he seemed to confirm it.

"But how could you have?" I asked. "Her museum is in London."

He gave me a rather hurt look. "You do not believe me." He took a swig of bourbon straight from the bottle, as if to console himself. "For your information," he said, pronouncing the words very carefully, "at that time she did not have *un musée*. She had a traveling exhibition."

"And you traveled with her?"

"*Oui*." He made a sweeping gesture with the bottle, slopping bourbon on the bedclothes. "All over *Angleterre*."

"What were you doing in England?"

"Getting these." He pulled up his trouser legs to display his mechanical limbs. "Which are hurting me at the moment." He unbuckled the leather straps, removed the appendages, and sighed. "*C'est meilleur.*"

"They didn't have wooden legs in France?"

"Not good ones. These were not so good, either, until I made a few improvements."

"How did you end up with Madame Tussaud?"

"I worked for *un charpentier*—"

"A carpenter."

"*Oui*. He was repairing some of Madame's exhibits—just the wooden parts. Madame and her son did all the wax parts." He laughed and took another slug of whiskey. "You know what the carpenter told me? He said he knew Madame's secret."

"Her secret?"

"The reason why the figures look so real." He leaned

forward, so close that I could smell the liquor on his breath. "You know what is underneath the wax?"

I shook my head.

"The dead person's skull."

A shiver went down my spine. "Really?"

Jacques shrugged. "That is what he told me."

"But if you made some of the figures, you must know for sure."

"Her son taught me how to sculpt with wax. I worked on the figure of Lord Byron. All I know is, we did not use Lord Byron's skull." He downed another gulletful of bourbon.

His words were becoming slurred and indistinct now, the way Otto's did when his voice box needed work. But I was determined to learn as much as I could, while he was in a talking mood. "How long were you with her?"

"*Quoi?*"

"How long did you work for Madame?"

"*Je ne sais pas.* A year, *peut-être.*"

"Why did you come to America?"

He paused with the bottle halfway to his lips and glared at me. "Have I ever told you that you ask too many questions?"

"Many times."

"Well, it is true." I feared that was the end of our conversation. But after another swallow of whiskey he wiped his mouth with his sleeve and murmured, "Something happened. An accident. The *gendarmes* were after me. Mr. Maelzel helped me to escape." Unexpectedly, he let out a hoarse laugh. "He had to smuggle me onto the ship. Can you guess where he hid me?"

I'm sure you have no trouble guessing, and neither did I. "Inside the Turk."

He nodded, and his long hair fell over his face. "*Il n'était pas difficile*, once I took off my legs."

I could also guess what sort of "accident" would have the police after him. Mulhouse's claim, that Jacques was wanted for murder, was apparently true—not that I'd ever doubted it. He seemed harmless enough now. He took one more swig of bourbon and then slowly sagged sideways, like a wax figure melting in the heat. I snatched the bottle from his hand just in time to prevent it drenching the bed.

In reality, there wasn't enough heat in the room to melt a block of ice, let alone a wax figure. December in Richmond was certainly more pleasant than December in Philadelphia, but the temperature often fell below freezing. At night I could pile on more blankets, but in the daytime, my new outfit didn't keep my scrawny frame nearly warm enough.

On my next afternoon off, I returned to Mr. Tindle's pawnshop and endured more of his puns while I picked out a woolen greatcoat roomy enough to fit over my back brace. I could afford a decent one; we were drawing such good crowds that Maelzel was actually paying me regularly.

As I handed Mr. Tindle the money for the coat, I thought of how Virginia had haggled with him on my behalf. Apparently he remembered, too. "I haven't seen your friend Miss Clam lately."

"She's not my friend," I muttered.

"Oh? I'm sorry."

I pulled the coat close around me. "So am I."

As I trudged back along Broad Street, I spotted— Oh, dear; I hate to even say the words, since I've worn them out already, but I don't know how else to put it: I spotted a *familiar figure* heading my way. No doubt you're thinking, Well, it can't be Virginia; that would be too much of a coincidence. It must be the Woman in Black. Or perhaps Mrs. Fisher—assuming she's *not* the Woman in Black. It can't be Mademoiselle Bouvier, since she's not a familiar figure. It could conceivably be Mulhouse. Or maybe it's Poe.

No, coincidence or not, I'm afraid it was Virginia. My heart thumped so hard it seemed to rattle my back brace. I made a quick detour to the other side of the street. I thought I had avoided her until I felt a tug on the sleeve of my coat and heard her voice, which sounded as sweet and childlike as ever. "Rufus? I almost didn't recognize you, all wrapped up in your coat that way."

I barely glanced at her. "What do you want?"

"Just to apologize. Well, and to explain—or try to." She shivered. "Can we go somewhere warmer?"

In my bitter mood I almost said, *How about the exhibition hall? You could get a really good look at the Turk.* But I didn't; I simply shrugged—as well as I could, anyway, in my back brace and heavy wool coat.

She took my arm, just as if we were still friends. "I was on my way to Mr. Tindle's to redeem some of our silverware, but it can wait." She led me to the Swan Tavern, where she ordered coffee for us. Aside from the woman at the bar, Virginia was the only female in the place.

"Are you sure you're allowed in here?"

"Of course. Eddy brings me here all the—" She broke off and stared down at her coffee mug. "I'm sorry. You don't want to hear about Eddy, I'm sure."

"You're right," I said. But I couldn't help asking, "Are you married to him?"

"I told you about that."

"But was it the truth?"

"I always tell the truth." She gave a rueful smile. "Just not necessarily *all* of it."

"You let me think we were friends."

"We are. Well, we could have been."

I shook my head. "If you hadn't wanted to know about the Turk, we never would have met."

She lowered her gaze again. "No. I suppose not. I really am sorry, Rufus. I didn't mean to hurt you. It's just that . . . well, Eddy—Mr. Poe—has done so much for me and Mama. When he asked me to do this, I couldn't refuse him. He's very curious about practically every subject under the sun, and I thought this was just one more thing. I had no idea he meant to write about it in *The Messenger*."

"*The Messenger?*" I had assumed he'd sell the story to the newspaper. Maybe it wasn't so bad, after all. "I don't suppose many people read this magazine of his?"

"Well, actually, yes. I think it has several thousand subscribers."

"Several *thousand?*" And if he did a piece about the Turk, that would guarantee him even *more* readers. I sank my head into my hands. "Oh, Lud. Maelzel is going to kill me."

"But it wasn't your fault."

"I was the one who let you in the hall."

"Does Mr. Maelzel know that?"

"It's not too hard to figure out."

She laid a hand on mine. Without her white gloves, her skin felt as cold as that of the plaster Venus. "I'm sorry, Rufus, truly I am."

"Prove it."

"How?"

"You can be very persuasive. Persuade Mr. Poe not to print the piece."

She smiled faintly. "All right. I'll try. But I don't know if it'll do any good. He says he has to increase the magazine's readership, or he'll be out of a job."

After several more anxious weeks went by, I began to hope that Virginia had successfully worked her wiles on her cousin. Then, one afternoon in January, Poe turned up unannounced. Jacques and Mr. Moody had gone to lunch together—I could just imagine how sullen and silent that scene would be—and Maelzel and I were draping cloths over the exhibits, to hide them from museum visitors. Maelzel didn't glance up at the intruder; he just gestured and said brusquely, "The museum is in those two rooms."

"It's Mr. Poe," I whispered.

"The devil take him," muttered Maelzel. But he greeted the man in a civil, even friendly fashion. No doubt he was hoping Poe would give us some free publicity in the newspaper or in his magazine. I, of course, was fervently praying that he wouldn't. As they talked, I went about my work, but I made sure my tasks kept me within earshot.

"I've attended your exhibition several times—" Poe was saying.

"Six times, in fact," said Maelzel.

"—and each time I'm struck by how fascinated people are with the chess automaton. I have to admit, I share that fascination."

"Some might even call it an obsession," Maelzel suggested wryly.

Poe ignored the comment. "From my observations, I've drawn a number of conclusions about the Turk. I've expounded upon them at some length in this article—" He produced a folded manuscript from the inside pocket of his topcoat. "—which I plan to publish in April, in the *Southern Literary Messenger.*"

Maelzel gave what might pass for a tolerant smile; I thought it looked a little strained. "Ah, yet another in a long string of half-baked theories about how the Turk operates."

Poe's smile was more confident—haughty, almost. "In all modesty, sir, I have to say that this one is fully baked. As you'll see, I've approached the matter the way a scientist might; I've laid out all the evidence, point by point, and then made my deductions from that evidence." He handed the manuscript to Maelzel, who regarded it as if it were a day-old fish that had begun to smell.

"What do you expect me to do with this?"

"I thought it only fair to allow you a chance to respond, to point out any flaws in my logic—though I doubt that you'll find many."

Maelzel laughed humorlessly. "Do not be so sure, Mr. Poe. I expect that I shall demolish your theory as easily as my machine demolished you at chess."

He had clearly struck Poe in a sore spot. The man's pale face went so hard, it might have been carved from wood. "It was no machine that defeated me, sir. It was a flesh and blood player." And for the first time, Poe looked in my direction.

CHAPTER 25

EXPECTED MAELZEL TO TURN ON ME, too, with an accusing and menacing gaze, and I tried to appear as ignorant and innocent as I possibly could. But he treated me the same way he usually did—as though I were beneath his notice. Instead, he glanced contemptuously at the manuscript. As he scanned the pages, the smirk on his face faded, to be replaced by a scowl. When he finished, he rolled the article into a tight cylinder and smacked it irritably against his palm. "Just what is it you want, Mr. Poe?"

"As I said, I want to give you a chance to respond, to *demolish* my argument if you can."

"You know I cannot."

"Then I'll print the piece as it stands." He stroked his mustache thoughtfully. "Unless . . ."

"Unless what?"

"Well, at the risk of sounding crass, sir, perhaps I could be persuaded not to."

Maelzel stared at him incredulously. "Are you attempting to *blackmail* me, sir?"

"Not at all. My idea was that, if I withheld the piece from our April issue, you might fill the space with an advertisement for your exhibition."

"Ah. And how much would such an advertisement cost me?"

"Shall we say . . . four hundred dollars?"

I groaned. That was a good year's wages, even for a skilled craftsman. Knowing how tight Maelzel was with his money, I could guess his response, and I was right. He took a step forward and seized Poe's shirtfront, as he so often did with me. "I have heard your idea. Now here is *my* idea. I recommend that you go home and begin working on another little piece for your magazine— your own obituary. Because if you print *this* piece, you are going to need it!" He jammed the pages into Poe's pocket and pushed him away so roughly that he stumbled and nearly fell.

Though Poe quickly disappeared, Maelzel's anger didn't. He turned it on me. "Obviously he knows that you are operating the Turk," he growled. "How could he possibly know that?"

"I—I have no idea. Maybe he was the one spying on

us?" I tried to put Fiona between myself and Maelzel, but he shoved her out of the way and advanced on me.

"He knows far more than he could have learned by simply spying. He describes almost exactly how the inside of the cabinet is set up, and how the arm mechanism works, and how the operator manages to stay unseen."

"He—he said he *deduced* it, by watching the Turk play!"

"I do not believe him. He could not know all that unless someone told him. Someone who knows the Turk inside and out. Someone like *you*." He jabbed a finger at my chest, but struck one of the bars of my brace, which made him even angrier. "How much did he pay you, boy?" he demanded.

"He *didn't* pay me, because I didn't say a word to him! I swear!" Perhaps you're thinking that I should have told him about Virginia; after all, *she* had betrayed *me*. But I couldn't bring myself to incriminate her; Maelzel might decide to get even with her, as he had with Mademoiselle Bouvier. Besides, Virginia couldn't have provided her cousin with all those details, either. She'd never seen the inside of the cabinet; she'd only seen me climbing out of it. Poe must have figured the rest of it out on his own.

"You are lying!" growled Maelzel. "I see it in your

face!" As if to wipe the lying look off my face, he struck me with the back of his hand. I staggered backward and collided with the Turk; the impact must have knocked loose the pin that held his arm in place, for the limb swung outward. As I backed away from Maelzel, it encircled me. *Oh, Lud,* I thought, *Now even Otto is betraying me.* I struggled so desperately to free myself that the arm bent backward and something inside it snapped. Something seemed to snap inside Maelzel, too. He lunged forward and, grabbing hold of my torture device, lifted me off my feet and flung me to the floor.

"The truth, boy!" he shouted, and kicked me in the ribs. Though the back brace deflected the blow, it still made me gasp with pain. "Tell me the truth!" Another kick, like a punctuation mark made physical. "You sold him my secrets!" And another kick. He was so furious now that he was out of control, like an automaton whose mechanism has gone awry. I knew that, if he kept it up, he would surely do me in, and there was no one there to stop him.

Then, suddenly, the blows ceased. I could still hear Maelzel grunting and cursing, but he didn't seem to be cursing me. I struggled to sit up; when I wiped the sweat and tears from my eyes, I saw Maelzel curled up on the floor, groaning and clutching his left knee. Jacques stood over him, with his crutch raised like a club. "*Ne bougez pas!*" he warned Maelzel. "Or I will break your other leg!"

Maelzel glared at his attacker for a long moment, then drew several deep breaths and said, in a voice that sounded almost calm, in a brittle sort of way, "This is the second time you have defended him and gone against me. I let it go the first time. This time I will not. You no longer work for me, Monsieur Jouy, and never will again. Get out."

Jacques lowered the crutch and nodded. "*Très bien.* As soon as I gather up my tools."

"You may come back for them, when I am not here. Leave now, and take the *verdammte Junge* with you."

Somehow I managed to stand and hobble to the door without help. Before Jacques closed the door behind us, I turned and took one last look at Otto. His dark eyes were fixed on me; his broken arm seemed to be reaching out to me, as if asking me to come back, or to forgive him. Or was he just trying to keep me in his clutches? That's the trouble with figures made of wood and wires and wax. They don't communicate very well.

I wouldn't see the Turk again for nearly seven years. I never saw Maelzel again at all. Eventually I did learn his fate, which was a sad one, and I'll reveal that in due time. I'm sure you're also curious to know who the mysterious Mrs. Fisher actually was, and what became of Virginia and Mademoiselle Bouvier and Monsieur Mulhouse. Be patient; I'll tell you all those things, too, before we're done. But first I have to tell you what became of me.

I had no desire to stay in Richmond, and neither did Jacques. That very afternoon, we boarded the mail coach for Philadelphia. If my situation had seemed bleak before, now it looked downright hopeless. I was out of a job and had no prospects of another. I had nowhere to live, no friends or family, and nothing to my name but a few dollars, the clothes (and the brace) on my back, and a sack containing my old, worn clothing and three books: Philidor's chess manual, *Elements of Phrenology*—which I had borrowed from Maelzel and never returned—and my father's journal, which I hadn't yet found the courage to open.

Jacques's possessions were nearly as scanty; his only baggage was an ironbound chest full of woodworking tools. The coachman wanted to put it on the roof, with the other luggage and parcels, but Jacques insisted on keeping it with him. Luckily there was plenty of room; though the coach could hold nine passengers, there was only one besides ourselves—a portly tobacco merchant who filled the air and my poor lungs with the acrid smoke of his own product.

"When you fetched your tools," I said, between coughs, "was Maelzel gone?"

"*Non*. But he gave me no trouble. He only warned me to keep my mouth shut about—" He glanced furtively at our fellow passenger. "*Eh bien*, you know what I mean."

"*Oui*. He was wrong about me, you know. I didn't tell Poe anything."

"I doubt you will ever convince him of that. *Alors*—" He reached into the pocket of his coat and drew out an envelope sealed with wax. "He told me to give this to you."

I examined it suspiciously. "What is it? A packet of arsenic?" I turned the envelope over. It was addressed to a Mr. Dunn at Nathan Dunn & Co., Philadelphia. When we lived at the Parsonage, I had heard my father speak rather distastefully of Nathan Dunn. As a Quaker, the man was expected to live modestly and simply, but he hadn't let that stop him from becoming one of the wealthiest merchants in Philadelphia. "Maelzel wants me to deliver this?"

Jacques nodded.

"He's too much of a miser to send it by post?"

"He says if you take it in person, this Mr. Dunn will find a place for you."

"But why would Maelzel recommend me for a job? He thinks I sold him out."

"Do not ask me. I know only what he told me."

The body of our coach was suspended on leather straps, which made the ride marginally more comfortable than our trip in the wagonette had been; I was grateful, for my ribs were aching from Maelzel's beating. The farther north we went, the colder the weather got and, even though I shrouded myself in the blankets provided by the stage line, I was shivering much of the time.

At least we didn't have to push the coach out of any mud holes; the road was frozen solid, which also meant that we made good time. Around midnight we arrived at Fredericksburg, where we put up at the Farmers' Hotel. The room cost far more than I would have liked, but it was clean and warm, and we didn't come away infested with lice or bedbugs.

Jacques sedated himself with bourbon as usual, and I made my bed on the floor as usual, just in case his sedative didn't work. After he became mellow, but before he became comatose, I said, "I never thanked you for saving my life."

"*Quoi?*"

"If you hadn't stopped Maelzel, he would have surely killed me."

Jacques gave a skeptical snort. "He can be *méchant*—cruel—but he is not a murderer."

"Really? What about Mademoiselle Bouvier?"

"What about her?"

"Well, she disappeared, didn't she? Mulhouse says that, if she sold the Turk's secret to someone, Maelzel might have done her in."

"Mulhouse is a fool."

"Then what did happen to her?"

"You are asking a lot of questions again, *Porcelet*." He took a long swig of whiskey and sighed. "Mademoiselle Bouvier was a fool, too. She did tell *un journaliste* that she operated the Turk. And Maelzel did get rid of her. But not in the way you think."

"How, then?"

"He sent her to Jamaica, as an indentured servant."

"Against her will? How could he do that?"

"He did not say. I suppose he drugged her."

I fished the blood-tarnished earring from my pocket. "Did this belong to her?"

Jacques rubbed his bleary eyes and squinted at it. "*Peut-être*. Where did you find it?"

"Behind the felt lining."

"Ah. No doubt she lost it when she set the cabinet on the fire. It must have caught on the machinery."

There was a long silence, during which I swallowed this information and Jacques swallowed more whiskey. Finally, I said, "And what about Mulhouse? He threatened to sell us out if Maelzel didn't give him more money."

"How do you know that?"

"I heard them arguing. Maelzel said that, if he did, he'd meet the same fate as Mademoiselle Bouvier."

Jacques shrugged. "All I know is, he was in Philadelphia when we left."

Another lengthy silence followed. I was waiting for Jacques to reach just the right stage of drunkenness before I spoke again. "Actually," I said, "Mulhouse never accused Maelzel of murdering Mademoiselle Bouvier."

Jacques was sober enough to catch the implication in my words. "Ah. So, he thought it was *me*."

"Well, he . . . he did mention the possibility. He said that—" I broke off, afraid of going too far.

Jacques filled in the blank I had left. "—that I killed someone back there, *en France*?" He wore his usual scowl, but he didn't really seem angry, just sort of . . . resigned, as if he'd known all along that his secret, like the Turk's, couldn't be kept hidden forever. "*Eh bien.* He is right."

CHAPTER

26

I CAN'T POSSIBLY TELL JACQUES'S STORY AS he told it to me, nor would you want me to. He mumbled so much and slurred his words so badly and used so many unfamiliar French words and expressions that I understood only about half of what he said. I didn't dare ask too many questions, for fear he might get disgusted and quit talking altogether. All I can do is take the bits and pieces and try to assemble them into something sensible, the way Maelzel's craftsmen took all those tiny figures and miniature buildings and constructed the Conflagration of Moscow.

I already knew that, after a year of touring England with Madame Tussaud, Jacques had returned to France, where he met Maelzel. That must have been around 1825, because the Battle of Trocadero, in which

Jacques lost his legs, took place in 1823. Though he had new wooden limbs, he couldn't fix the damage done to his mind. Nearly every night he relived the horrors of the battle in his dreams.

Maelzel was having nightmares, too, but they were of the financial sort. Apparently someone else owned the Turk at that point, and Maelzel was supposed to be making payments on it. But you know how much he hated parting with his money. To make matters worse, the Turk was out of commission, thanks to Mademoiselle Bouvier's clumsiness.

Before Maelzel hired her, she had been an actress, but her stage career had ended when she damaged her vocal cords somehow. She was slight enough to fit into the cabinet easily and clever enough to master the endgames quickly; more importantly, she was willing to work for next to nothing. But of course she ended up costing Maelzel far more than he anticipated, when she accidentally set his star attraction on fire.

Maelzel searched for someone to help him repair the machine and found Jacques. The Frenchman's handicap had made him practically unemployable so he, too, was willing to work for a pittance. And since his violent nightmares had gotten him booted out of one boardinghouse after another, he was happy to sleep in the workshop, where he wouldn't disturb anyone.

Maelzel had decided to give the Turk a voice, and

Jacques threw himself into the task. If he worked hard enough, he could block out the memory of his brief, catastrophic military career. But at the end of each day, he was drawn to those raucous, run-down taverns near the Paris docks, where soldiers and sailors gathered to squander their pay on drink and women. It was the only place he could mingle with men who understood what he'd gone through and what he was going through now, who saw him not as a cripple but as a comrade.

Not that he sat around swapping war stories and singing indecent songs. Mostly he kept to himself, nursing a single beer or coffee for hours. It was better than returning to the workshop and lying there waiting for the dreams to come. One evening, to his surprise, he heard someone speak his name and looked up to see Otso, the Basque who had fought alongside him at Trocadero, who had bound his bleeding stumps and carried him to safety.

With no more wars in the offing, Otso had grown tired of army life and mustered out. Now he was drifting about aimlessly, with no money and no prospects, not even a place to lay his head. Jacques had been warned not to let anyone into the workshop, but this wasn't just anyone. It was his closest companion, the man who had saved his life. He offered to let Otso stay the night, provided he was gone when Maelzel arrived the next morning.

The Basque was good company; he even made Jacques laugh with his outrageous accounts of all the adventures he'd had, all the women he'd seduced, all the pompous officers he'd played tricks on. When they finally turned in, Jacques had the feeling that, for once, he might not have his usual, terrible dream.

And he didn't. Instead, he relived an incident that had taken place a few days before the fateful battle. He'd gone off in the woods to relieve himself and was attacked, not by the enemy, but by a fellow Frenchman, a starving deserter bent on stealing his rations.

There was no warning, just a sudden blow to the back of his head that brought him to his knees. He felt someone yanking at the strap of his haversack. When he clung to it stubbornly, the deserter knocked him flat on his back and then, straddling his body, closed a hand around his windpipe. Jacques tried to call for help, but the man clamped the other hand over his mouth. Just before he lost consciousness, Jacques managed to fumble his bayonet out of his belt and thrust the point between his assailant's ribs. The man cried out and toppled sideways.

Jacques sat up, gasping for breath. Everything was dark. He fumbled around with one hand and felt, not rain-soaked leaves, but a mattress damp with sweat. He was not in some godforsaken woods in Spain, but in Maelzel's Paris workshop. His other hand clutched an implement that was slick with blood. But it was not a bayonet; it was one of his woodworking chisels. And the man who lay groaning next to him was not the French deserter. It was Otso.

"Ah, Jacques," the Basque whispered, "c'est moi." Oh, Jacques, it's me. They were the last words he ever spoke, and they had been echoing in Jacques's brain ever since: *Ah, Jacques, c'est moi.*

Later on, when he could think more clearly, Jacques tried to reconstruct what had happened. He had probably shouted aloud, as he often did in the grip of one of his nightmares. Perhaps Otso feared that someone would hear the noise and investigate. Not wanting to get Jacques into trouble, he had tried to silence his friend by clamping a hand over his mouth.

Though Otso's death was an accident, Maelzel knew that the police wouldn't see it that way. The following day, he packed up his automata and other exhibits and booked passage on a packet ship for New York, taking with him Mademoiselle Bouvier and Jacques—who, as you know, was concealed inside the Turk. With one blow, he had rescued Jacques from the gallows and himself from bankruptcy. The Turk's owner could hardly collect rent when both the machine and Maelzel were on the other side of the Atlantic.

❖ ❖ ❖

When we boarded the post coach in the morning, Jacques was his usual sullen, silent self. It was as if his rambling confession of the night before had never happened—and in truth, I'm not sure he even remembered it. I wish I could say the same. The awful scene he described haunted me for years. That's the trouble with being so all-fired curious; sometimes you find out things you'd rather not know.

We stayed that night at an inn near Alexandria, and the following night somewhere outside Baltimore. Each time, when Jacques brought out his bottle of bourbon, I took a long walk and didn't return until I was sure he would be dead to the world. I didn't care to hear any more confessions.

After four days of cold, tedious travel, we reached Philadelphia, and there we parted ways. "What do you plan to do?" I asked Jacques.

"I plan to find someplace," he growled, "where no one will ask me any questions." With that, he hobbled off.

"Thank you!" I called after him—for, though he had treated me roughly, he had also saved me from Maelzel's abuse and straightened my bent back. He made no sign that he heard me.

If Mr. Dunn was going to find a place for me, as Maelzel promised, I wanted to look presentable when I presented myself to him. With my last remaining dollar, I rented a chilly room in a boardinghouse, where I washed myself and my linens. The clothing took so long to dry that I lost patience and donned them while they were still damp. Then I set out for the offices of Nathan Dunn & Co.

As I've said, Mr. Dunn was a very prosperous merchant, so I expected his headquarters to be rather grand. It was, in fact, a very ordinary room with rows of high desks at which clerks perched uncomfortably on stools. Well, it *would* have been ordinary, if not for the exotic array of Oriental art and artifacts that sat or hung about the place: silk kimonos, lacquered boxes, ivory fans, jade Buddhas, porcelain vases, Japanese paintings—souvenirs of his many trading trips to the Far East.

The man himself was much like his establishment: quite plain and ordinary in appearance, as befits a Quaker—except that in the lapel of his drab gray sack coat he sported a silver stickpin in the shape of a dragon. There was nothing grand about his manner, either. I expected him to treat me as Maelzel had—as though I were hardly worth bothering with. Instead, he greeted me cordially, showed me to his private office, and offered me a seat while he opened the sealed letter I had brought. I was very glad to sit, for the coach trip had left me thoroughly exhausted.

It took him only a few moments to read the message. He perched on the edge of his desk, a thoughtful expression on his face. "How long did thee work for Mr. Maelzel?"

"Most of a year," I said.

"Hmm. And what were thy tasks?"

Even though the Turk's secret was out, or would be as soon as Mr. Poe published his piece, I didn't think it wise to reveal my role as the machine's operator. "I swept the floors and helped repair the exhibits."

"So, thee can work with thy hands? Good, good. There is always a demand for craftsmen's apprentices." He stood and donned a broad-brimmed hat and a great-coat that was as drab as his suit. "I'm done here for the day. I may as well take thee there in my carriage."

He didn't say where he was taking me and, for once, I asked no questions. I was grateful to have any sort of position at all. Whoever my new employer was, he could be no worse than Maelzel. I was so worn out from my weary journey that I didn't feel much like talking, in any case. Mr. Dunn's carriage had a very soft seat, a fur rug to pull over me, and a soothing rocking motion; in a matter of minutes, I was sound asleep and didn't wake until we reached our destination.

At first, I wondered whether I actually *was* awake, for it felt more like a bad dream—a dream in which I climbed from the carriage and discovered that, instead of taking me to meet my new employer, Mr. Dunn had delivered me to the House of Refuge.

CHAPTER

27

IT WASN'T UNTIL I TWISTED MY ANKLE ON the uneven cobbles and felt a jolt of pain that I realized it was no dream. "Why did you bring me here?" I demanded, but the words didn't have the force I intended them to; they came out in a hoarse whisper.

"Mr. Maelzel instructed me to," said Mr. Dunn, taking hold of my arm. "Thee was in the House of Refuge when he took thee on, and, since thee did not prove suitable, he said I should return thee here."

There was a time when I would simply have accepted my fate, as I had been taught to do. But that time had passed. "No!" I protested. "I won't go back to being a pawn!" Pulling away from him, I turned and headed for the main gate, which was still hanging open.

But my body wouldn't cooperate. My movements

seemed painfully slow and labored, the way they some-times do in dreams. My legs felt as though they were made of wood and wires, and I couldn't manage to operate them properly. I stumbled again, and this time I did more than just twist an ankle; I went flying face-first onto the cobblestones—or at least I started to. I don't remember actually hitting the ground; I suspect that Mr. Dunn caught hold of my back brace at the last second and saved me.

Well, I say saved, but what he actually did was con-demn me, just as that merciless magistrate had done many months before. I later learned that Mr. Dunn was more than just a merchant; he was also one of the directors of the House of Refuge. I suppose he thought he was doing the best thing for me; I would have a roof over my head, after all, and food in my belly, and a chance to learn reading and writing and a trade of some kind. Never mind that I could already read and write, probably better than he could, that the food was mostly inedible and the work intolerably dull, and that I would share the roof over my head with boys who found great delight in tormenting me.

Of course, none of this was going through my head at the time. That's because, for the next several days, I was out of my head with fever. When I became foggily aware of my surroundings again, I was lying on a hard cot in the infirmary and someone was leaning over me, someone with only one arm. "Ezra?" I murmured.

"Yep, 'tis me. Or what's left of me. I never expected to see you here again. What happened?"

"It's a long story," I started to say, before I was seized by a fit of coughing.

"Sorry," said Ezra. "I reckon you shouldn't try to talk. You've got pneumony, or so they say. How d'you feel?"

"Not bad," I said, which set off another spate of coughing.

"Oh, now, don't give me none of that *accept your fate with good grace* bunkum. Anybody can see you feel just awful."

I nodded.

"Well, that's all right. You just lie there till you feel better, and even when you do, don't you tell 'em so. You'll get treated a lot better in here, and fed a lot better, too. After they took my arm off, I played sick for two whole weeks before they caught on."

Now, as you know, when a character in a novel has a high fever, as soon as the fever breaks the doctor always says something like, "Well, he's out of the woods now." But I wasn't a character in a book, and I wasn't out of the woods, or even on the fringes. I'd just passed through a little clearing, you might say, and before long I was lost again. Each time I rallied a little, the nurse seized the opportunity to dose me with calomel.

It made me vomit so violently that I thought I'd turn myself inside out. As I later learned, that's what calomel is meant to do—though I can't imagine why you'd want to take someone as sick as I was and make them even sicker.

Ezra was right about the food being better; unfortunately, I couldn't keep any of it down. With each day that passed, I grew a little weaker. I couldn't even find the strength to cough; the nurse had to turn me over and pound on my back to clear my lungs. My brain seemed as feeble as my body; when I tried to play mental chess, after half a dozen moves I lost track of where the pieces were.

Each afternoon, Ezra managed to escape his chores long enough to pay me a visit. I'm afraid I wasn't very good company, but he talked enough for both of us. Despite his last disastrous attempt to escape, he hadn't given up on the idea. In a low voice, he filled me in on his new scheme, which involved a hot-air balloon, I think—though that may just have been a product of my addled brain.

I had other visitors from time to time but, as far as I can tell, they were all imaginary. My father even turned up several times. Though he seemed intent on conveying some message to me, I never could make out what it was. I thought perhaps he'd discovered that there really was an Afterlife and was welcoming me to it. I feel sure I would have joined him, too, if I'd stayed in that infirmary much longer.

But one evening—or it may have been morning; in my fevered state I had no sense of time—two strange men appeared. They lifted my limp body from the cot, laid me gently on a stretcher, covered me with blankets, and carried me outdoors, where they slid me into the back of a van and hauled me away. I was so far gone that I supposed the vehicle was a hearse, and I was headed for the graveyard.

The prospect didn't worry me particularly. I would have been more alarmed had I known what my real destination was: The Friends' Asylum for the Insane. I was vaguely aware that I was being placed in another bed, and that it was more comfortable than the infirmary cot, but that was all.

Well, not quite all. Just before I drifted into unconsciousness, I noticed—forgive me for using this threadbare phrase one more time—a familiar figure bending over me. I assumed I was hallucinating again, for in my faint, fogbound vision the woman resembled the mysterious, black-clad Mrs. Fisher.

I have no memory of the days that followed; I know only what I've been told: that the doctors and nurses at the Friends' Asylum gave me the best of care. There were no more debilitating doses of calomel, only beef tea and red wine diluted with water, fed to me a spoonful at a time by my friend in the dark dress who, they say, never stirred from my bedside.

You may wonder why someone I scarcely knew would be so concerned about my welfare. Well, I wondered the same thing—as soon as I was able to wonder anything at all. Actually, the first thing I wondered was how I could possibly still be alive. The second thing I wondered was where I'd been taken, and why. Only then did my thoughts turn to Mrs. Fisher. She was still sitting in a chair, not three feet away. When I turned my head and gazed at her through crusted, half-open eyelids, she smiled and put a hand to my forehead.

"The fever is gone," she said.

"Does that mean I'm out of the woods?" I murmured.

"I think so."

I went on gazing at her face for a long while, trying to recall whether we had met before, and drew a blank. We had encountered each other, of course, just not face-to-face. She had a pleasant countenance—a little melancholy and careworn, but attractive and intelligent and kind all the same. She clearly didn't mind my staring at her. In fact, she gave as good as she got. But she didn't appear puzzled at all about my identity; she seemed to know exactly who I was.

"I'm sorry," I said, finally. "Do I know you?"

"No. Not really." I expected her to go on, to offer some explanation for her presence there. And she did seem about to speak several times, but each time she simply sighed, as if she couldn't find the right words. After a bit, she leaned over and picked up something from the little table next to the bed. It was my father's journal, which I had left in its paper wrapping all this time. It was no longer wrapped. She opened it to a page near the back and handed it to me. "This will explain better than I can," she said. Then she stood and, as softly as a shadow, left the room.

I rubbed the crust from my eyes and peered at the page. Luckily my father wrote in a very bold and expansive hand; otherwise I couldn't have hoped to make out the words. Though the journal entry was fairly short, by the end of it his handwriting was growing unsteady, as if he was having trouble holding the pen.

My dear boy,

By the time you read this, I will be in—I nearly said in Paradise, but I'm not so certain of that as I once was. At any rate, I'll be gone to wherever it is we go after death, even if it is only under the ground. I can't depart this world, though, without revealing to you the secret that I have suffered with, like a festering wound, these many years. I thought I was doing right to keep it from you, but I'm no longer so certain of that, either. I suspect that you are stronger than I ever gave you credit for.

I have led you and everyone else to believe that your mother, my beloved Lily, died soon after you were born. The truth is, she lived for some months afterward—though not with us. You see, she had always been subject to melancholy moods; after giving birth, she descended into that deep state of melancholia that some doctors term depresssion, and nothing anyone did could rouse her from it.

We were not well off financially at that time, to put it mildly. Her wealthy parents, who had always disapproved of me, claimed that her condition was a result of having to live in such poverty, and they insisted on taking her home with them. I thought it would be for only a short while, so I consented. But there she sank into such despair that, fearing for her life, they committed her to a mental hospital—they would not say which one. I tried my best to find her, but they must have admitted her under a false name.

A few months later, I received a brief, impersonal note from her parents, informing me that she had taken her own life. I was not even permitted to attend the funeral. Perhaps I was wrong to hide all this from you, and if so I ask your forgiveness. I just felt you had enough burdens to bear; I didn't want to saddle you with another, even heavier one. I told no one else, either, for the stigma of insanity would surely have been attached to you.

I regret that I leave you no inheritance of any kind, only this sad and rather shameful secret. But as I said, I've come to believe that you are strong enough to make your own way in the world after all. And I do leave you one other thing, for what it's worth—a father's love.

P.S. If the worth of my scientific theories should ever be recognized within your lifetime, and my book reprinted, please add to it the notes in this journal.

My hands trembled, the way my father's must have when he set down those last shaky sentences. The journal slipped from my grasp and, bouncing off the bedclothes, fell to the floor. Mrs. Fisher bent to retrieve it. I hadn't even been aware of her presence; she came and went as quietly as a ghost. I reached out shakily and touched her to reassure myself that she was flesh and blood. She closed her hand around mine; I felt the warmth of her skin, and the faint throb of her pulse.

"I still don't understand," I whispered.

She turned her hand over and pulled up the sleeve of her dark dress so I could see the rough scar that marred her thin wrist. "I did try to take my life," she said. "But I didn't succeed."

"Then you're—?"

Have you ever seen a rainbow splashed across the sky in the middle of a downpour? Well, when my mother smiled and, at the same time, her eyes overflowed with tears, that's what it made me think of. "Yes," she said. "Oh, yes."

CHAPTER

28

I HAD NEVER HAD A MOTHER BEFORE; I didn't know how to behave toward her. So I did what I've always done—I asked a lot of questions. Well, not all at once. I was still as weak as the watered-down wine they fed me, and I couldn't concentrate for more than a few minutes before drifting off, so I had to be content with one question and one reply at a time. As a result, I reconstructed my mother's story the same way I did Jacques's—by collecting pieces and assembling them into a complete picture.

My grandparents had committed her to that very institution, the Friends' Asylum for the Insane. To avoid having any scandal attached to the Raybold family name, they registered her under the alias of Mrs. Fisher. Thanks to the kind and attentive care she got, her condition steadily improved; after only a few months, she was able to return home—to the Raybold home, I mean, not ours. Her parents believed that, if she went back to my father, she would surely descend into depression again, so they kept her a virtual prisoner. They hired a companion for her, a formidable figure named Miss Armstrong, who was more like a jailer. My mother tried more than once to escape, but each time Miss Armstrong brought her back, and each time the amount of freedom they allowed her became less and less.

Finally she grew so despondent and so desperate that she took a razor to her wrist. I'm not sure whether she actually meant to do herself in, or whether it was merely a means of getting herself sent back to the Friends' Asylum. That was the one question I didn't ask her.

It was at this point that her parents sent my father the false report of her death. They convinced my mother, in turn, that I had died—not much of a stretch, considering how sickly I was—and that my father had given up on her—also an easy thing to believe, since he had made no contact with her.

She languished in that hospital for years, alternating between bouts of the deepest melancholy and periods in which she seemed quite normal. But even in her most hopeful moments, she refused to return to the prison of her parents' home. The hospital was happy enough to keep her, as long as the Raybolds paid the bill.

And then—apparently around the same time my father published his fateful tome—both my mother's parents contracted cholera and died; that was the end of the money, and the end of their control over her. She had herself released from the hospital, rented out the Raybold estate, and had been living on the considerable income from it ever since.

"Why didn't you come to the Parsonage?"

"I did. It just took a while to get up the nerve. After all, I believed that Tobias wanted nothing to do with me, and I thought that you were . . . Well, by the time I finally found the courage, you were gone."

"Then it *was* you I saw, haunting the place like a ghost."

She gave a wan smile. "I'm sorry I ran off. I had no idea at that point who you were. It wasn't until I followed you about for a while that things began to fall into place." She leaned over and kissed my forehead. "That's enough for now. You get some rest."

"You, too," I said, and heaved a weary sigh. "It's hard work, coming back from the dead."

"Yes," she said. "It certainly is."

When I could muster enough strength to sit up, my mother brought in a chess set, which gave us a sort of common ground on which to meet and get acquainted. Earlier, I criticized novelists who assure us that, when a fever breaks, the patient is out of danger. Well, those same novelists would have us believe that, though a mother and child have been separated since birth, it doesn't matter; the moment they are reunited they will instantly love and understand each other. I wish that were true. But sharing the same experiences is just as important as sharing the same blood, and after being on different paths for so long, it was awkward trying to walk side by side.

"I thought that if I played you while you're down and out," she said, "I might stand a chance of winning."

"The first time we played, you won," I reminded her.

"Only because you let me."

"How did you know it was me operating the Turk?"

She shrugged. "A mother's intuition." The phrase brought to mind Virginia, who once spoke of "woman's intuition." My face must have betrayed me, for my mother said, "What's wrong?"

"Nothing. Just a little pain in my chest."

"Do you want to stop playing?"

"No, no. Not when I'm winning. How did you *really* know?"

She gave me an exasperated look. "You ask a lot of questions."

"So I've been told." We played in silence for a few minutes, and then I tried again. "So, how did you really know?"

"Know what?"

"About the Turk."

She sighed in resignation. "I didn't. Not until I had a talk with Mr. Mulhouse."

"Mulhouse? You *know* him?"

"I've met him. Twice, in fact. Once in Philadelphia and once in Richmond."

"He's in *Richmond*?"

"He arrived a few days after you left. Maelzel needed someone to run his machine, and Mulhouse needed the work."

"So he told you where to find me?"

"Yes. For all his faults, Mr. Mulhouse is a gentleman, and no gentleman would keep a boy and his mother apart."

"And he told you the Turk's secret?"

"Not in so many words. But he let a few hints drop. Laudanum tends to loosen a person's tongue." With a smile of satisfaction, she captured one of my rooks.

"Where did you learn to play chess?" I asked.

"It was part of my therapy."

"They taught you well," I said.

And then I took her queen.

❀   ❀   ❀

It was another two weeks before I got back on my feet. Even then I was short of breath and weak in the knees. The muscles in my back had weakened, too, and I stoically strapped myself into the torture device again. Thank goodness one thing, at least, had gotten stronger—the bond between my mother and me.

She had been occupying a single room in a boardinghouse, but now she took more spacious lodgings and brought me there to live. She was not entirely well, any more than I was; she still suffered from melancholia, and often retreated to her room. Her doctor recommended a change of scene; when I was able to travel, we sailed for Europe. We did a sort of Knight's Tour of the Continent, globe-trotting from one chess tournament to another and never landing in the same place twice. I didn't win any tournaments, but I did win a fair amount of money from players who overestimated their own skill and underestimated mine.

When we returned to Philadelphia in the fall of 1838, I learned from Mr. Peach at the Chess Club that Maelzel's automata and dioramas were being auctioned off.

"Why? Has he gone bankrupt?"

"Worse than that. He died. And your friend Mulhouse as well."

"Both of them? How?"

"Yellow fever, is what I heard. They were putting

on an exhibition down in Mexico. Or was it Panama? Someplace tropical and unhealthy, anyway."

I later found out that it was, in fact, Cuba. I'm afraid I didn't mourn Maelzel very much, but Mulhouse's passing did sadden me. In a very trying time, he was the nearest thing I had to a friend.

I attended the auction, and was tempted to bid on the Turk, but our European jaunt had left us short of funds. He was bought for four hundred dollars by a Dr. John Mitchell—who, as curious and coincidental as it may seem, had once been physician to none other than Edgar Allan Poe, when the poet was living in Philadelphia.

Unfortunately for Dr. Mitchell, poor Otto had lost his air of mystery, thanks to Poe's exposé. What's more, the doctor never managed to find anyone who could operate the Turk properly. Eventually, he donated the machine to Dunn's Chinese Museum, a popular Philadelphia attraction. Since my story is so rife with coincidence, you will not be surprised to learn that the museum's owner was the very same Mr. Dunn who had stuck me in the House of Refuge.

Though a Turk may be considered more or less Oriental, Otto never quite fit in there. I often considered stopping by and paying my compliments to him, but I didn't really care to stir up memories of my miserable apprenticeship. Then, in 1843, I learned that Mr. Dunn was moving his museum from Philadelphia to London. Knowing that I might not have another chance, I decided to look in on Otto, for old times' sake.

I wished I hadn't. He was, as they say, but a shadow of his former self. Mechanically, he seemed sound enough, and though the cabinet was a little the worse for wear, it had been recently polished. But his garments were faded and worn, and his chessboard had been replaced by one with squares that contained letters of the alphabet and numbers, plus a few words. A copper speaking tube projected from the top of the cabinet. Around Otto's neck hung a sign that read:

Th e Swa mi
SEES ALL, KNOWS ALL
5 CENTS PER QUESTION

A gaggle of giggling children from a nearby girls' school were gathered around, gawking, but they apparently had no money. "Excuse me, ladies," I said, and, stepping forward, deposited a half dime in the slot indicated. Otto lifted his head and his dark eyes stared, as unsettlingly as ever, into mine. He seemed surprised to see me, but no doubt I was only imagining it.

Apparently Mr. Dunn had found someone capable of operating the machine, at least well enough to spell out a few words. The Turk's hand rose from its resting place and moved, with only a little hesitation, to the word *Bonjour*. A gasp went up from the little girls. "*Bonjour*," I said, into the speaking tube. "Are you ready for my question?"

The Turk's finger selected the square that read *Oui*.

"*Bon. Est-ce que vous jouez aux échecs encore?*" Do you still play chess?

This time the Turk paused for a long moment before responding. And then, one letter at a time, he picked out a word: *P. O. R. C. E. L. E. T. ?*

"*Oui. C'est moi.*"

The girls, who had lost interest by now, darted off like a flock of sparrows. The Turk moved his hand to spell out another word: *B. A. C. K. ?*

"Yes, I'm back. Oh, you mean how *is* my back?"

Oui.

"A little stiff from time to time, but straight as a die. Well, almost. How's yours? From sitting in there, I mean."

M. A. L.

"I know the feeling. I suppose you've removed your legs, in order to fit in there better?"

Oui.

"You're keeping the Turk in shape, I see. Do you ever let him play chess?"

A pause, then: *T. O. O. M. A. N. Y. Q.*—

"I know, I know. But that's what you're here for, isn't it, Swami? To answer questions?"

Another pause, in which I could almost feel the sullenness. *Oui.*

"All right. You don't have to answer all those other questions, just this one. Do you . . . do you still have those nightmares?"

An even longer pause. *Oui.*

"I'm sorry to hear that. You know, the last time I saw you, I tried to thank you. I don't think you were listening then. But now you have no choice, do you? Thank you for protecting me, and for building the back brace, and I hope you have a good life. *Au revoir.*" I shook the Turk's mechanical hand and walked off without waiting for a reply; I knew there wouldn't be one.

CHAPTER

29

O H, DEAR. I'M NOT DOING SUCH A
good job of weaving my tale, am I? Though
I meant that to be the final chapter, I realize
now that I've left a few loose ends. Well, I did warn
you that I wasn't an accomplished storyteller.

For one thing, I still haven't gotten around to telling
you what became of Virginia Clemm—or Virginia Poe,
I should call her, for she did marry her now-famous
cousin. There's a good reason why I've been avoiding
the topic: her fate is a sad one, and I'd just as soon not
dwell on it. But it would be unfair to you, the reader,
to ignore it altogether.

For all his faults, Mr. Poe was a devoted husband; by
all accounts he and his young bride were quite happy,
except for having no money. But after they moved

back to Philadelphia in 1837, Virginia became ill with consumption—tuberculosis, to use the more modern term—and, at the tender age of twenty-four, she died.

You may also be curious to know about Fiona—the nanny, I mean, not the automaton—and about Ezra, my friend from the House of Refuge. You recall the Mr. Peach I mentioned, who frequented the Chess Club? Well, he hired Fiona to work in his shop; a year later, to everyone's surprise—perhaps even his—he married her.

As for Ezra, he lived up to his promise and his nickname by escaping yet again—though not by hot-air balloon, as I imagined. He built a sort of ladder out of yarn and kindling wood and climbed over the wall. Mr. Dunn was so impressed with the boy's cleverness and determination that he made Ezra an apprentice clerk.

There's one more character whose fate I suppose I must reveal, though it's nearly as tragic as poor Virginia's.

I may have implied that, when Mr. Dunn moved his Chinese Museum to London, he took all his exhibits with him, including Otto—or the Swami, as he was now known. I wish that were true. But the fact is that, after nearly three-quarters of a century of celebrating and challenging and speculating about the Turk, the public had lost interest in him. So many bona fide mechanical marvels had come upon the scene lately—the telegraph, the sewing machine, the steam locomotive, the electric motor—and they were actually useful and practical. A machine that could play chess or tell fortunes seemed somehow frivolous, little more than an especially clever toy.

Though I didn't know it at the time, Mr. Dunn left the Turk behind, to gather dust and mold in a back room of the museum building. With its Oriental exhibits gone, the building's main hall was hired out for concerts and lectures and political conventions and flower shows and other such mundane events.

I didn't learn Otto's whereabouts until a full decade later. My mother and I spent much of that time in Europe, traveling from one tournament to another; I faced some of the world's best players and, in all modesty, acquitted myself pretty well. By 1854, we were back in Philadelphia, where I was hired by the Chess Club to be their resident chess master.

As luck would have it, our old friend Mr. Peach once again provided me with information about the Turk. He had recently made an inspection tour of the old museum building, with an eye to purchasing it, and had discovered Otto languishing in one of the storage rooms.

"How did he look?" I asked.

"Well," said Mr. Peach, "it was quite dark in that

back room, so I wheeled him out into the main hall, where the light was better. I must say, he looked rather shabby and forlorn. The mice had made a nest in his turban."

I couldn't bear to think of my clockwork comrade sitting there, useless and abandoned; I knew all too well what that felt like. I made up my mind that I would contact the building's owner as soon as possible and offer to buy the automaton.

I never got the chance. The following day was the Fourth of July—a time when, in the city that calls itself the Birthplace of America, the machinery of business and commerce grinds to a halt, to make way for blaring brass bands and dwindling ranks of weary-looking war veterans and throngs of cheering flag-wavers. But the ones who relish the holiday most are the pyromaniacs—and at that time they numbered in the thousands, all of them equipped with devices that flamed and sparkled and exploded.

By the morning of the Fifth, the city's streets looked like a battleground where two enemy forces had met, armed only with Crowns of Jupiter and Stars of Co-lumbia. You might think that, after an entire day of this, the citizens of Philadelphia would have been fed up with fireworks. And most undoubtedly were, but when evening came there were still scattered booms and bangs in every neighborhood.

The noise put me on edge and made it hard to sleep. In my half-awake state, I kept imagining that I was hearing artillery fire, the sort that must have surrounded Jacques at Trocadero, and at any moment a shell might rip through the roof and blow some part of me away.

Just when things seemed to have settled down, there was another disturbing sound—the tolling of church bells. Not the relaxed, rhythmic peal that summons you to church on Sundays, but the urgent clanging that signals a fire. Through my open window, I heard running feet and panicky voices shouting: "Where is it?"

"The National Theatre, someone said!"

The theatre lay right next door to the museum building where Otto was imprisoned. I sprang out of bed and into my clothing. In the hallway, my mother was emerging from her room, wrapping a robe around her. I rushed past her, ignoring her cry of "What's happening?" and burst out the front door—and was very nearly run down by a fire engine hauled by four burly smoke eaters, eager to be first on the scene and get the glory. Even though they were winded, they let out great guffaws, as though it were all a huge lark and running me over would only have added to the fun. They were followed by four more men pulling the hose cart.

When I reached the site of the conflagration, the

firemen, instead of battling the fire, were battling a rival hose company for the right to hook up to the nearest fireplug. Meanwhile, the National Theatre was blazing away, throwing off brands that threatened to ignite the buildings around it. At last, the firemen began manning their seesaw-like pumper. I detoured around them and made for the old museum building, which was separated from the theatre only by a narrow alleyway.

The alley was already filled with burning debris, and the flames had begun to swarm up the wall of the museum. Somewhere on the other side of that wall sat the Turk, unable to do a thing to save himself. I glanced desperately around, looking for some way of breaking into the building. A few yards away, a young smoke eater was leaning on his fire ax, grinning, as though this were just another fireworks display.

I strode over to him. "I need your help, my friend! There's someone inside the museum!"

The fellow scowled, as if my interruption were spoiling the show. "That building there?"

"Yes! Can you break down the door?"

"If you reckon it's necessary. I don't care to be arrested for destroying property."

"It'll be destroyed in any case, won't it?" I gestured toward the museum's roof, which was now ablaze.

Despite my attempts to hurry him, the fireman

hacked at the door in such a leisurely way that, by the time we were inside, a section of the roof had caved in, and the ceiling of the main hall was on fire. In the light from the flames, I could barely make out the Turk at the far end of the smoky room.

"Why's he just sitting there?" demanded the firefighter. "Why don't he make a run for it?"

"He can't walk! We'll have to help him!" I scrambled to the Turk's side and, grabbing hold of the cabinet, started pushing it toward the door. The young smoke eater, meanwhile, just stood there, gaping, obviously wondering what to make of the machine. Before I got halfway to the door, a blazing rafter descended from the ceiling. It crashed into one side of the cabinet and sent me sprawling.

The fireman rushed forward at last and yanked me to my feet. "It's no good!" he shouted, between bouts of coughing. "We got to get out of here!"

"We can't leave the Turk!"

"It ain't a real person! We are!" He seized the back of my shirt and propelled me, stumbling and choking, toward the door.

Once we were outside, I broke away from his grasp. Taking several lungfuls of fresh air, I turned and peered into the interior of the hall. Though the cabinet was aflame and the ermine-trimmed robe had begun to smoulder, the Turk was still sitting upright, his fierce eyes glaring at me accusingly, as if astonished that I would leave him there, at the mercy of the flames. Clearly he didn't share my father's belief that we should accept with good grace whatever befalls us.

And then, slowly, his expression began to change, to one of profound sadness. His mouth went slack, his mustache drooped, great tears streamed down his cheeks—or so it appeared. It took me a moment to realize what was really happening: the wax from which Otto's face was fashioned had started to melt. A patch of it sloughed off, then another, revealing bit by bit what lay beneath the wax—something white and smooth, like bone; in fact, if I hadn't known better, I might have mistaken it for a human skull.

And if I hadn't known better, I might have imagined that the faint sound I was hearing, through the crackle of the flames and the crash of falling rafters, was a human voice. It wasn't, of course; it was only the Turk's mechanical voice box, activated by the hot air that rose from the burning cabinet and up through the chimney of his hollow chest. It was trying to form the words it had been designed to utter: *Échec et mat.* But the heat had warped the delicate mechanism, and instead the Turk, as he perished, seemed to be sighing, *Ah, Jacques, c'est moi. Ah, Jacques, c'est moi.*

MOST OF MY HISTORICAL NOVELS have featured one or more actual, well-known personages from the past. This book is no exception. Edgar Allan Poe makes an appearance, of course, and P. T. Barnum has a cameo role. What you may not realize is that I've included an even more famous historical figure—the Turk. Though he's more or less unknown today, for nearly two centuries he was a worldwide celebrity.

You've probably never heard of Johann Nepomuk Maelzel before, either, but he was a celebrated character in his own right, not only as the man who displayed the Turk, but as the inventor of a device essential to many generations of musicians—the metronome. Well, actually, he didn't invent it so much as steal the design from another inventor. He also tried to claim credit for Beethoven's composition *Wellington's Victory*.

Though he clearly wasn't the most admirable of men, Maelzel wasn't quite as unpleasant as I've portrayed him. His contemporaries describe him as "polite" and "amiable," the "prince of entertainers." But for the purposes of the story, I've given him a darker side.

I've made Mr. Poe a bit more of a scoundrel than he was in real life, for the same reason; though he was moody and eccentric and had a drinking problem, he probably wasn't unscrupulous. He did write an exposé of the Turk, but it wasn't based on "ill-gotten information," only on deduction—a method that figures prominently in his detective stories "The Murders in the Rue Morgue," "The Mystery of Marie Roget," and "The Purloined Letter." (You can read his *Messenger* article about the Turk online at http://www.eapoe.org/works/essays/maelzel.htm.)

William Schlumberger, alias Mulhouse, was a real person, too, who operated the Turk from 1826 until his death in 1838. Though the elusive Mademoiselle Bouvier is my own creation, Maelzel did, in fact, use an unnamed young Frenchwoman as his operator for a short time. The character of Jacques is fictional but, again, based on fact—or rather on a story that claims to be fact, involving a Polish officer who lost his legs in a revolt against the Russians; he was supposedly smuggled out of Russia inside the Turk.

Neither Reverend Goodspeed nor his controversial *Development of Species* actually existed, but there were a number of naturalists and other scientists who tackled the topic of evolution—also known as "descent theory," "continuity theory," and "transmutation"—well before Darwin.

Though I've taken a few liberties with the characters, the locations in the book and the details of early nineteenth-century life are as accurate as I could make them with the help of dozens of histories, biographies, and contemporary accounts.

Immerse yourself in yet another world of colorful characters, villainy, and drama in **The Shakespeare Stealer.**

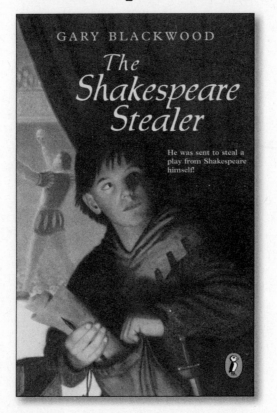

I never knew my mother or my father. As reliably as I can learn, my mother died the same year I was born, the year of our Lord 1587, the twenty-ninth of Queen Elizabeth's reign.

The name I carried with me throughout my youth was attached to me, more or less accidentally, by Mistress Mac-Gregor of the orphanage. I was placed in her care by some neighbor. When she saw how small and frail I was, she exclaimed "*Och*, the poor little pigwidgeon!" From that unfortunate expression came the appellation of Widge, which stuck to me for years, like pitch. It might have been worse, of course. They might have called me Pig.

Of my life at the orphanage, I have made it a habit to recall as little as possible. The long and short of it is, it was an institution, and institutions are governed by expediency. Mistress MacGregor was not a bad woman, just an overburdened one. Occasionally she lost her temper and beat one of us, but for the most part we were not mistreated so much as neglected.

The money given us by the parish was not enough to keep one child properly clothed and fed, let alone six or seven. We depended mostly upon charity. When someone felt charitable, our bellies were relatively full. Otherwise, we dined on barley mush and wild greens. When times were hard for others, they were doubly so for us.

It was the dream of each child within those dreary walls that someday a real family would come and claim him. Preferably it would be his true parents—who were, of course, royalty—but any set would do. Or so we thought.

When I was seven years of age, my prospects changed, as some say they do every seven years of a person's life— the grand climateric, I have heard it called. That orphan's dream suddenly became a reality for me.

The rector from the nearby hamlet of Berwick came looking for an apprentice and, thanks to Mistress MacGregor's praise, settled on me. The man's name was Dr. Timothy Bright. His title was not a religious one but a medical one. He had studied physick at Cambridge and practiced in the city of London before coming north to Yorkshire.

Naturally I was grateful and eager to please. I did readily whatever was asked of me, and at first it seemed I had been

very fortunate. Dr. Bright and his wife were not affection-
ate toward me—nor, indeed, toward their own children.
But they gave me a comfortable place to sleep at one end of
the apothecary, the room where the doctor prepared his
medicines and infusions.

There was always some potion simmering over a pot of
burning pitch, and one of my duties was to tend to these.
The pitch fire kept the room reasonably warm. I took my
meals in the kitchen. Though the situation was hardly
what we orphans had secretly hoped for, it was more or less
what I had expected—with one exception. I was to be
taught to read and write, not only in English but in Latin,
and not only in Latin but also in a curious abbreviated language of Dr. Bright's own devising. *Charactery*, he called it.
It was, to use his own words, "an art of short, swift, and secret writing, by the which one may transcribe the spoken
word as rapidly as it issues from the tongue."

His object, I soon learned, was not to offer me an education so much as to prepare me to be his assistant. I was to
keep his scientific notes for him, and to transcribe his
weekly sermons.

I had always been a quick student, but I was never
quick enough to suit the doctor. He had some idea that his
method of stenography could be learned in a matter of
mere months, and he meant to use me to prove it.

I was a sore disappointment to him. It was an awkward
system, and it took me a full year to become reasonably
adept, and another year before I could set down every word

without begging him to speak more slowly. This vexed him, for once his ample mouth was set in motion, he did not like to stop it. To his mind, of course, the fault lay not with his system but with me, for being so thickheaded.

I never saw him write anything in this short hand himself. I am inclined to think he never mastered it. As I grew confident with the system, I began to make my own small improvements in it—without the doctor's knowledge, of course. He was a vain man. Because he had once written a book, a dry treatise on melancholy, he felt the world should ever after make special allowances for him. He had written nothing since, so far as I knew, except his weekly sermons. And, as I was soon to discover, not always those.

When I was twelve, and could handle a horse as well as a plumbago pencil, the doctor set me off to neighboring parishes each Sabbath to copy other rectors' sermons. He meant, he said, to compile a book of the best ones. I believed him until one Sunday when the weather kept me home. I sat in on Dr. Bright's service and heard the very sermon I had transcribed at Dewsbury a fortnight before.

It did not prick my conscience to know that I had been doing something wrong. We were not given much instruction in right and wrong at the orphanage. As nearly as I could tell, Right was what benefited you, and anything which did you harm was Wrong.

My main concern was that I might be caught. I had never asked for any special consideration, but now I asked Dr. Bright, as humbly as I could, to be excused from the task. He blinked at me owlishly, as if not certain he had heard me properly. Then he scratched his long, red-veined nose and said, "You are my boy, and you will do exactly as I tell you."

He said it as though it were an unarguable fact of life. That discouraged me far more than any threat or show of anger could have done. And he was right. According to law, I was his property. I had to obey or be sent back to the orphanage. As Mistress Bright was fond of reminding me, prentices were easily come by and easily replaced. In truth, he had too much invested in me to dismiss me lightly. But he would not have hesitated to beat me, and heavily.

There was a popular saying to the effect that England is a paradise for women, a prison for servants, and a hell for horses. Prentices were too lowly to even deserve mention.

Eventually our sermon stealing was discovered. The wily old rector at Leeds noticed my feverish scribbling, and a small scandal ensued. Though Dr. Bright received only a mild reprimand from the church, he behaved as though his reputation were ruined. As usual, the blame fell squarely on my thin shoulders. My existence there, which had never been so much to begin with, went steadily downhill.

As I had so often done in my orphanage days, I began to wish for some savior to come by and, seeing at a glance my superior qualities, take me away.

In my more desperate moments, I even considered running away on my own. As I learned to read and transcribe such books as Holinshed's *Chronicles* and Ralegh's *Discov-*

7

ery of Guiana, I discovered that there was a whole world out there beyond Yorkshire, beyond England, and I longed to see it with my own eyes.

Up to now, my life had been bleak and limited, and it showed no sign of changing. In a new country such as Guiana, I imagined, or a city the size of London, there would be opportunities for a lad with a bit of wherewithal to make something of himself, something more than an orphan and a drudge. And yet I held no real hope of ever seeing anything beyond the bounds of Berwick. Indeed, the thought of leaving rather frightened me.

I was so ill-equipped to set out into that world alone. I could read and write, but I knew none of the skills needed to survive in the unfamiliar, perhaps hostile lands that lay beyond the fields and folds of our little parish. And so I waited, and worked, and wished.

If I had had any notion of what actually lay in store for me, I might not have wished so hard for it.

When I was fourteen, the grand climateric struck again, and my fortunes took a turn that made me actually long for the safety and security of the Brights' home.

In March, a stranger paid a visit to the rectory, but it was not some gentleman come to claim me as his heir. He was, in fact, no gentleman at all.

The doctor and I were in the apothecary when the housekeeper showed the stranger in. Though dark was almost upon us, we had not yet lighted the rush lights. The frugal doctor put that off as long as possible. The flickering flames of a pitch pot threw wavering, grotesque shadows upon the walls.

The stranger stood just inside the doorway, motionless and silent. He might have been taken for one of the shadows, or for some spectral figure—Death, or the devil— come to claim one of us. He was well over average height; a long, dark cloak of coarse fabric masked all his clothing save his high-heeled leather boots. He kept the hood of the cloak pulled forward, and it cast his face in shadow. The only feature I could make out was an unruly black beard, which curled over his collar. A bulge under the left side of his cloak hinted at some concealed object—a rapier, I guessed.

We all stood a long moment in a silence broken only by the sound of the potion boiling over its pot of flame. Dr. Bright blinked rapidly, as if coming awake, and snatched the clay vessel from the flame with a pair of tongs. Then he turned to the cloaked figure and said, with forced heartiness, "Now, then. How may I serve you, sir?"

The stranger stepped forward and reached under his cloak—for the rapier, I feared. But instead he drew out a small book bound in red leather. When he spoke, his voice was deep and hollow-sounding, befitting a spectre. "This is yours, is it not?"

Hesitantly, the doctor moved nearer and glanced at the volume. "Why, yes. Yes it is." I recognized it as well now. It was one of a small edition Dr. Bright had printed up the year before, with the abundant title, *Charactery: An Art of Short, Swift, and Secret Writing.*

"Does it work?"

"I beg your pardon?"

"The system," the man said irritably. "Does it work?"

"Of course it works," Dr. Bright replied indignantly. "With my system, one may without effort transcribe the written or the spoken word—"

"How long does it take?" the man interrupted.

Dr. Bright blinked at him. "Why, as I was about to say, one may set down speech as rapidly as it is spoken."

The man gestured impatiently, as if waving the doctor's words aside. "How long to *learn* it?"

The doctor glanced at me and cleared his throat. "Well, that depends on the aptitude of the—"

"How *long*?"

The doctor shrugged. "Two months, perhaps. Perhaps more." Perhaps a lot more, I thought.

The stranger flung the book onto the trestle table, which held the doctor's equipment. A glass vessel fell to the floor and shattered.

"Now see here—" Dr. Bright began. But the man had turned away, his long cloak swirling so violently that the flame in the pitch pot guttered and smoked. He stood facing away a moment, as if deep in thought. I busied myself cleaning up the broken beaker, content for once to be a lowly prentice with no hand in this business.

The black-bearded stranger turned back, his face still shadowed and unreadable. "To how many have you taught this system of yours?"

"Let me see . . . There's my boy, Widge, here, and then—"

"How many?

"Well . . . one, actually."

The hooded countenance turned on me. "How well has he learned it?"

Dr. Bright assumed his false heartiness again. "Oh, perfectly," he said, to my surprise. He had never before allowed that I was anything more than adequate.

"Show me," the man said, whether to me or the doctor I could not tell. I stood holding the shards of glass in my hand.

"Are you quite deaf?" the doctor demanded. "The gentleman wishes a demonstration of your skill."

I set the glass in a heap on the table, then picked up my small table-book and plumbago pencil. "What must I write?"

"Write this," the stranger said. "I hereby convey to the bearer of this paper the services of my former apprentice—" The man paused.

"Go on," I said. "I've kept up wi' you." I was so intent on transcribing correctly and speedily that I'd paid no attention to the sense of the words.

"Your name," the man said.

"Eh?"

"What is your *name*?"

"It's Widge," the doctor answered for me, then laughed nervously, as if suddenly aware how odd was the name he had been calling me for seven years.

The stranger did not share his amusement. "—my former apprentice, Widge, in consideration of which I have accepted the amount of ten pounds sterling." He paused again, and I looked up. For some reason, Dr. Bright was staring openmouthed, seemingly struck dumb.

"Is that all?" I asked.

The man held out an unexpectedly soft and well-manicured hand. "Let me see it." I handed him the table-book. He turned it toward the light. "You have copied down every word?" I could not see the expression on his face, but I fancied his voice held a hint of surprise.

"Aye."

He thrust the table-book into my hand. "Read it back to me."

To the unschooled eye, the scribbles would have been wholly mysterious and indecipherable:

Yet I read it back to him without pause, and this time I was struck by the import of the words. "Do you—does this mean—?" I looked to Dr. Bright for an explanation, but he avoided my gaze.

"Copy it out now in a normal hand," the stranger said.

"But I—"

"Go on!" the doctor snapped. "Do as he says."

13

It was useless to protest. What feeble objection of mine could carry the weight of ten pounds of currency? I doubted the doctor earned that much in a year. Swallowing hard, I copied out the message in my best hand, as slowly as I reasonably might. Meantime my brain raced, searching for some way to avoid being handed over to this cold and menacing stranger.

Whatever the miseries of my life with the Brights, they were at least familiar miseries. To go off with this man was to be dragged into the unknown. A part of me longed for new places, new experiences. But a larger part clung to the security of the familiar, as a sailor cast adrift might cling fast to any rock, no matter how small or barren.

Briefly, I considered fleeing, but that was pointless. Even if I could escape them, where would I go? At last I came to the end of the message and gave it up to Dr. Bright, who appended his signature, then stood folding the paper carefully. I knew him well enough to know that he was waiting to see the color of the man's money.

In truth, I suppose I knew him better than I knew anyone in the world. It was a sad thought, and even sadder to think that, after seven years, he could just hand me over to someone he had never before met, someone whose name he did not know, someone whose face he had never even seen.

The stranger drew out a leather pouch and shook ten gold sovereigns from it onto the table. As he bent nearer the light of the pitch pot, I caught my first glimpse of his features. Dark, heavy brows met at the bridge of a long, hooked nose. On his left cheek, an ugly raised scar ran all the way from the corner of his eye into the depths of his dark beard. I must have gasped at the sight of it, for he turned toward me, throwing his face into shadow again.

He thrust the signed paper into the wallet at his belt, revealing for an instant the ornate handle of his rapier. "If you have anything to take along, you'd best fetch it now, boy."

It took even less time to gather up my belongings than it had for my life to be signed away. All I owned was the small dagger I used for eating; a linen tunic and woollen stockings I wore only on the Sabbath; a worn leather wallet containing money received each year on the anniversary of my birth—or as near it as could be determined; and an ill-fitting sheepskin doublet handed down from Dr. Bright's son. It was little enough to show for fourteen years on this Earth.

Yet, all in all, I was more fortunate than many of my fellow orphans. Those who were unsound of mind or body were still at the orphanage. Others had died there.

I tied up my possessions with a length of cord and returned to where the men waited. Dr. Bright fidgeted with the sovereigns, as though worried that they might be taken back. The stranger stood as still and silent as a figure carved of wood.

When he moved, it was to take me roughly by the arm and usher me toward the door. "Keep a close eye on him, now," the doctor called after us. I thought it was his way of expressing concern for my welfare. Then he added, "He can be sluggish if you don't stir him from time to time with a stick."

The stranger pushed me out the front door and closed it behind him. A thin rain had begun to fall. I hunched my shoulders against it and looked about for a wagon or carriage. There was none, only a single horse at the snubbing post. The stranger untied the animal and swung into the saddle. "I've only the one mount. You'll have to walk." He pulled the horse's head about and started off down the road.

I lingered a moment and turned to look back at the rectory. The windows were lighted now against the gathering dark. I half hoped someone from the household might be watching my departure, and might wish me Godspeed, and I could bid farewell in return before I left this place behind forever. There was no one, only the placid tabby cat gazing at me from under the shelter of the eaves.

"God buy you, then," I told the cat and, slinging my bundle over my shoulder, turned and hurried off after my new master.